In New Granada

W. H. G. Kingston

"In New Granada"

BY

W.H.G. Kingston

1879

Chapter One.

Introductory—My father's history—Enters the navy as a
surgeon—Learns Spanish—Appointed to the "Zebra," in the
Pacific—Takes Dicky Duff under his charge—A shooting
expedition on shore—Captured by Spaniards on coast of
Guatemala with Dicky and Paul Loro—Carried to Panama—
Meets an old friend, who takes him to Guayaquil—Visit Loja
to inspect Peruvian bark—Meets Dr Cazalla—Accompanies
him to Popayan—He marries Miss Cazalla, who becomes
my mother; and Richard Duffield marries her niece, an
heiress—They both settle at Popayan.

The circumstances which led my father, Dr Andrew Sinclair, to settle
in New Granada—the land of my birth—are of so romantic a
character, that I cannot better preface an account of my own
adventures in that country than by narrating them.

My grandfather, Duncan Sinclair, after whom I was named, was a
member of an old Covenanter family in Dumfriesshire, and was the
parent of six sons,—all of whom, with the exception of the eldest,
who inherited the estate, had to seek their fortune in the world. My
father was his fourth son. Having gone through a medical course at
the University of Edinburgh, where he gained not only a knowledge
of his profession, but of science generally, he entered the Royal Navy
as an assistant-surgeon, and was ultimately promoted to the rank of
surgeon. Among his many other talents, he possessed that of
acquiring foreign languages, and he spoke French and Spanish
remarkably well; though at the time he learned the latter—from a
wounded Spanish prisoner, whose life was saved by his skill—he
little thought how useful it would prove to him. After visiting many
parts of the world, adding greatly to his store of information, he was
appointed to the *Zebra* sloop-of-war of eighteen guns, which soon
after sailed for the Pacific.

Among the youngsters on board was a midshipman named Richard
Duffield,—generally known, however, as Dicky Duff. He was the

orphan son of an old messmate, who had been killed in action. The brave lieutenant's last thoughts, as he lay mortally wounded in the cockpit, the guns still thundering overhead, were about his son.

"The boy's mother is dead, and when I am gone he'll not have a friend in the world. Doctor, will you look after him? I know you will!"

"Don't let any doubt about that trouble you. I'll act a father's part towards your boy as well as I am able," was the answer.

My father faithfully fulfilled his promise; and when the boy was old enough, he got him placed on the quarter-deck, and generally managed to take him to sea with himself. Richard Duffield was grateful for the kindness shown him, and became much attached to his protector, with whom he had many tastes in common.

My father, whenever he had an opportunity, was in the habit of going on shore with his gun, to obtain specimens of the birds and beasts of the country; while he also frequently brought off a bag of game for the benefit of the commander and his own messmates. On such occasions he was generally accompanied by Dicky Duff, who had become as good a sportsman as himself.

On one occasion, when the *Zebra* was off the coast of Guatemala in Central America, my father, having obtained a boat from the commander, left the ship, taking with him Dicky Duff, and their constant attendant, Paul Lobo, an African seaman, and a crew of six men. No inhabitants appearing, the boat was hauled up on the beach, and the crew amused themselves at leap-frog and other games, while my father and his two attendants proceeded some way inland. Having had very good sport, and filled their bags, my father sent back the midshipman and Paul to the boat with the game, while he continued shooting, hoping to obtain some more birds.

He had been thus employed for some time, and was thinking of returning, when the sound of several shots reached his ears. These were followed by a regular volley, and he had too much reason to fear that the inhabitants had attacked the boat. Instead, therefore, of returning to her, he made his way directly towards the shore. Emerging from the forest, which reached almost to the water's edge, he saw the boat at some distance off, with a party of men on the beach firing at her. His hope was that Dicky and Paul had already got on board before the boat shoved off. The distance was considerable, but still he hoped to be able to swim to her; so, leaving his gun and ammunition, with the game he had shot, under a tree, he plunged into the water. He had got some distance from the shore when he found that he was discovered, by seeing a shot strike the water not far from him. On looking round, what was his dismay to perceive Dicky and Paul in the hands of the Spaniards! He could not desert them, and consequently he at once turned and swam back, hoping that by explaining their object in visiting the shore he might obtain their release. But no sooner did he land than the Spaniards rushed down and seized him. In vain he expostulated. "He and his companions belonged to a ship of war, and they wished to be able to boast that they had made three prisoners." They told him, however, that if he would make signals to the boat to return, they would give him and his younger companions their liberty. On his refusing to act so treacherously, they became very angry, and bound his hands behind him, as well as those of Dicky and Paul. The seamen at once pulled back to the ship, when the captain sent a flag of truce on shore to try and recover his surgeon and midshipman; but the Spaniards refused to give them up.

After being kept prisoners for some time, they were sent down to Panama. Here, though strictly guarded, they were not ill-treated; and when it became known that my father was a surgeon, many persons, of all ranks, applied to him for advice. He was thus the means of effecting several cures, by which he obtained numerous friends. Indeed, he might here have established a good practice, and have comfortably supported himself and his companions; but he was anxious, for Dicky's sake especially, to return with him to the ship. There was no place, however, nearer than Cartagena, at which it was customary to exchange prisoners; and how to get to it, was the difficulty.

He had been kept a prisoner for some months, when, passing through the streets, he met his old acquaintance, Don Tomaso Serrano, from whom, while Don Tomaso was a prisoner on board his ship, he had learned Spanish. They immediately recognised each other, and expressed their pleasure at meeting. Don Tomaso, on hearing what had befallen my father, told him that he was in command of a man-of-war schooner, and was about to proceed in her to the southward. "Although I cannot obtain your liberty," he said, "I have sufficient influence to get leave for you and your companions to come on board my vessel and proceed with me as far as Guayaquil. I have friends there, whom I hope to interest in your favour; and by their influence you will, I hope, be able to obtain permission to land and travel across the country to Honda, from whence you can make your way down the river to Cartagena. It is a round-about route, but it may prove the shortest in the end. You will have an opportunity, too, of seeing a beautiful region; and you cannot fail, I am sure, to be hospitably treated wherever you go."

My father at once closed with Don Tomaso's offer, and was allowed to go on board the schooner, accompanied by Dicky and Paul. Having obtained a considerable sum of money, he was able to dress both of them, as well as himself, in Spanish costume, so that they did not attract attention; and as both he and Paul spoke Spanish perfectly, they were generally taken for natives. Though still prisoners, the party were treated with the greatest kindness, and enjoyed as much liberty as they could desire.

Heavy weather coming on, the schooner ran into the port of Buenaventura. Beyond the bay, opening into it, is a lagoon of considerable extent. On one side is the town, a great part of which is built on piles at the water's edge. The place has but little to recommend it; indeed, there are scarcely a dozen houses of any size, while the rest of the buildings have a miserable appearance both without and within. Above the town stands the church, —a building of no architectural pretensions, and greatly resembling a barn. Buenaventura is the port of a considerable district, embracing the valley of the Cauca. The climate, however, owing to the constant damp and heat, which produce intermittent fevers, prevents foreigners from residing here; indeed, it rains nearly every day in the year.

PORT AND ROADSTEAD OF BUENAVENTURA

Most of my father's time on shore was occupied in visiting persons suffering from ague, and in prescribing for them. What a blessing, indeed, can a clever medical man prove in such regions! He is like a heaven-sent messenger carrying relief to the sick and suffering.

The weather moderating, the schooner continued her voyage, and at length reached Guayaquil, the port of Quito, to the south of which it is situated, at the head of the Gulf of Guayaquil. Here Don Tomaso proved as good as his word, and obtained leave from the governor for my father to travel with his attendants through the country.

While on shore at Guayaquil, he heard that in the region of the little town of Loja, three days' journey off, grew in the greatest profusion the cinchona, or Peruvian bark tree, at that time but comparatively little known in Europe. Although my father was well acquainted with the beneficial effect produced by the bark in cases of intermittent fever, he was anxious to ascertain, by personal examination, the other peculiarities of the tree. He obtained leave, therefore, from the governor, to proceed in the first instance to Loja.

That place he reached without difficulty. On his arrival in the town, he found that a Spanish doctor was residing there for the same object, but that he was now laid up by a severe attack of illness, unable to continue his researches. My father immediately called on him, and found that he was no other than Doctor Cazalla, a physician widely celebrated for his scientific knowledge and talents. Introducing himself as a medical man, my father offered to prescribe for his brother physician, and in a short time had the satisfaction of restoring him to health. The two doctors then set out together on an expedition of botanical research, in which both Dicky and Paul accompanied them.

The time thus spent together having resulted in the establishment of a warm friendship between my father and the Spanish doctor, the latter prevailed upon him to visit Popayan, his native place, on the way to Cartagena. Their journey over that mountain region amid which Chimborazo towers to the sky, was interesting in the extreme. I have often heard my father speak of it. Popayan was at length safely reached, with the botanical treasures they had collected; and here my father was induced to remain for some time, in order to assist his friend in their arrangement. Before their labours came to an end, my father and Dicky were taken seriously ill. It now became the turn of the Spanish doctor to attend to them. He, however, was aided in his task by two ladies,—his sister and a young niece; the latter taking Dicky under her special charge. The result was that my father married the doctor's sister, and Dicky fell desperately in love with his niece. The war with Spain was by this time over, and the *Zebra* had returned to England, so my father and his young charge, believing that they had little prospect of getting on in the navy, determined to remain where they were. As Doctor Cazalla was engrossed in scientific pursuits, he gladly yielded up his practice to my father, his brother-in-law, whose fame as a physician was soon established in the town and throughout the surrounding district.

Richard Duffield, for I ought now to give him his proper name, in the course of a few years married Dona Maria, the girl who had so affectionately tended him, and who proved to be the heiress to a nice estate in the neighbourhood, to the improvement of which, when he became the proprietor, Richard devoted his time and attention; while Paul Lobo remained with my father as his personal attendant and general factotum.

Chapter Two.

Our studies interrupted—Don Juan de Leon—A ride to visit Don Ricardo, accompanied by Hugh and our tutor, Mr Laffan—Description of Popayan—Tyrannical treatment of New Granada and Venezuela by the Spaniards—Previous struggles of the colonists for liberty—Fearful cruelties inflicted on them by the Spaniards—My uncle, Dr Cazalla, a known Liberal—His dangerous position—How Mr Laffan became our tutor—Juan expatiates on the perfections of Dona Dolores, and invites me to accompany him on a visit—Pass a party of Indians—Don Ricardo's hacienda—Fruits of New Granada—Invited to stay—Juan, our tutor, and I serenade Dona Dolores—The interview—Dona Dolores endeavours to arouse Juan's patriotism—Music victorious—A heroine—Juan devotes himself to the cause of freedom.

"Holloa! mio amigo Señor Duncan, come down! I want to have a talk with you. You can spare a few minutes from your books."

Leaving the table at which I was seated with my brother Hugh and our tutor, Mr Michael Laffan, I went to the window, which looked out into the court of our house at Popayan, when I saw that the person who had hailed me was our friend Don Juan de Leon. He had just ridden in, mounted on a fine black horse, his special pride; and as he gracefully sat his steed, he looked a remarkably handsome young fellow. His costume, too,—a broad-brimmed sombrero, a feather secured to it by a jewelled buckle, a richly-trimmed poncho or capote over his shoulders, broad leggings, ornamented with braiding and tags, and large silver spurs,—became him well.

"Come down, Duncan, I want to speak to you," he said, beckoning to me.

Having obtained permission, I descended to the courtyard with a hop, skip, and jump. After shaking hands, I begged him to come in, as I was sure the ladies of my family would be glad to see him.

"I have no time now," he answered; "I hope to pay my respects to-morrow."

"What have you to say to me?" I asked.

"I want you to come with me to visit your friends Don Ricardo and Dona Maria at Egido. You can easily obtain a holiday from Señor Miguel. As the ride is a long one, I shall be glad of your companionship. You will have no objection either, I am sure, to enjoying the bright smiles of your sweet little cousin, Dona Rosa, their daughter."

Don Ricardo, I should explain, was our old friend Richard Duffield; and Señor Miguel was Mr Michael Laffan, our tutor.

"She is not my cousin, though we are both half British, and our fathers are old friends. But confess, Juan, that you have another object in going to Egido. You will have no objection either to pay a visit on your way to Dona Dolores Monteverde, and to bask in her sweet smiles," I rejoined, repeating his words. "However, as Mr Laffan would say, 'Amicus certus in re incerta, cerniter' (A true friend is discovered in a doubtful matter), I shall be very glad to accompany you, and be of any service in my power, if I can obtain leave."

"Thank you, Duncan. Go then and obtain leave, although I thought you were old enough to act as you might think fit in a matter of this sort," said Juan. "I have a little commission to perform at the other end of the town, and will shortly return for you. You are sure to obtain leave, so I can depend upon having your company."

Lighting a cigarillo, he rode off down the street. My father was out, so I went to my mother in order to have her sanction, in case Mr Laffan should prove obdurate. Juan was a favourite of hers, as well as of everybody who knew him, so when I told her of his request she made no objection.

"Then I'll tell Mr Laffan that I have your leave," I observed.

"And that you have mine too," exclaimed my young sister Flora; "for I want you to carry a packet to Rosa, and a note with my love, and tell her she must come here soon and stay with us."

While I ordered my horse, and put on my riding costume, Flora wrote and sealed her note, which I promised faithfully to deliver with the packet she entrusted to my care. On going to Mr Laffan to beg that he would excuse me from my studies for a few hours, he exclaimed, looking out of the window —

"It's a mighty fine day. Hugh and I will be ready to take a ride with you. I can instruct him in orthography, geography, botany, and the natural sciences, as we go along."

Hugh was delighted to go, and undertook duly to receive all the instruction our worthy tutor could impart to him on the way. Though my brother was still very young, he was a capital horseman, and would make nothing of riding a dozen leagues or more in a day. I was in doubt, however, whether Juan would be particularly pleased to have Mr Laffan's company; but such an idea never occurred to our good tutor, who was not inconveniently troubled with bashfulness. I knew, however, that he would be welcomed at the house of Don Ricardo, who esteemed him for his many sterling qualities.

Hugh and Mr Laffan were ready almost as soon as I was, and when Juan returned we were all three mounted in the courtyard, prepared to accompany him.

"I did not know that you were coming, Mr Laffan," he said, lifting his hat and bowing politely; "but it will afford me great pleasure to have your society."

Our tutor replied in wonderfully curious Spanish, into which he could not help occasionally introducing a few Irishisms, for the purpose, as he used to say, of adding pepper to his remarks.

Without delay we set off, Juan and I riding together, Mr Laffan and Hugh following; and I saw by our tutor's gestures, after we got clear of the town, that, faithful to his promise, he was imparting information in his usual impressive manner, which Hugh was endeavouring with all his might to take in.

POPAYAN.

While we ride along, I will describe the region and the city in which I was born, and some of the principal events which had occurred since my father settled there, up to the present time.

In the western half of New Granada are three ranges of lofty mountains, into which the main branch of the Andes is divided, extending from Quito northwards to the Caribbean Sea; a fourth branch, running close to the shores of the Pacific, extends towards the Isthmus of Panama. These four ranges form three valleys, elevated, however, a considerable distance above the sea. Throughout that to the east runs the magnificent river Magdalena; the next is watered by the Cauca, of equal length; and the third valley by the Atrato, of less extent, which runs into the Gulf of Darien. At the head of the centre valley—that of the Cauca—is situated Popayan, the capital of the province of the same name, in the midst of a beautiful plain, almost surrounded by two streams, which finish their course about a league below it, when they fall into the fine river Cauca. This river then runs to the northward through the rich and charming valley of the Cauca. Nothing can be more delicious than the climate of this region, the inhabitants being never oppressed by excessive heat, or annoyed by extreme cold. Rain, however, falls during the last three months of the year, and also in April and May; but even at that period the mornings are fine, as the showers seldom come on until two or three o'clock in the afternoon, and continue during the night. The plain, or I may call it the wide valley of Popayan, lies between two ranges of lofty mountains. On one side are the Cordilleras, with Purace, eternally covered with snow, rising above them; and on the west side is another range, which separates the valley from the province of Buenaventura. In the midst, surrounded by trees, appears Popayan, with its numerous churches and large convents, distinguished at a considerable distance by their whiteness. It is one of the most ancient towns in that part of the continent. Its founders, companions of Sebastian Belalcazar, made it the capital of the province, establishing a bishopric, a college, and numerous religious institutions. Although its buildings might not be greatly admired in Europe, the inhabitants are proud of them; and justly so, when the difficulties under which they were erected are remembered. Every article used in their construction had to be brought either on the backs of men or mules; and there were few native craftsmen capable of performing the necessary work. Many families proud of their ancient descent were settled in the town, and its society was therefore superior to that of any of the surrounding places. In Popayan is a large square, of which I shall have to speak by-and-by, with the cathedral on one side, and the residences of some of the principal people in the town occupying the other sides. There were, besides, several churches, four convents, and two nunneries. To the north of the city, towards the Cauca, is the handsomest bridge in that part of the country. From the town, in the early part of the morning, when the sun shines on them, can be seen the Cordilleras of Chicquio, and at a less distance rises the Paramos of Puxana and Soltana, presenting a magnificent appearance.

This description may give a faint idea of the beautiful scenery amid which I was born. Although I was accustomed to it from my earliest days, I nevertheless admired it more and more as I grew older. Though my father and Richard Duffield had not intended to settle in America when they married, their wives, who were attached to the country, exerted all their influence to induce them to stay, so they finally made up their minds to abandon their native land. The doctor, having been so long a prisoner, was supposed to be dead, and he had no difficulty in retiring from the service; while the midshipman very easily discharged himself.

At the time I speak of, Liberal principles had been making rapid progress in the country among persons of all ranks. For years the colony had groaned under the tyranny and narrow-minded policy of the mother country. As she produced wine, oil, and silk, the inhabitants of New Granada and Venezuela were not allowed to cultivate either the vine, the olive, or the mulberry, under the idea that they would thus be compelled to consume the produce of Spain. Attempts were made from time to time to establish manufactories, which were invariably destroyed by the orders of the Spanish Government. At length, when Spain herself became enslaved by the French, the colonists took the opportunity of throwing off the galling yoke, and New Granada and Venezuela declared their independence. The Spanish standard was cut down and destroyed, while the tricoloured flag was hoisted in numerous towns and fortresses. The inhabitants of the two vice-royalties flew to arms, and, under the leadership of General Miranda, the Royalists were defeated in Venezuela. No sooner, however, had Spain been liberated by the success of the British arms over Napoleon's generals in the Peninsula, than she made use of her recovered liberty again to enthral the hapless colonists. Simon Bolivar, who had hitherto taken no active part in the revolution, was at length won over to espouse the cause of Freedom; and a congress having been assembled at Caracas to organise a new Government for the state of Venezuela, he proceeded to England for the purpose of endeavouring to induce the British Cabinet to aid the cause of Liberty. Finding, however, that the English had resolved on maintaining a strict neutrality, though they had ample excuses for interfering in the cause of humanity, he returned in disgust to Caracas.

Sometimes success attended the Patriot arms, sometimes the Royalists were victorious. At length a dreadful earthquake occurred. I remember it well. Fear was inspired by the terrible destruction it caused to life and property. In the three cities of Caracas, La Guayra, and Merida, twenty thousand persons perished. The priests, monks, and friars, who in general were the main supporters of Spanish tyranny, knowing that with the advancement of Liberal principles their power would be decreased, if not overthrown, declared this catastrophe to be a judgment on the revolutionists. About twelve hundred of the Royalist prisoners who were confined in the fortress of Puerto Cabello, of which Bolivar was then commandant, having broken loose, murdered some of the garrison, and by the treachery of the officer on guard took possession of the citadel. Bolivar, with a band of followers, narrowly escaped destruction; and General Miranda, who was at Vittoria, on hearing that this important place, with all its stores, arms, and ammunition, was deserted, capitulated in despair to Monteverde, the Royalist general; and being sent in irons to Spain, he there died — shortly afterwards — in a dungeon.

The whole country was now once more entirely in the hands of the Royalists, who inflicted the most fearful cruelties on the hapless inhabitants. On pretexts the most trivial, old men, women, and children were arrested, their houses plundered, and they themselves maimed in the most horrible way, or massacred as rebels.

I have been speaking chiefly of Venezuela. The Liberals in New Granada suffered similar reverses; but, in consequence of the inaccessible nature of many parts of the country, the Patriots, although defeated, were able to take refuge in positions from which they could not be driven by the Spaniards; and many, under various leaders, remained in arms, prepared for the moment when they might again attack the Royalists with a prospect of success, and drive them, as they had vowed to do, from the country.

The bloodthirsty monster, General Murillo, had at this time his headquarters at Santa Fé de Bogotà, the capital of New Granada. Our own city of Popayan had not altogether escaped, but it was at present comparatively tranquil, though people lived in dread of what a day might bring forth. Murillo was attempting to stamp out Liberal principles by the destruction of every man of science and education in the country, being well aware that ignorance and superstition were the strongest supporters of Spanish tyranny. My father, as a medical man and an English subject, hoped to escape annoyance; though our uncle, Dr Cazalla, owing to his known Liberal principles and scientific attainments, was well aware that his position was critical in the extreme. Though on his guard, he was too bold to fly. My father often urged him to leave the country, but his reply was, "I will remain, to forward, by every means in my power, the cause of liberty, and endeavour to advance the true liberties of the people among whom I live." My father steadily pursued his professional duties, attending equally on the Royalists and Liberals, by both of whom he was highly esteemed, — though those who knew him best were well aware that his sympathies were all on the side of Freedom.

However, my object is not so much to describe the political events which occurred in the country, as to narrate my own adventures, and those of my relatives and friends. My father had often intended to send my brother and me to England for our education; but my mother was unwilling to part with us, and suggested, instead, that an English tutor should be procured, who would give us the instruction we required. My father remarked that it was not only the knowledge we should obtain by going to England which would prove of value, but the training and general education we should receive at an English school. He had made up his mind to act as he thought best, notwithstanding our mother's objections, when he was called in to visit an English traveller who had lately arrived at Popayan, accompanied by a secretary—Mr Laffan—for whom he seemed to entertain a warm regard. His malady increased, and my father soon saw that his hours were numbered, and told him so. The dying man acknowledged that his funds were nearly exhausted; that he was waiting remittances from England, but that it might be long before they arrived, if they ever came at all; and he was greatly concerned as to what would become of his attendant, who would thus be left in a foreign country without the means of leaving it, or of obtaining support. My father had not been favourably impressed by the appearance of Mr Laffan, who was tall and gaunt, with awkward manners and ungainly figure; but after some conversation he found him to be a man of considerable attainments and intelligence, and apparently thoroughly honest and trustworthy.

On the death of the unfortunate gentleman, my father found his companion plunged in the deepest grief.

"He was my best friend, sir, the truest I ever had in the world; and now he's gone and left me all alone among savages, or little better, by the way they murder each other; and we may call them heathens, too, when we see them bow down to stocks and stones."

My father, feeling for the poor man, inquired whether he would be willing to act as tutor to two boys. On receiving this proposal, Mr Laffan started up and pressed my father's hand, and while the tears ran down his cheeks, assured him that he would gladly devote his life and energies to the task, hoping that my father would have no cause to regret having entrusted us to his charge.

Having seen his former patron placed in the grave, Mr Laffan took up his abode in our house, and well and faithfully fulfilled the duties he had undertaken—although, it must be confessed, in a somewhat curious fashion—and we soon became as much attached to him, I believe, as he was to us. He gave us not only mental, but physical training; for, in spite of his gaunt figure, he was a first-rate horseman, and thoroughly understood the sword-exercise, a practical knowledge of which he imparted to us. He was a good shot and a keen sportsman; and although he seldom spoke of himself, he had, I discovered, seen a good deal of service, and had honourable wounds to show. He was a devoted Liberal, and detested tyranny in every shape and form. As may be supposed, we admired his principles, which, indeed, were those of our father and uncle, and all the members of our mother's family.

As I have said, Juan and I rode on, while Mr Laffan and Hugh followed close behind us. Our road lay between lanes bordered by hedges of the prickly pear, and gardens filled with fruit trees of every description; while before us rose the Cordilleras, adding much to the beauty of the scenery. Before we had ridden far, Don Juan confessed to me that, besides paying a promised visit to my friends, his object was to see Dona Dolores.

"She is beautiful and good, and full of sense and spirit, so unlike the greater number of my countrywomen," he exclaimed; "I believe there is nothing that she would not dare and do."

"I quite believe all you say of her, Juan," I answered; though I confess I did not admire the young lady quite as much as my friend did. According to my taste, her manner was somewhat too determined and forward—shall I call it?—although I could not exactly say that she was masculine in her appearance, or wanting in feminine attractions; and I had no doubt that she could be soft and tender on occasion.

"But does Dona Dolores return your love?" I asked.

"I hope so; I have no reason to believe that she dislikes me," he answered, "though I own that she treats me sometimes as if I were a mere boy. But perseverance conquers all difficulties. My great desire is to convince her of the sincerity of my affection, and that I am worthy of her love."

"I should think that she would soon be convinced of that," I observed, looking up at Juan, of whom I thought a great deal; he was a man, I fancied, to whom any girl would willingly give her heart.

"I have determined to visit her to-day, after paying my respects to Don Ricardo and Dona Maria, and to learn my fate. Will you accompany me, Duncan? I dare say that, if I give you a sign, you will find an excuse for leaving us together while I plead my cause."

I, of course, said that I was perfectly ready to do as Juan wished, although I did not think my presence would be necessary.

We had got more than half-way to Egido, when we overtook a large party of Indians returning from Popayan to their own village. At their head marched one of their number playing the tabor and pipes, to which they kept admirable time. The men were a remarkably fine-looking set of fellows; and the women were handsome, with good figures. The former, who carried long lances, wore kilts, and on their heads blue cloth caps trimmed with scarlet, ornamented with gold lace somewhat the worse for wear. Their bearing, also, was bold and independent. They saluted Don Juan in a familiar way, and he laughed and joked with them as we passed by.

"These men would make good soldiers, if they could be got to join the Liberal cause," observed Mr Laffan.

"But you'll not get them while they live under the influence of their priests," answered Juan. "The friars try to persuade the people that the Liberals are in league with Satan, and that if they join them they will do so at the peril of their souls. They eyed you three very suspiciously," he continued; "for the friars tell them that all Englishmen have tails, like monkeys, and horns on their heads, and that they are addicted to eating babies when they can get a supply."

"You should try and disabuse them of such notions, Don Juan," said Mr Laffan.

"I!—it is no business of mine. I let the people think as they like—it does no harm."

"It always does harm to allow people to believe a falsehood, and we should oppose it with truth," observed Mr Laffan.

Don Juan laughed, and commenced trolling forth a jovial song as we rode along, as if he did not like to be lectured by our tutor.

On arriving at the hacienda, we found that Don Ricardo was out; but Dona Maria received us very kindly, and servants immediately came forward to take charge of our horses. My little cousin Rosa, as we always called her, received me with smiles as I delivered Flora's package, and gave her the message she had sent. She was a beautiful blue-eyed girl, with a rich colour, inheriting the naturally fair complexion of her father, with her mother's beauty; for Dona Maria was one of the prettiest of the young people in that part of the country—still looking almost like a girl. Without inquiring whether we would have them, she immediately ordered the usual refreshments, wine, cake, and fruit, with some cups of coffee, to be placed on the table; to which, after our ride, we did ample justice. Mr Laffan complimented Dona Maria on the fruits produced on the estate. Indeed, when I afterwards left my native valley, I learned to appreciate them, by comparison with the productions of other regions. Nothing, indeed, can surpass the flavour of the chirimoya, a fruit sometimes double the size of a cocoa-nut, tasting like a mixture of strawberries, cream, and sugar, with a fragrance far superior to any mixture. Then the caymato (in shape like a lemon, but far sweeter, with scarcely a touch of the acidity of the lemon), a species of lime, and the pomegranates, oranges, and strawberries, one of which was a mouthful, and figs unsurpassed in any other country. Then there was the mamei, a fruit as large as a water-melon, very nice, fresh, and not to be despised when preserved. Then there were several sorts of pine apples, and a variety of melons. Indeed, the climate of this region is especially favourable to the production of fruit, as the thermometer seldom falls below 68 degrees, and never rises much above 76 degrees. Then the wine and the lemonade were delightfully cooled by ice; an ample supply of snow being constantly brought down from the mountain of Purace, distant little more than a day's journey.

In a short time Don Ricardo came in, and welcomed us in a hearty, sailor-like fashion. He still retained his nautical manners and appearance, as well as his seamanlike habits. He was broad-shouldered, of moderate height, with a fine brow and an open countenance, and the light blue eye of the Anglo-Saxon. We always called him Uncle Richard, and he treated us as his nephews.

"You'll stop, now you have come," he said, shaking us all by the hand; "I've been looking for you for many a day. We must have some hunting and shooting. I will send over and let your father know that I have laid an embargo on you, so that he must not expect you until you appear. You can study as hard as you like in the evening, or whenever we are in the house, and Mr Laffan will give you lectures on natural history while we are on our excursions. Juan, mio amigo, you must remain also; we have plenty of room, and can hang up a dozen hammocks, or fifty for that matter; I have hooks provided on purpose in the hall."

FRUITS OF NEW GRANADA.

Juan did not even make a show of refusing, for fear that the invitation might not be pressed. I suspect that Uncle Richard was well aware of his admiration for Dona Dolores, who was a distant cousin of Dona Maria's. She was an only daughter, and heiress of a fair estate close to Egido.

Mr Laffan making no objection, Don Ricardo despatched a messenger, as he had promised, to our father, and we remained with clear consciences.

The house itself, I may here say, was a long low building, of two stories only in one portion, round which ran a broad verandah. It possessed no pretensions to architectural beauty, but was very neat and comfortable inside, and even elegant on the garden front.

DON RICARDO'S HOUSE.

Before dinner Don Ricardo took us out to see the gardens and farm. In the former, the fruits I have already described were growing in profusion, besides vegetables of all sorts. In one direction spread out fields of Indian corn of luxuriant growth. In the meadows were cattle and sheep with beautiful white fleeces and long tails, while numbers of horses were seen galloping about at liberty.

"I sincerely hope the Spaniards will not pay a visit to this place," observed Mr Laffan to me, as Uncle Richard and Juan were walking on ahead; "they would soon make a clean sweep of these cattle and the corn-fields."

This estate was only one of many others of a similar character scattered over the country, but probably Egido benefited by the energy and perseverance of its owner. My father used to remark, that Dona Maria was twice as rich as she would have been had she married a countryman with an estate double the size of her own. The people also were well looked after, having nice cottages, well thatched, and kept clean and tidy. Uncle Richard's plan was to go about giving prizes to those who had the best-kept huts. He had a school for the children, too, where they were taught to read the Bible, notwithstanding the objection at first raised by the parish priest— who was, however, at length induced to read it himself. He one day came to Uncle Richard and acknowledged it to be the best book for all who could read. Although the honest padre at first sided with the oppressors of his country, he now became an earnest Liberal, but avoided taking any open part in politics, and confined himself to instructing the people. Uncle Richard was no theologian, and had never had an argument in his life with Padre Vincente. His custom was simply to open the Bible and point to certain parts, and say, "Read that; if this book was written by God's command—and I am sure it was—that's what he says, not I." Padre Vincente might not have called himself a Protestant, but he certainly preached the gospel, and the people under his charge were the best conducted and happiest in the neighbourhood.

On our return to the house, we found dinner ready. Dona Maria, during our absence, had been busy superintending its preparation; and if the table did not groan with delicacies, the feast was as good a one as we could have desired to eat. Mr Laffan, Hugh, and I showed, at all events, that we enjoyed it, though Juan was unusually silent, and ate but little. There was something on his mind, which came out after dinner.

"Duncan," he said, "I want you and Señor Laffan to assist me in giving Dona Dolores a serenade, as soon as the shades of evening come on. You sing, and he plays the guitar. I understand that Dona Dolores is fond of music, although she tells me that I trifle away my time by practising it."

Uncle Richard laughed when Juan told him what he was going to do. "If I were a bachelor I would accompany you, although such kind of singing as yours is somewhat out of my way. I don't think, however, that the young lady would be charmed by 'Cease, rude Boreas,' 'One night it blew a hurricane,' 'On board of the Arethusa,' or such other songs as I used to sing afloat."

We had no difficulty in procuring a couple of guitars. Juan took one, Mr Laffan the other, and as soon as it began to grow dark we set out. We soon approached the front of Dona Dolores' residence. It was a two-storied building, with a balcony on one side overhanging the road some little way from the entrance-gate.

Juan and I were walking together, Mr Laffan bringing up the rear, when suddenly the former stopped and grasped my arm. "I see some one on the balcony," he whispered. "It must be she—how fortunate! She would consider it rude to go away when once we begin; let us lose no time."

We cautiously approached.

"Suppose it is only her old duenna, Señora Ortes!"

"Nonsense!" answered Juan. "I can discern the outline of her figure; no other form can possess such grace."

I thought that Juan's imagination assisted him in this respect, as I could only just distinguish that a female was seated on the balcony. As we drew near, however, I began to suspect that it was Dona Dolores herself, but her head at the time was turned away, as if addressing some one.

Stepping softly, so that we might not be discovered until we at once burst into song, we approached the house. Juan led the way; I kept close under the wall, having no guitar; while Mr Laffan stood at a little distance. Juan gave the signal, and we commenced the song. It was in praise of a lady resembling Dona Dolores in all particulars, and the love and devotion of one whose affection she had won, but appeared to regard with disdain.

Dona Dolores—for it was she—leaned her head on her hand as she listened to the music, which was such as to attract any female ear. I will not speak of my own powers; but Juan's voice was full and rich—indeed, he was one of the best singers I ever heard; and Mr Laffan did his part on the guitar.

We had continued for some time, when Dona Dolores leaned forward and said, "I will not pretend to be ignorant as to who you are. You desire to speak with me; and I am willing to see you. You are welcome to come in, with your young friend, whose voice I recognise."

THE SERENADE

Don Juan poured out his thanks, and expressed his readiness to take advantage of the permission given him.

Dona Dolores had said nothing of Mr Laffan; perhaps she had not perceived him, or in the dark had mistaken him for me, as I had been concealed under the wall—although our figures were very different. At all events, it was very evident that he would be one too many. Of this he was perfectly well aware himself, and as we went round to the front entrance he whispered,—"I'll go back and tell Don Ricardo that you have the honour of an interview, and will soon return;" and without another word he hastened along the road.

We made our way to the front gate, which was opened as we arrived by Señora Ortes, who had been directed by her mistress to let us in.

"Dona Dolores awaits you in her sitting-room," she said; "you are welcome."

She led the way into the house. We found Dona Dolores with a female friend, somewhat older, seated in a well-furnished room, with a couple of guitars on a sofa beside them. Some books were on a table, very seldom to be seen in a lady's apartment in that country; while one of the walls was ornamented with swords and daggers, guns and pistols—giving a somewhat odd appearance to a lady's boudoir.

Dona Dolores looked handsomer than ever, and I could not be surprised that she had won my friend's heart. She smiled as we approached and saluted her. Don Juan having told her where we were staying, and a little ordinary conversation having taken place, they both looked, I thought, as if they wished that the other lady and I were at a distance. We, at all events, supposing such to be the case, retired to the other end of the room, to examine some artificial flowers, which the young lady told me she had learned to make at the nunnery of the Encarnacion at Popayan. She then confided to me that she had once intended to be a nun, but, after a little experience of a conventual existence before she had taken the vows, thought better of it, and had returned to her friends; adding, "And perhaps some day I may accept a husband, should a suitable one be presented to me."

While we were speaking, she saw my eye directed towards the arms on the walls.

"They are all in good order, and intended to be used," she observed. "My friend thinks it a good place to keep them in, as no one would imagine that they were placed there otherwise than for ornament. The time may come, however, and that before long, when they may do good service to our country."

Although my companion continued to speak, as if to engage my attention, I could not help hearing the conversation that was going on between Don Juan and Dona Dolores. In ardent tones he declared his love and devotion, and vowed that his happiness in life depended on her becoming his wife.

"I will not deny, Don Juan, that I return the love you bestow on me; but this arises from the weakness of my woman's nature. Notwithstanding this, I tell you that nothing shall induce me to marry a man who is not ready to sacrifice his life and property to obtain the enfranchisement of our beloved country from the tyrannical yoke of her oppressors. You have hitherto led an indolent life, regardless of the sufferings of our people. Not until I see you boldly come forward and nobly devote yourself to the cause of freedom, will I promise to become your wife. When that freedom has been won, and the Spaniards, the hated Godos, have been driven into the sea—"

"But that may not be for many years, my beloved Dolores!" exclaimed Don Juan; "am I to wait so long before I enjoy the unspeakable happiness of calling you mine?"

"If you and other young men of wealth and position in the country, who ought to set the example to other classes, hang back, that glorious object may never be accomplished, and I shall die a maiden;

for I swear to you I will never wed while our country remains enslaved," exclaimed Dona Dolores in a firm tone.

My companion's tongue here went rattling on at such a rate, that I did not hear what more was said for some time; but it was evident that Dona Dolores was expatiating on the duty of all patriots to struggle on, in spite of every difficulty, until the power of the Spaniards was overthrown.

At length Don Juan exclaimed,—"Your arguments have prevailed, Dona Dolores: from henceforth I will emerge from the useless life I have hitherto led, and will devote my life to the cause of Freedom. You shall have no reason to complain of your pupil. I trust that you will hear of such deeds as you would have me do; and you may be sure that I shall ever be found in the van of the battle, when the foe are to be encountered. Your approval, and the reward I look for, will spur me on to acts of valour."

As he spoke I looked round. Dona Dolores had given him her hand, which he was pressing to his lips; and I heard her say,—"I will trust you, Juan; and you may rest assured that I will not depart from my promise."

As my companion had no longer any excuse for remaining where we were, she returned to the side of her friend. Dona Dolores had taken up her guitar, and running her fingers over the strings, sang a few verses of a patriotic song, which greatly affected Juan, and at the same time roused in my heart a desire to take a part in the struggle for freedom in which all classes throughout the country were eager to engage. It was well-known that, when once it began, it would be to the knife, as the Spanish generals showed no mercy to those who fell into their power—neither sex, rank, nor age were spared. As we spoke of the atrocities which had been committed, the eyes of Dona Dolores flashed fire. She pressed her lips together, and looked towards the wall on which the weapons hung.

"Every man and youth—ay, every woman who has a spark of patriotism—must take a part in the glorious work!" she exclaimed.

Rising from her seat, she took a sword from the wall. "Here, my Juan, let me gird you with this weapon; and when once you draw it, swear that it shall never again be sheathed until the standard of Liberty waves throughout the length and breadth of the land, and every Spaniard is hurled into the ocean which bore him to our shores."

Don Juan, kissing the jewelled hilt of the weapon, swore as Dolores wished, and with a triumphant smile she buckled it to his waist.

My enthusiasm being aroused, I dare say I too looked as if I wished to be presented with a sword.

"You must wait a while," observed Dona Dolores, divining my thoughts; "you are not yet your own master, and I would not compromise your excellent father."

The remark showed that the speaker possessed good sense and judgment as well as patriotism.

At last I reminded Juan that Don Ricardo would be expecting us, and we took our leave of the two ladies—my admiration for Dona Dolores greatly increased by the visit we had paid her.

I expected that Juan would break out enthusiastically in her praise, but he did not utter a word during our walk home; his thoughts were evidently occupied by the new duties he had undertaken. He had hitherto passed his time in superintending his mother's estate, or enjoying such amusements as offered. He would now have to lead a life full of dangers and hardships.

"I congratulate you on finding Dona Dolores at home," observed Uncle Richard when we arrived.

"Yes, we had that honour," said Juan, endeavouring to hide the sword which he had received—he had given me his to carry. I observed that he placed it carefully against the wall, and covered it with his cloak.

DOÑA DOLORES

Supper was now announced, but Juan spoke very little during the meal. Mr Laffan, however, conversed for all the party; rattling away, as he could do when he had had a glass or two of good wine to raise his spirits, and listening, apparently with rapt attention, to Uncle Richard's sea stories and jokes, though he had heard them fifty times before. Dona Maria, too, spoke English very fairly, having learned it from her husband; and Juan could understand what was said, though he was bashful about speaking.

We retired at an early hour to our hammocks, as we were to start betimes the next morning, on our expedition.

Chapter Three.

A shooting expedition—Snaring parroquets—The dominie and the tiger-cat—A deer shot—The dominie proves that he is a man of courage—Blow-pipes and poisoned arrows—A jaguar hunt—Stories about jaguars—A fearful thunderstorm—The stricken tree—Reach home—A discussion on Liberty—Set out on a second expedition—Reach a hot spring—Visit to an old Cacique—The last of his race—Promises to aid the Patriot cause—Vinegar river—The dominie tastes the water—Uncle Richard's farm—Return homewards—Paul Lobo meets us with bad news—Our night-ride to Popayan—Dona Dolores enlists the dominie—We reach Popayan—Arrangements made for the safety of our family—The dominie and I remain with my father.

I was in doubt whether Juan would accompany us. When I asked him, he replied that he wished to have some conversation with Don Ricardo, and that he should have an opportunity of speaking to him as we rode along. Leaving our own horses in the stable, we were supplied instead with active little mules, better calculated for climbing up and sliding down the steep declivities. We had a dozen couples of dogs, not quite as large as greyhounds, but of the same species.

"They will run down any of the wild animals found in these forests, as well as the danta, or wild ass—the black bear, red leopard, tiger-cat, the deer, and fox; though it is necessary to follow them closely, since, not being well broken-in, they will devour their prey, if they have an opportunity, before the hunter comes up," observed Uncle Richard, as we were about to start, our canine companions barking and yelping round us.

We had not gone far when we saw an Indian in a large field of maize near the road, engaged in snaring the red-headed, green parroquets, which are here very numerous, and do much mischief to the crops of corn. The snares are very simple, being composed of a line of horsehair, a slip-knot, and a loop, in the centre of which a little maize is sprinkled as a bait. As soon as the bird pitches on the grain, the Indian draws the line with a sudden jerk, and catches the bird by the legs. Just as we arrived he had caught one, which Hugh cried out he should like to have. On this the man brought it to him; but the bird fought so vigorously to obtain its liberty, and gave Hugh so severe a bite on the finger, that he was glad to let it go.

We had dismounted in order to enjoy a draught of water from a fountain which bubbled out of the hill-side, and to pluck some oranges from a grove irrigated by it. Mr Laffan had gone to a little distance, and we saw him stretching up to reach some fruit from a bough overhead, when he uttered a cry, or rather a howl to which an Irishman alone can give vent; and his foot slipping on a root which projected above the soil, down he came stretched at full length. But he was not inclined to lie long on the ground; and springing up, off he scampered. At the same instant a tiger-cat leaped out of the tree; while a covey of partridges, which had been nestling in the grass close by, rose with a loud "wurr," still further alarming the dominie.

"Get your guns! get your guns!" he shouted. "There's a huge tiger, or a jaguar, or a beast of some sort, close at our heels; he'll be after seizing some of us, if we are not on our guard."

As he spoke we saw the tiger-cat, quite as much frightened as Mr Laffan, scampering off in the opposite direction; and a hearty laugh, in which we all indulged, assured our friend that no danger was to be apprehended. Before we could get our guns ready, both partridges and tiger-cat had disappeared.

The air was pure and invigorating, and the scenery, made up of forests, mountains, and streams, was magnificent.

At length the dogs found a deer, to which, as it started off along the side of the hill, we all gave chase. Over fallen logs, gullies, and streams we galloped, finding it no easy matter to keep up with our nimble four-footed companions. Juan was the most active among us; holding his rifle in his hand ready for a shot, he at length got ahead. I saw him lift his weapon and fire, and as he did so the deer leaped several feet in the air and fell over dead. We soon had it flayed and cut up, when it was placed on the back of one of the mules brought for the purpose.

Several other deer were started, and I had the satisfaction of killing one with my own rifle; but Juan was the most successful.

The dominie, although he did not at first quite recover his nerve, had before long an opportunity of displaying his skill and courage. The dogs, which were ahead, were heard barking loudly.

"That's not deer," observed Uncle Richard; "it must be some savage animal at bay."

We were hurrying forward—having, I should have said, dismounted from our mules—the dominie on this occasion leading, when, with a loud roar, a huge jaguar leaped from its covert, scattering the dogs on either side, and making directly toward us. Mr Laffan, dropping on his knee, and holding his rifle like an infantry soldier about to receive a charge of cavalry, waited until the jaguar was within twelve yards of him, when he fired. The creature bounded on, and I trembled for our friend's safety; but in an instant, rising, he sprang on one side, and drawing his hunting-knife he struck it into the shoulder of the savage animal, right up to the hilt, when the jaguar rolled over with one convulsive struggle and was dead.

We all congratulated the dominie on his skill and coolness.

"I'm not in the habit of howling when I see a beast, but I was just now thinking to pick an orange, when the tiger-cat sprang at my throat. Faith! it was a little more than I bargained for," he answered, laughing.

"It is certainly what any of us would have done; though few would have met a jaguar with the same coolness as you have exhibited," observed Uncle Richard.

AN INDIAN SPORTSMAN

We arrived at length at a neatly-thatched cottage near a hacienda, belonging to a farmer who employed Indians chiefly in the cultivation of his fields. He was absent, but an old Indian who had charge of the house begged us to enter and consider it as our own. As the sun was high and the heat increasing, we were glad to find shelter beneath its roof. Here we spread the viands which had been brought in a pannier on the back of one of the mules.

Several of the Indians possessed blow-pipes, from which they projected arrows not more than eight inches in length; and with these we saw them bring down a number of parroquets and other birds in rapid succession. Scarcely had a bird been touched than, after fluttering for a few moments, it fell dead. The arrows, we found, were poisoned; and the Indians told us that the poison was produced from the moisture which exudes from the back of a small green frog. They declared that, to obtain it, the frog was put near a fire, and in the moisture which quickly appeared on its back they dipped the tips of their arrows. So speedy is the poison, that even a jaguar or puma which has received the slightest wound soon becomes convulsed and dies. Instead of feathers, a little cotton is wrapped neatly round the lower end of the arrow, to make it go steadily through the air: and at about an inch from the point it is spiral.

The major-domo told us that the farm, being at a distance from others, was frequently attacked by jaguars, which carried off pigs, calves, and sometimes even mules, although horses and the larger animals were generally too wary for them. He took us to a remote spot, to show us a trap which had been set for catching the jaguars. It was in a small circular plot of ground, enclosed with strong stakes of considerable height, to prevent the entrapped jaguar from breaking through or leaping over. A doorway is left for the jaguar to enter. Above this is suspended a large plank of wood communicating with one on the ground, over which the jaguar on entering must tread, and it is so contrived that as he does so the portcullis falls and shuts him in. A live pig is fastened by a rope in the centre of the enclosure as a bait. An Indian is always on the watch at night in a tree near the spot, and the moment the jaguar is caught he gives the alarm, and his companions assemble and despatch it with firearms and lances. Previous to our visit, a male and female jaguar had been caught together, but before the labourers could assemble they had almost eaten up the poor pig.

As we had already as much venison as we could carry, we agreed that we should like to go out with the old Indian factor, Quamodo, and hunt jaguars under his guidance, with as many of his people as he could collect. By the time luncheon was over, therefore, he had provided a party of Indians, armed with long lances, and a number of sturdy-looking dogs very unlike our own high-bred animals— which, being unfit for the purpose, were left behind under the charge of their keepers.

We proceeded some distance through the forest, the dogs advancing in regular order like riflemen skirmishing, so that there was no chance of a jaguar being passed without their discovering him. After keeping on for about a couple of miles, the dogs stopped and began to bay loudly; whereupon the old Indian told us to halt, with our arms ready for action, while the lance-men moved forward. The dogs, encouraged by their masters' voices, continued to advance; and we soon caught sight of a jaguar thirty yards in front of us, seated on his haunches, prepared for fight. Several of the more daring dogs now sprang forward, but two paid dearly for their boldness; for the jaguar striking them with his huge paw, they soon lay dead at his feet. The Indians now allowed the dogs to attack the jaguar. Taught wisdom by the fate of their companions, however, they assaulted him in the rear, rushing in on his haunches, biting him, and then retiring. This continued for some time. Although the jaguar saw the men, he had first to settle with his canine enemies; and the efforts he made to keep them at a distance apparently considerably exhausted him. The Indians then shouted and threw sticks towards him, in order to irritate him and make him spring upon them; and having got up to within twenty yards of him, they next presented their lances in such a position that, when he might spring, they would receive him on the points. Suddenly he began to move; then he sprang, moving in a semicircular line, like a cat and uttering a tremendous roar. The lance-men kept their bodies bent, grasping their lances with both hands, while one end rested on the ground. I thought that the jaguar would have killed the man at whom he sprung, but the Indian was strong of nerve as well as of limb, and the point of his lance entered the jaguar's chest, when the others immediately rushed forward and despatched the savage brute with their weapons.

Old Quamodo told us how it sometimes happens that a hunter unfortunately fails to receive the jaguar on his lance; and in many instances he is torn to pieces before he can be assisted. His only resource on such an occasion is his manchette, or long knife, —by means of which, if he can stab the jaguar, he may possibly escape. Quamodo also narrated how, upon one occasion in his youth, when he was very fond of jaguar hunting, he only slightly wounded an animal with his lance, and the jaguar, closing with him, knocked him down with his paw. Keeping his presence of mind, however, he drew his long knife with one hand, while he seized the throat of the jaguar with the other. A desperate struggle ensued, and he received several severe wounds from the claws and teeth of the creature. As he rolled over and over he made good use of his knife, stabbing his antagonist until the jaguar sank down dead from loss of blood. He managed to crawl home, and recovered. He declared that as soon as he was well again he went out hunting, and killed a couple of jaguars, in revenge for the injuries he had received.

On another occasion, while out hunting, he fell asleep on a bank, exhausted by fatigue. Suddenly he was awakened by a tremendous blow on the side of the head. His natural impulse was to start up and shout lustily, when he saw a huge jaguar standing close to him, about to repeat the salute. His cries were heard by his companions, who were at a short distance, and they hastened to his assistance. The jaguar, however, was probably not very hungry, for before he could use his manchette, or his friends come up, the creature bounded off, leaving the hunter with the top of his ear torn away, and an ugly scratch on his head. Still the old Indian was of opinion that the jaguar seldom attacks human beings unless first molested by them.

We encountered and killed another animal, much in the same way as the first; and having secured their skins, we returned to the farm, and afterwards set off on our way home. As we emerged from the forest we saw that clouds of inky blackness were collecting rapidly overhead, and spreading across the whole valley.

"We must push forward, for we are about to have a storm, and no slight one," observed Uncle Richard. "Fast as we may go, however, we shall not escape the whole of it."

Scarcely had he spoken when a flash of the most vivid lightning darted from the sky, wriggling along the ground like a huge snake.

"It's well that we are in the open country; but even here we may be overtaken by one of those flashes—though Heaven grant that they may pass us by," said Uncle Richard.

The flashes were succeeded by the most tremendous roars of thunder, as if the whole artillery of heaven were being discharged at once. The animals we rode stopped and trembled, and when urged by the spur dashed forward as if running a race for their lives; indeed, it was no easy matter to sit them, as they sprang now on one side, now on the other. In a short time the rain came down in torrents, every drop, as the dominie declared, "as big as a hen's egg." As a natural consequence, in a few seconds we were wet to the skin, though that mattered but little.

While we were passing a lofty and magnificent tree, about fifty yards off, a flash darted from the sky, and a fearful crash was heard. The next instant the tree was gone, shivered to the very roots, while the fragments of its branches and trunk strewed the ground around. No shelter was at hand; indeed, unless to escape the rain, it would have been useless, for the strongest building would not have secured us from the effects of such a flash. Our great object was to keep away from any trees which might attract the lightning.

The storm was still raging when we arrived at home, where we found Dona Maria and Rosa in no small alarm about us,—thinking more of our safety than their own. They had closed all the windows and doors—as they said, to keep the lightning out; although in reality it only prevented them from seeing the bright flashes. The trembling mules were sent round to the stables; while Uncle Richard produced various articles from his wardrobe with which to clothe us.

The ladies laughed heartily as we made our appearance at the supper-table. Hugh was dressed with one of Rosa's petticoats over his shoulders, which she declared gave him a very Oriental look. The dominie had on a flowered dressing-gown of Uncle Richard's, with a pair of loose drawers, and a sash round his waist. Juan wore a red shirt, a sky-blue dress coat, and a pair of shooting breeches; while I was rigged out in an entire suit belonging to our host, a world too wide, and much too short.

The storm had by this time ceased, though the thunder, as it rolled away down the valley, was occasionally heard.

The ladies were amused by the account of our adventures, especially on hearing of the alarm of Mr Laffan at the unexpected appearance of the tiger-cat Uncle Richard having proposed music, Dona Maria and Rosa got their guitars and sang very sweetly.

"Now let us have a dance," cried our host, jumping up; "old Pépé plays the fiddle, and we have another fellow who is an adept with the pipes."

The persons named were sent for. The first was a grey-headed old man, half Spaniard, half Indian; the latter a young man, a pure-blooded Indian. The merry strains they struck up inspired us all; even the dominie rose and began to snap his fingers and kick his heels. Don Ricardo setting the example, we were soon all engaged in an uproarious country dance; while every now and then we burst into laughter, as we looked at each other, and criticised our costumes.

Pretty well tired out, we soon turned into our hammocks, Uncle Richard having proposed another excursion on the following day.

On getting up in the morning, we found all the females of the family already on foot, busily engaged in various household duties. Dona Maria, habited in a somewhat *dégagé* costume, was superintending the baking of Indian corn bread, which was done in the most primitive fashion. Some of the girls were pounding the grain in huge mortars with pestles, which it required a strong pair of arms to use; others were kneading large masses of the flour in pans, which were then formed into flat cakes, and placed on a copper "girdle" with a charcoal fire beneath, where they were quickly baked. They gave us some of the cakes to stay our appetites, just hot from the "girdle," and most delicious they were.

Having taken a turn round the fields, where the labourers were assembling to commence work, we returned to an early breakfast. As Mr Laffan had seen but little of the country, Uncle Richard proposed that we should visit some interesting places in the neighbourhood. Juan excused himself; he very naturally wished to pay his respects to Dona Dolores, and soon afterwards rode off.

"He is desperately in love, there's no doubt about that," remarked Dona Maria. "Dolores will make much of him, for she is equally attached to him, though she will not acknowledge it. She is a fine spirited girl—a devoted Patriot. She converted her father, who was rather disposed to side with the Godos for the sake of a quiet life; but she roused him up, and he is now as warm in the cause of liberty as she is."

"Are you not a Patriot, Aunt Maria?" I asked.

"I side with my husband, and he is an Englishman."

"But Englishmen love liberty and hate tyranny, if they are worthy of the name of Britons," I answered; "and I hope we shall all be ready, when the time comes, to fight for freedom."

"But we may lose our property and our lives, if the Spaniards prevail," she remarked.

"They must not prevail; we must conquer!" exclaimed Uncle Richard, who just then came in.

HOUSEHOLD DUTIES.

"Has Dona Dolores won you over?" asked Dona Maria of her husband.

"She is a noble creature, and sees things in their true light," answered Uncle Richard. "While the Spaniards have the upper hand, through keeping the people in subjection by their soldiers, and their minds in darkness and superstition through the teaching of the priests, our country can never flourish. All progress is stopped. Our agriculture is stunted, our commerce crippled, and no manufactures can exist."

"That's just what Dona Dolores says," observed Aunt Maria.

"And she says the truth," answered Uncle Richard. "I for one am resolved to aid the Patriot cause; and you, my dear wife, will acknowledge that I am acting rightly. You cannot wish to see our children slaves; and what else can they be, if, for fear of the consequences, we tamely submit to the yoke of Spain?"

I remembered this conversation in after-days, when Uncle Richard showed how fully he kept up to the principles he professed, and Dona Maria proved herself to be a true and faithful wife.

After Uncle Richard had transacted some business, we set off on our expedition, mounted on mules, for the road we had to traverse was rough and uneven in the extreme. We had several small rivers to cross, which, in consequence of the storm of the preceding day, had become torrents, and almost carried our mules off their legs. The beds of the streams, too, were full of large stones, which had fallen down from the mountains. In these torrents swimming is of no avail, as the water rushes on with irresistible force, carrying everything before it. Sometimes in the descent of the hills the mules sat on their haunches, gliding down with their fore-feet stretched out in the most scientific fashion.

At length, sliding down a steep descent, we arrived at the hot spring, which issues from an aperture about three feet in diameter, at the bottom of the valley—the water bubbling up very much like that in a boiling pot. Around the brink of the aperture is an incrustation of brimstone, of a light colour, from which we broke off several pieces and carried them away. The dominie put in his finger to test the heat of the water, but drew it out again pretty quickly.

"You will not find me doing that a second time!" he exclaimed, as he put his scalded finger into his mouth to cool it.

We had brought some eggs, which were boiled hard in little more than three minutes.

Mr Laffan having carried away some of the water, afterwards analysed it, and found it to be composed of sulphur and salt. On being exposed to the sun, the sulphur evaporated, and left pure white salt fit for use.

After leaving the spring, we continued some way further towards the Rio Vinaigre, or Vinegar River. On our road we passed several Indian huts perched on the summits of precipices which appeared perfectly inaccessible; but, of course, there were narrow paths by which the inhabitants could climb up to their abodes. They naturally delight in these gloomy and solitary situations, and had sufficient reasons for selecting them: for they were here free from the attacks of wild beasts or serpents, and also from their cruel masters the Spaniards, who were accustomed to drag them away to work in the mines, to build fortifications, or to serve in the ranks of their armies.

Dismounting, we climbed up a zig-zag path, to pay a visit to one of these Indian abodes which was less difficult to reach than the rest, although a couple of well-armed men, supplied with a store of rocks, could from the summit have kept a whole army at bay. The hut was the abode of an old Indian, the descendant of the chief of a once powerful tribe. We found him leaning against the sunny side of his house, and holding on to a long staff with which he supported himself. He was dressed in a large broad-brimmed hat, a poncho over his shoulders, and sandals on his feet. His projecting, dropping lower jaw exhibited the few decayed teeth he had in his head, which, with his lustreless eyes, made him look the very picture of decrepitude. He brightened up and rose, however, as he saw Uncle Richard,—with whom he was acquainted, and who had frequently shown him kindness,—and welcomed us to his abode.

The thatched hut was diminutive, and full of smoke, as there was but one small hole in the roof by which it could escape. Some distance behind it, and separated by a wide chasm, over which a bamboo bridge had been thrown, was a wide level space, with mountains rising above it, on which sheep and goats were feeding—the fields fenced round by a shrub called el lechero, or milk-tree, which derives its name from a white liquid oozing out of it when a branch is broken off. This liquid, however, is sharp and caustic. The sticks, about six feet in height, throw out young shoots like the osier, and when pruned become very thick, and form an excellent fence. Within the enclosure were growing patches of wheat, potatoes, and Indian corn, as also the yuca root, from the flour of which palatable cakes are formed. This mountain plantation was cultivated, the old man told us, by the faithful followers of his tribe. He had no children; he was the last of his race.

Uncle Richard had an object in paying the visit. The old Indian had considerable influence over the inhabitants of the surrounding hills, and he wished to stir them up, when the time should come, to join the Patriot ranks.

"I am too old myself to strike a blow for liberty," said the old man; "but often, as I gaze over yonder wide valley, and remember that once it belonged to my ancestors, that by the cruelty and oppression of the Godos my people are now reduced to a handful, and that the sufferings and death of thousands of my people rest on the heads of our oppressors, my heart swells with indignation. Si, Señor Ricardo, si. You may depend on me that I will use all the influence I possess to arouse my people, but I fear that we shall be able to send scarce fifty warriors into the field—many of them mere youths, although they have the hearts of men."

After some further conversation, Uncle Richard left a present with the old cacique, and we bade him farewell.

AN AGED INDIAN

On reaching the foot of the cliff we met several Indians, who, having observed us from neighbouring heights, had come down to ascertain the object of our visit. Uncle Richard spoke to them, although not so openly as he had done to the chief. The men had a peculiarly serious cast of countenance; not one of them smiled while with us, but they appeared good-tempered, and were perfectly civil. Their eyes were large, fine, and full of expression; and two or three girls who were of the party were decidedly good-looking, which is more than can be said of Indian maidens in general. Each man was accompanied by a dog, of which he seemed very fond. Round their huts we saw abundance of fruit, and several fat pigs, so that they were evidently well off for provisions.

It is wonderful how long these Indians will go without food by chewing coca leaf, which is far more sustaining and refreshing than tobacco.

"Those men would make sturdy soldiers, and fight bravely," observed Uncle Richard, as we rode away.

Our destination was a small valley, through which the Rio Vinaigre makes its way towards the Cauca. We left our animals at the top of the hill, as the descent was so steep and slippery that it would have been impossible to ride down it. As it was, we could scarcely keep our legs, and the dominie more than once nearly fell head over heels.

Uncle Richard, by-the-by, had not told our worthy friend the character of the river-water. He had brought a cup, formed from a gourd, which answered the purpose of a "quaich," as it is called in Scotland; and we made our way down to the edge of the stream, where he could dip out a cupful. The water appeared bright and sparkling, and the dominie, who was thirsty after his walk, put it to his lips and took a huge gulp. Directly afterwards he spat it out, with a ridiculous grimace, exclaiming—

"Rotten lemons, iron filings, and saltpetre, by all that is abominable! Ah, faith! there must have been poison in the cup."

THE WATERFALL

"Wash it out and try again," said Uncle Richard; "although, I tell you, I believe the cup is perfectly clean."

The dominie made a second attempt, with the same result.

"You find it taste somewhat like vinegar?" asked Uncle Richard.

"Indeed I do," answered Mr Laffan. "Is it always like this?"

"Yes," said Uncle Richard; "it comes in its present state out of the mountain, and you were not far from the truth in your description, as when analysed it is found to be acidulated, nitrous, and ferruginous. So completely does it retain these qualities, that in the Cauca, several leagues below where it falls into that river, not a fish is to be found, as the finny tribe appear to have as great a dislike to it as yourself."

The dominie, to satisfy himself, carried away half a bottle, for the purpose of analysing it on his return home.

Proceeding up the valley, we visited, in succession, three waterfalls, one of which came down over a perpendicular cliff, with a descent of a couple of hundred feet. We then bent our steps homewards, stopping by the way to dine and rest our animals at a farm belonging to Uncle Richard, and which it was one of the objects of our excursion to visit. The building was entirely of wood, with wide projecting eaves, supported by posts united by a railing, which gave it a very picturesque appearance. Around the house was an enclosure for the poultry, of which there was a great profusion. Indeed, it would have been difficult for a hen-wife to know her hens. Outside this was another enclosure for cattle and horses. In a smaller paddock were several llamas, which are not indigenous to this part of the country. They had been brought from Upper Peru, where they are used as beasts of burden, and were here occasionally so employed. It was a pretty rural scene.

"It's lovely, it's lovely! In truth, it reminds me of Old Ireland, barring the palm-trees, and the cacti, and the chirramoyas, and the Indian corn, and those llama beasts," exclaimed Mr Laffan. Then looking at the Indian women who were tending the poultry, he added, "And those olive damsels. Ah, young gentlemen, you should see my own fair countrywomen, and you would acknowledge that through the world you couldn't meet any beings so lovely under the blue vault of heaven—whatever there may be above it in the form of angels; and they are as modest as they are good."

Mr Laffan continued to expatiate on the perfections of green Erin's Isle, its mountains, lakes, and rivers, a theme in which he delighted, until his eyes glistened, and his voice choked with emotion, as he thought of the country he might never again see.

Uncle Richard having inspected the farm, and examined some of the horses, we mounted our animals and proceeded homewards. We were approaching the house, when we caught sight of Paul Lobo galloping towards us from the direction of Popayan.

"What is the matter?" exclaimed Uncle Richard, observing his excited manner.

A RURAL SCENE

"El señor doctor want to see you, Massa Duncan, in quarter less no time. Says he, You Paul Lobo, get on horseback and bring him here."

The horse stood panting for breath, its nostrils covered with foam, showing at what a rate he must have ridden.

"Why does he want to see me?" I asked anxiously. "Is he ill, or my mother or Flora?"

"No, no! dey all berry well; but el señor doctor got news from Cauca, and berry bad news too. De Spaniards enter dere, and cut de t'roats ob all de men 'cept what ride or run away, and de women as bad, and dey come on quick march to Popayan; do de same t'ing dere, no doubt."

"That is indeed bad news," I said. "We will get our horses and return home to-night; they are fortunately fresh. You must change horses, Paul, and go with us, after you have had some food."

"We must endeavour to oppose them, if it can be done with any chance of success," exclaimed Uncle Richard, who had just then come up. "I will accompany you, Duncan, and ascertain what your father advises. We will let Señor Monteverde and Dona Dolores know, in case they may not have received the information."

We immediately entered the house, and Uncle Richard sent off a messenger to the Monteverdes, where he supposed Juan would be found.

While we had dinner, and prepared for our ride, Paul took some food, and was again ready to start when the horses were brought round.

Dona Maria was much agitated on hearing the news. "Do nothing rash, my dear Richard," she said to her husband. "It is impossible to withstand the Godos."

"Nothing is impossible to brave men fighting in a just cause," answered Uncle Richard.

Embracing his wife and Rosa, to whom we had already bidden farewell, he joined us in the courtyard, where we sat our horses ready to start. We had a long ride before us in the dark, the road being none of the best, but our steeds were sure-footed, and we were well accustomed to them.

We had got to some distance, when we heard the tramp of horses coming along a road which led from the Monteverdes' house, and Dona Dolores, with her father and four domestics, all armed, came up. She sat her steed, as far as I could judge in the fast gathering gloom, like a person who had thorough command over it. She rode up to me, as if desirous of speaking; and I took the opportunity to inquire for my friend Juan, observing that he had not returned to Don Ricardo's.

"He has gone home to commence the career which, I trust, he will from henceforth follow," she replied. "He will endeavour to raise and arm the men on his property, as well as others from the surrounding villages. We were already aware that the Spaniards were advancing up the valley, and had been engaged in sending information in all directions to arouse the Patriots, and to counsel them to take up arms in defence of their homes and families. We may count on you, Señor Duncan? Young as you are, you may render essential service to our glorious cause, though your arm may not yet be strong enough to wield a sword."

"I believe I could make very good use of one, if necessary," I answered, somewhat piqued by her remark. "Juan would tell you that I can hold my own, even against him."

"I am glad to hear it," she observed.

"We must not count the cost, dear as that may be," I said; "but I shall be ready to yield up my life, and everything I possess, could I be sure that victory would be gained by the sacrifice."

"We may count on you, then, as a Patriot?"

"Yes, most certainly, as you can on Don Ricardo."

"And upon your tall tutor? I don't know his name."

I told her his name, and she immediately rode up alongside Mr Laffan. We were ascending a hill too steep to gallop up, which enabled us to hold this conversation. What the patriotic young lady said to the dominie I did not at the time know, but, whatever his previous sentiments were, her enthusiastic eloquence soon won him to the cause she had espoused.

On reaching the level ground, we galloped forward as hard as our horses could go, led by Uncle Richard. Our worthy tutor kept by the side of Hugh, about whom he seemed to have no little anxiety; but my young brother sat his horse as well as any of us, and assured Mr Laffan that he need not be troubled about him. Dona Dolores, with her father, followed close behind Uncle Richard, and whenever we were obliged to pull up she spoke with her usual earnestness to one or other of the party, as if eager to make the best use of the time in impressing her ideas on others. She did not disdain to speak even to Paul Lobo.

"I do what massa el señor doctor does," was the reply.

She found, at last, that she could make nothing of Paul—who was, however, as great a lover of liberty as any of us.

Crossing the bridge, we at length entered the city, where the streets were even more quiet than usual. We scarcely met a single person as we rode up to our house. It was perhaps as well that we did not, for the appearance of so large a party might have roused the suspicions of some of the Spanish authorities.

My father came in from visiting a patient at the moment we arrived. Dona Dolores and Señor Monteverde had, I should have said, parted from us, and gone to the house of a friend. My father seemed somewhat surprised at seeing Uncle Richard with us, but said he was very glad that he had come. We found supper on the table waiting us; and as soon as the servants had withdrawn, my father addressed me, and told us the particulars of the news he had received.

"This city will not be a safe place for women and children, or any one else, in a short time," he observed. "Those who have duties to perform must remain at their posts. I have numerous patients whom I ought not to and will not desert. I therefore sent for you, Duncan, to take charge of your mother and sister, and to escort them to your Uncle Richard's, where you can watch over their safety. I know that I can rely on Mr Laffan to assist you."

"Indeed, sir, you may," he replied; "while I have an arm to strike a blow, I will fight for the ladies."

"I hope that while they are in my house they will run no risk, removed as it is from the city," said Uncle Richard; "and if you will entrust them to my keeping, I will take care of them, along with my wife and daughter. Duncan and Mr Laffan may be of use here."

Uncle Richard then began to tell my father the plans which had been formed for preventing the Spaniards from entering the city.

My father stopped him. "I desire not to be acquainted with anything that is going forward. It is my duty to endeavour to heal the sick and wounded, in the character of a physician and a non-combatant. I may remain unmolested, and be able to serve the cause of humanity. As for Duncan and Mr Laffan, I will reconsider my intentions. I will, however, accept your offer as regards my wife and Flora, and place them under your care."

It was finally arranged that my mother and sister, with their female attendants, and Hugh, should set off the next morning, escorted by Uncle Richard; and that Mr Laffan and I should remain until, in the course of events, it might be decided what was best to be done.

Chapter Four.

My mother and sister leave Popayan with Uncle Richard—
Mr Laffan and I accompany them—Lion given to me—Meet
Juan and his troop—Hear an inspiriting address from Dona
Dolores—A political ball at Don Carlos Mosquera's—Dona
Dolores warns me against Captain Lopez—She enlists
numerous recruits—The dominie shows that he has had
military experience—Drilling the levies—The citizens
employed in erecting fortifications—The enemy approach—
Preparations for the defence—The summons to arms—The
city attacked—Mr Laffan and I join Don Juan—The enemy
driven back—A sortie—The enemy attacked—Guns
captured—Return in triumph to the city.

During the night information was received that the Spaniards, two
days before, had entered Bouga, on the Cauca, leaving us in no
doubt that they were advancing up the valley, and might be
expected in our neighbourhood in the course of three or four days—
perhaps even their cavalry might appear sooner, as they probably,
thinking there was no force to oppose them, would push on ahead of
the main body. My father therefore kept to his resolution of sending
off my mother and sister; and the next morning at daylight, after a
hurried breakfast, the horses and mules were brought round to the
courtyard, ready to start. My mother and sister, and the female
attendants, rode the mules; the rest of the party were mounted on
horseback. It was settled that Mr Laffan and I should accompany
them to Egido, as we could without difficulty be back before
nightfall.

Our uncle, Dr Cazalla, came to see our mother off.

"I wish that you would accompany us, my dear brother," she said.
"If the Spaniards take the place, you are certain to be annoyed and
persecuted, even should no worse consequences follow."

"No, no; I must stay at my post, as your husband intends doing. We must set a good example. If the principal people run away, what may be expected of others?"

My mother's entreaties were of no avail, so Uncle Richard, finding that all was ready, gave the word to move on.

We proceeded as fast as the mules could travel, and by noon arrived at Uncle Richard's hacienda, where Aunt Maria and Rosa gave my mother a warm reception.

"We shall here, I trust, be safe from the Spaniards; but if we hear of their coming, we must take to the mountains, where even they will be unable to find us," said Dona Maria.

"But what will become of the house and estate?" asked my mother.

"We must leave that matter in God's hands," answered Dona Maria. "If the fruit trees are cut down, and the corn destroyed, he can restore them. The Godos cannot prevent that."

As soon as our horses had baited, the dominie and I prepared to start on our return. I embraced my mother and sister affectionately, and bade farewell to dear little Rosa and Aunt Maria. We knew not what might occur before we should meet again. I had, while staying at the house, admired a fine dog called Lion, which had grown from a puppy into a noble animal since I first saw him. The creature had taken a great fancy to me, too, and this had been observed by Uncle Richard.

"I make you a present of him, Duncan," said Uncle Richard; "he will prove faithful, I am sure, and may possibly be of service."

Lion was a species of hound, with a thick tawny coat and large paws, possessing prodigious strength. He was good-tempered and obedient, but at the same time it was very evident that he could fight desperately with those powerful jaws of his. Patting his head, I told him that he was to accompany us, and he seemed fully to understand me. The dominie was already mounted. Lion looked at Uncle Richard when he saw me getting on horseback, as if to ask if he was to go. Uncle Richard nodded, and pointed to me. So Lion set off, keeping close to my heels all the way, clearly understanding that I was in future to be his master.

Mr Laffan was as eager to get back to the town as I was, in order to hear the news. We were still about half a league from Popayan, when we saw, in an open space near a wood, a considerable body of men, some on horseback, others on foot, with flags fluttering above their heads. As we approached, one of them rode out to meet us, in whom I recognised Don Juan, though much changed in appearance. Instead of his civil garb he was dressed in military fashion, with a long lance in his hand, a carbine at his back, and pistols in his holsters.

"I have not been idle, you see, Duncan," he observed, after we had greeted each other. "I have raised fifty fine fellows, and hope to have a hundred more mounted and armed in a day or two. If every gentleman will do the same, we shall soon collect a Patriot force sufficient to drive back the Spaniards."

We rode forward with him to see his troop. The larger number were mounted, but there were some infantry armed with long guns—tall, sinewy fellows, dressed in broad-brimmed hats, loose trousers, and coats fastened by pouch belts round their waists. The horsemen also wore large sombreros, leggings and huge spurs, and tight-fitting jackets; and they were armed with spears and swords of various lengths. Some had pistols, others carbines, but the lance was the principal weapon.

We rode together into the town,—the infantry, who wore only sandals on their feet, keeping up with the horses. We were passing down one of the streets on our way to a convent which the authorities had turned into barracks, when a lady appeared at a balcony. Juan reined in his steed, and ordered his men to halt. I recognised Dona Dolores. My friend bowed low, with a look of pride on his countenance. Dona Dolores smiled, and addressed a few encouraging words to the men, reminding them of the cruelties which had often been inflicted by the hated Godos, urging them to fight bravely, and not to sheathe their swords until they had driven their foes into the sea. The men cheered, and Dona Dolores saying she would no longer delay them, we rode on.

The dominie and I parted from Juan at the next turning, and soon reached home. Finding that my father was just setting out to attend a large party given at the house of Don Carlos Mosquera, one of the principal inhabitants of the place, Mr Laffan and I hurriedly dressed and accompanied him. Though ostensibly a ball, the real object was to bring persons of Liberal principles together, of both sexes. As many of the upper classes took a warm interest in the cause of freedom, nearly all the ladies of the influential families were there, with their husbands and fathers. I was surprised, also, to see several parish priests, who were as warm in the cause as any other person. Indeed, one of these padres had donned a semi-military costume, and announced his intention of aiding his countrymen with his sword. Those who knew him best said that he could fight as well as he could preach.

I soon met Dona Dolores and her father. She smiled, and beckoned me to her.

"I was glad to see you just now with Don Juan, and I hope that you will obtain your father's leave to join his corps," she said.

I replied that I would gladly do so, but that at present my father wished me to remain with him at Popayan.

While we were speaking Don Juan joined us, when Dona Dolores complimented him on his zeal and activity in so soon getting together a body of men.

"We have got the men, the arms, and the horses, but we all require what cannot so readily be obtained—the necessary discipline," he answered. "I myself require to learn the duties of an officer, for, except that I can use a sword and lance, I know little of military affairs."

"You will soon learn, Juan," said Dona Dolores in encouraging tones; "you must obtain an expert instructor, and your own natural talents will point out to you how to act on most occasions."

Just then a military officer approached and bowed to Dona Dolores. I saw an expression of scorn pass over her countenance, unobserved by Juan, who, saluting the officer, addressed him as Captain Lopez.

"The very man I want," observed my friend. "I have just raised a body of men, who require to be disciplined. You have had experience; you must join me, if you do not already belong to a regiment."

I did not hear the answer given by Captain Lopez, but Dona Dolores, turning to me, said, "He is not to be trusted; a mean-spirited fellow, though a great boaster. You must tell Juan not to accept his services."

This Captain Lopez was, I afterwards found, a rejected suitor for the hand of Dona Dolores. With her clear perception, she had discovered that he did not possess the qualities she could admire.

Juan and Captain Lopez had gone to some distance, and were engaged in eager conversation. During this time several persons had come up and asked Dona Dolores to dance; but she declined, saying that she was in no mood for such an amusement. She contrived, however, to keep most of them by her side for some time, while she urged on them the duty of joining the Patriot cause. I left her surrounded by a number of gentlemen, and went to look after Juan, to whom I wished to repeat the remarks I had heard from Dona Dolores. I found him at length in an alcove, still talking with Captain Lopez. The captain's countenance, as I watched him at a little distance, impressed me very unfavourably. There was a scowl on his brow, and a peculiar wrinkle about his lips, which made me feel that I for one would not trust him; and I hoped that my friend would not be induced to do so either.

I waited until the captain quitted Juan, to whom I then went up, and told him what Dona Dolores had said.

"She is too probably right, for she has wonderful perception of character; but, unfortunately, I have engaged Captain Lopez to come and drill my men, and I cannot now well put him off without his considering himself insulted. However, I will remember the warning I have received, and not trust him too much. I intend to bear the whole expense of the corps myself, and am anxious to get some smart young officers. I wish that you would join us, Duncan. You would soon learn your duties; they come almost by instinct to some people."

"If I can get my father's leave, depend upon it I will," I answered; "and as Mr Laffan has seen some service, I have no doubt that he will assist you. Perhaps he himself will join. I suspect that he would be as well able to drill your corps as Captain Lopez."

Several gentlemen present had been engaged in raising men; and, I was told, there were already upwards of two thousand troops in town, though few of them were sufficiently disciplined to meet the enemy. Other Patriot leaders were scouring the country round to obtain recruits, and these, in small parties, were coming in during the night.

In spite of the serious aspect of affairs, the people at this ball danced as much as ever. The card-tables were also filled, but the players stopped very frequently, forgetting the game to discuss matters of importance. I understood that there were men on the watch at the doors, to give notice should any foes to the Liberal party make their appearance.

"I found, on our return home, that my father was pretty well satisfied with the enthusiasm exhibited by the people generally.

"Bloodshed I fear there must be, for the Spaniards fancy that they can overthrow liberty with a few blows, and are determined to stamp it out; but they are mistaken," he observed.

From dawn the next morning, till nightfall, the new levies were undergoing drill in the great square. I saw Juan at the head of his men, and Captain Lopez drilling them.

"Don't you think you can give my friend Juan a helping hand?" I said to Mr Laffan, who had accompanied me.

"Faith, it's not impossible!" he exclaimed, his eye brightening. "If he asks me, I'll try to brush up my knowledge of such matters."

I told Juan what the dominie had said, when he at once came forward and begged that he would take charge of a part of his men.

"Is it the cavalry or the infantry?" asked Mr Laffan.

"The cavalry are the most important," answered Juan. "Here is a spare horse at your service."

Mr Laffan at once leapt into the saddle, and going to the head of the men, formed them into line. To my surprise, he gave the proper orders in Spanish without hesitation, and soon showed that he had had no little experience as a cavalry officer. He kept the men at work for three hours without cessation, after which they were dismissed for breakfast. Captain Lopez cast a scowl at us as he passed on his way to his quarters, without deigning to compliment Mr Laffan on his proficiency. Juan accompanied us home to breakfast, and afterwards we returned to the square, when, to my surprise, the dominie took the infantry in hand, and drilled them for four hours in a still more thorough way even than he had done the cavalry.

"If we had but a few British sergeants and corporals, we should make something of these fellows in a few weeks," he observed. "I would be mightily obliged to the enemy if they would but wait till then; we should by that time be able to give a good account of them."

Don Juan, as might have been expected, begged Mr Laffan to join his corps, offering him the command of either of the companies.

"I am engaged to the doctor, and cannot quit his service unless he dismisses me," he answered; "but, while I have the opportunity, I will gladly drill your men for as many hours as they can stand on their legs. Some years have passed since I have done any soldiering, and it makes me feel young again to be so engaged."

While the levies were drilling, the townspeople—including old men, women, and children—were employed, under the few officers who had any knowledge of engineering, in throwing up batteries and forming entrenchments round the town. In some cases the walls were strengthened by the aid of a machine, consisting of a large square bottomless box, into which the mud was thrown, and then beaten down hard. A number of these boxes were used at a time, and it was extraordinary with what rapidity a strong wall could thus be erected. The mud was brought in carts, in baskets, and in various other ways, and thrown into the box. Additional strength was gained by forming a slope on the outer side. A number of guns buried on a former occasion by the Patriots, to conceal them from the Spaniards, were also dug up, and mounted. Night and day the people worked, for every hour gained added to the strength of the place, and increased the prospect of successfully resisting the enemy.

There were several known Royalists in Popayan, who had hitherto remained quiet; and many of them, on seeing the preparations made for the defence, hurriedly left the town. Many Liberals also sent off their families, to avoid the risk to which they would be exposed. Among the Royalists I met the Bishop of Popayan, Don Salvador Ximenes, mounted on a splendid horse, and attended by his secretary and several ecclesiastics—who, but for their hats, I should have taken for military officers, for they were all armed to the teeth, and had a decidedly martial aspect. My father knew the bishop well, while I had often seen him. Though a somewhat small man, he was remarkably well-made, and had a good-natured, open countenance, with sparkling grey eyes. His secretary was a tall, good-looking fellow, with a broad pair of shoulders, but bearded like a pard, and looking little like a priest; indeed, he had formerly been a captain of dragoons in Spain, until he followed the bishop out to South America. Don Salvador had been canon of the cathedral at Malaga when Buonaparte invaded Spain. On that occasion, throwing off his ecclesiastical garb, he had assumed the rank of a colonel, and by his preachings and exhortations he had aroused the Spanish peasantry to resist the French. On the restoration of Ferdinand the Seventh to the crown of Spain, the *ci-devant* colonel was created Bishop of Popayan, then in possession of the Spaniards, where he had made himself very popular among all ranks, notwithstanding his political opinions.

On meeting the martial-looking bishop and his companions, I felt sure that his departure foreboded no good to the Patriot cause. I bowed to him as I passed, and he gave me a nod of recognition, although he was well aware that I was not a member of his flock.

I at once rode on to Don Carlos Mosquera's house, to inform him of the departure of the bishop, should he not be acquainted with it.

"Let him go," he answered. "He will do more harm to liberty inside the town than he will do without; and we cannot imprison him. If he comes as an enemy, a bullet may put a stop to his intrigues."

I frequently met Dona Dolores on the parade-ground, riding a handsome horse, and attended by her father, Juan, and others. She on several occasions addressed the men, especially the new recruits, and urged them to be faithful to the noble cause in which they were engaged. She also occupied herself in writing to Patriots in various parts of the country, or to persons whom she hoped to win over.

While the citizens were working away in the town, scouts were sent out, that we might have early notice of the approach of the enemy. Several days elapsed, however, without any news of their approach, and this afforded time for fortifying the city and increasing the number of its defenders. So confident did the Patriots at length become, that it was proposed to march out and encounter the enemy in the open country; but wiser counsels prevailed. Our men were ill-disciplined, and we had no field-artillery.

A WALL-MAKING MACHINE

Upwards of a week had passed, when the scouts brought in the information that the Spaniards were advancing. Still two or three days must elapse before they could reach Popayan. The interval was spent in strengthening the fortifications, and otherwise preparing for the defence of the city. Provisions were brought in, and gunpowder and shot manufactured, while the drilling of the men went on as energetically as at first. White men, Indians, and blacks, all seemed to take a real pleasure in their duties. The army was certainly a motley one, both in costume and colour, composed as it was of men of every shade from white to black—the dark, however, predominating; several of the officers were black, and others had Indian blood in their veins, if they were not pure Indians. Where all fight for liberty, however, the only qualifications required for command are talent and courage. Not a few even of the highest rank could neither read nor write.

My father, I may here say, had half consented that I should join Don Juan's troop, and had given leave to Mr Laffan to act as he felt inclined.

The enemy had now got within three leagues of the city. Some deserters who came in—or rather, I should say, some Liberals who had made their escape from the Royalist ranks—informed us that they were not at all prepared for the resistance they would meet with, as they were not aware that the city was so strongly fortified and garrisoned.

Each night we went to bed expecting that the next day might be that of battle; but I was one morning awakened by hearing all the bells in the city ringing. I jumped up, and going to Mr Laffan's room, found him dressed, and in the act of buckling on his sword—afterwards sticking a brace of pistols in his belt.

"I intend to join Don Juan," he said; "if I fall, Duncan, you will not forget the instruction I have given you. Good-bye, my boy; do you stay quietly at home."

"Not if I can help it," I answered. "Wait but five minutes. My father will not refuse me permission to assist in defending the walls."

I was quickly ready, and came downstairs to find my father.

"You cannot let me play a girl's part and stay at home!" I exclaimed. "Do let me go."

"I am afraid I should not be right in hindering you. May Heaven protect you!" answered my father.

"Thank you, thank you," I replied, as if the greatest possible favour had been granted me; and I set off with Mr Laffan.

Mounting our horses, we rode to the lines, near which we found Juan's troops.

"I hope we shall have an opportunity of making a sortie," exclaimed the dominie; "we will put the Spaniards to the right-about if we get the chance of taking them in flank."

While our servants held the horses, we went into the nearest battery, from whence we could see the Spaniards advancing to the attack. By the way in which they came on, it was clear that they expected to enter an unwalled town; and our batteries were so concealed that the enemy did not discover their existence until close up to them, when we opened upon them with every gun at once. Their artillery replied, but their shot struck our embankments; while ours flew into the midst of their ranks, creating confusion and dismay. Their infantry, however, advanced, firing rapidly, and several of the defenders were hit; but this only increased the ardour of the rest. The whole south side of the city was a blaze of fire, both parties rapidly exchanging shots. The enemy, however, soon saw that this general style of assault would not succeed, and concentrated their efforts on the batteries defending the chief entrance; but again and again were they driven back.

I had gone with Mr Laffan towards the eastern side, when, by means of our glasses, we saw a large body of men, accompanied by artillery and cavalry, making their way round, intending apparently to attack the city on the other side. On my conveying the information to our general, Don Juan offered to lead out his men, and proceed by some by-paths through a wood, so as to fall suddenly on the flank of the force—hoping to capture the guns and put the enemy to flight. This offer was accepted.

"You will accompany me?" said Juan to the dominie and me.

"With all the pleasure in the world," was the answer; and in another moment we were riding out to the southward of the city—the part Juan had selected for the ambush. We were followed by a body of infantry, who were to support us, for without them we could not secure the fruits of our hoped-for victory.

The dominie was in the highest spirits, and could scarcely restrain himself from shouting out in his glee. Every now and then he gave a flourish with his sword, as if well acquainted with its use.

On we dashed, over all impediments—our light-footed infantry not far behind. We had just time to reach the wood where we were to remain concealed, and to give our horses breathing time, when we heard the approach of the Spaniards. We waited in perfect silence until their cavalry had passed, when, Juan giving the signal, we dashed out from our cover, taking them completely by surprise. The gunners were cut down, almost before they had time to draw their swords; after which we immediately charged upon the infantry, who, though they received us with an ill-directed fire, were at once thrown into confusion. Meantime the enemy's cavalry had wheeled about as fast as the narrowness of the road would permit them, and came charging down upon us to attempt to recapture the guns; but our infantry, who had now come up, poured in a hot fire, by which a third of their saddles was emptied. Unable to ascertain our numbers, they must have imagined that they were being attacked by a large force, and a panic seizing them, the survivors galloped off to the south, leaving their guns in our hands, while the infantry, whom we pursued, fled in disorder towards the main body. We followed, sabring all we overtook; when Mr Laffan advised Juan to return, lest an attempt might be made to retake the guns, the most important fruit of our victory. Our foot-soldiers, however, had in the meantime harnessed to them some of the slain troopers' horses, and when we got back we found they were already half-way to the city. In half an hour we were triumphantly entering it; and dragging the guns up to the batteries, we made use of them against their late owners.

In less than an hour after this the Spaniards were in full retreat. Patriotic shouts rose on all sides, and the bells rang forth joyous peals, while every man congratulated his neighbour on the victory gained.

Don Juan did not fail to receive a reward for his gallantry in the approving smiles of Dona Dolores. It was his first battle, and he had given proof that he was a brave and intelligent leader. Congratulations were offered him on every side, and all predicted that he would ere long become one of the chiefs of the Republic.

Chapter Five.

Aroused by alarm-bells—Country-houses seen on fire—
Anxiety about Uncle Richard's—Retreat of the Spaniards—
Mr Laffan and I ride out to Egido—Find the Monteverdes'
house burned to the ground—Egido destroyed—What has
become of the inmates?—Proceed in search of them—No
tidings—Inquire of some peasantry—Obtain recruits—
Pursued by Spanish cavalry—Almost overtaken—We reach
the town—Juan chases the Spaniards—Fresh troops arrive—
Anxiety about our family and Uncle Richard's—Paul Lobo
sets out to find them—We hear that the Fastucians, headed
by the Bishop of Popayan, are advancing to attack us—Our
army marches to meet them—The Bishop sends a flag of
truce proposing terms—I and others accept an invitation to
dine with the Pastucian officers—Fearful treachery—Captain
Pinson and my other companions killed—I leap from the
window and mount my horse—A ride for life.

Rejoicings for the victory we had gained were taking place when I
returned home, wearied by the fatigues I had gone through. My
father was out attending to the wounded, of whom there were large
numbers, besides which many of the defenders had been killed. It
was still dark when I was aroused by the ringing of the alarm-bells,
and dressing hurriedly, I ran to Mr Laffan's room. He also had got
up; and taking our horses from the stable, we rode out to ascertain
the cause. We found people in every direction hastening to the
ramparts. On reaching the top of an embankment, we saw fires
blazing up in several directions to the north and east.

"These must be country-houses and farms which the Spaniards have
set on fire," observed my companion.

Several persons whom we found on the spot were of the same
opinion. Probably the cavalry who had escaped to the southward
had returned, and, in revenge, had set fire to all the residences they
passed; or detachments had been sent from the main body to lay

waste the country. As the more distant fires were in the direction of Egido, and Señor Monteverde's hacienda, I felt very anxious about our family.

Had they had time to escape? I knew too well that the Spaniards spared neither sex nor age. My hope, however, was that Uncle Richard would have been on the watch, and have left the house in time—though that, too probably, had fallen a sacrifice to the vengeance of the Spaniards.

In a short time I encountered Juan, who was anxious to march out and attack the enemy; but the general, he said, had prohibited him from doing so, "as his men were as yet too ill-disciplined for such an undertaking, and would most certainly be defeated."

The alarm that another assault was about to be made proved false, as scouts sent out reported that the enemy were still upwards of two leagues from the city. When daylight returned no Spaniards were in sight, nor could any signs of them be seen from the highest point in the city.

Just as Mr Laffan and I returned home my father came in, tired out by the arduous labours in which he had all night been engaged. On my telling him of the fears I entertained of what had happened at Egido, he, after some hesitation, gave me leave to ride out and ascertain if the inmates had escaped.

"I will go with you, Duncan," said Mr Laffan; "two heads are of more value than one, and so are two swords, and if we fall in with enemies we shall have a better chance of cutting; our way through them."

Anxiety concerning the fate of my mother and sister overcame my father's scruples, so, mounting our horses, Mr Laffan and I rode out through the eastern gate. Our steeds were accustomed to the road, and we put them to their best speed.

We had gone about two-thirds of the way, when Mr Laffan reined in his horse, observing, —"We may be riding right into the middle of a detachment of the Spaniards, if we go along at this rate. More haste, less speed! A good soldier should feel his way, when an enemy is likely to be in the neighbourhood."

We accordingly advanced more cautiously than we had done at first, except when we could see our way for some distance ahead. Our road ran not far from the residence of Señor Monteverde; and in regard to it our worst apprehensions were fulfilled. The house had been burned to the ground, the garden and the surrounding fields destroyed. I regretted that I should have such sad intelligence to convey to Dona Dolores. A glance was sufficient to show us what had been done, and as we galloped on our anxiety increased lest Egido should have shared the same fate.

"We must be prepared for the worst," said Mr Laffan, as he pointed to a column of smoke which ascended above the trees in the direction of Egido.

In a few minutes we reached the spot where the house once stood entire; its blackened walls alone remained, the interior filled with heaps of still smouldering embers. The enemy had indeed made short work of it. We found that the stables had escaped, but the horses had been carried away, and not an animal of any description remained; nor could we see any person moving about from whom to obtain information. We searched the out-houses, which were not harmed, and the ruins, as far as the hot embers would allow, but we could discover no traces of bodies.

"The inmates must have got away before the enemy arrived," I exclaimed.

"I truly hope so," answered Mr Laffan, but he did not look very confident.

"If they escaped, they would take the road to the mountains," I suggested. "Let us ride on in that direction; we may possibly meet with some one who has seen them. I cannot bear to return to my father without some more hopeful information than we possess."

The dominie not objecting, we rode on. However he very frequently stood up in his stirrups to get a look round, fearing that we might be riding into the lion's mouth.

We had gone some distance when we caught sight of a group of persons collected on a slight elevation, from whence they could obtain a view over the plain. When they first discovered us, they showed some disposition to conceal themselves, but on observing that we were but two persons of fair complexion their fears apparently vanished, and they remained waiting our approach.

I immediately inquired whether they had seen any fugitives from the Spaniards making their way to the mountains.

"Yes, señor; many and good cause they had to run, for the Godos put to death all they caught. We ourselves got away just in time from our cottage, which the cruel barbarians burned. They would have killed us had we remained."

I then asked if they had seen Don Ricardo—who was, I thought, probably known to them—with a party of ladies, either on foot or horseback.

One of two men to whom I more particularly addressed myself answered that they had, about daybreak, seen a party who had got some way up the mountains, but they were too far off to enable them to distinguish who they were. More definite information they could not give us.

They were fine tall fellows, dressed in the universal broad-brimmed hat, ponchos over their shoulders, and loose trousers—with, of course, bare feet; while they were smoking in the most unconcerned manner, as if they took their misfortunes lightly.

FUGITIVES.

"Are you not disposed to punish those, who have destroyed your farm?" I asked.

I then told them of the corps which were being raised, and invited them to join. Their eyes brightened when I spoke of the possibility of driving the Spaniards for ever from the country. A woman who was with them, and who had remained seated beside a basket of provisions, started to her feet.

"Yes," she exclaimed; "we shall never enjoy peace or prosperity until that has been accomplished! Pépé! Mariano! you will fight—we will all fight—for so good a cause."

They agreed to come into the town after they had gone back to their farm and endeavoured to recover any of the cattle, pigs, or poultry which had escaped.

"There is little chance of that; the thieves will have carried off everything," observed the woman.

As we could gain no further information from these persons, we resolved to try and make our way up the mountains, in the hope of either finding our friends, or hearing from other fugitives where they had taken shelter; but although we fell in with a few more people, our inquiries proved unsuccessful.

We had ridden some distance, when the dominie, who could see well ahead, exclaimed. "We shall either have to hide ourselves or ride for it! Those men are, I suspect, Spanish cavalry."

To hide ourselves, owing to the nature of the ground, was scarcely possible, and almost before we had turned our horses' heads, the enemy, for such undoubtedly they were, had discovered us. Our animals, too, from the rate at which we had come, were somewhat fatigued. We had only stopped once, to allow them to drink at a fountain.

"We must gallop for it," said Mr Laffan, "or we shall chance to be shot or made prisoners by the Spaniards. Keep a firm hand on your rein, and do not spare either whip or spur. On we go." And digging spurs into our horses' flanks, we galloped forward in the direction of the town, with the Spaniards in full pursuit.

There were a dozen or more of them, but they were too far off to fire with any chance of hitting us. We had a fair start, too, but our horses might come down, or we might encounter another party in front; still, neither of us were inclined to yield until every hope of escape was gone.

"On, on!" cried the dominie, feeling for the pistols in his holsters, so that they might be ready at any moment. "I intend to shoot one or two fellows if they come near us,—and you must do the same, Duncan; but it will be better to keep well ahead of them."

But the Spaniards' horses were fresh, and, led by a well-mounted officer, they were gaining on us. At last they got near enough to fire, and several bullets whistled through the air; but we were still too far ahead to run much risk of being hit. The sound had the effect of reanimating our horses, however, and they redoubled their efforts, their nostrils snorting, their mouths and bodies covered with foam. At length the towers and steeples of the city appeared in sight. If we could lead the Spaniards up to the walls, they might, we hoped, be cut off. We shouted, therefore, in order to attract the attention of the sentinels. Fortunately we had been observed, and so were the enemy, for as we got in sight of the gate it opened, and out dashed a body of horse, led by Juan. It was now the turn of our pursuers to fly, and as we looked over our shoulders we saw them wheeling round. At length pulling rein, we stood on one side, while Juan and his troop dashed by. I should have liked to have accompanied him, but our steeds, having once stopped, could only just stagger on into the city.

In a short time Juan returned, having cut down eight or ten of the Spaniards, when he had to gallop back on finding himself in the presence of a vastly superior force.

The troops in the city, flushed with their success, were eager to be led out against the enemy; but as they were chiefly raw recruits, the general firmly refused to comply with their wishes. The scouts brought back word that the enemy were retiring rapidly, although in good order, to the northward. The object of this retrograde movement we could not at first ascertain, but concluded that it was in consequence of other Patriot forces gathering in their rear, and they were afraid of being cut off from the capital.

Our numbers now daily increased. The two peasants, Pépé and Mariano, whom we had met, arrived with twenty companions, — tall, stalwart men, who, with others like them, made excellent infantry. Two regiments of fairly disciplined troops also arrived, partly officered by Englishmen and other foreigners; and it was now said that we should be able to take the field, if necessary, to attack the Spaniards.

My father had, in the meantime, been fearfully anxious about Uncle Richard's and our own family, but with the information the dominie and I brought him his mind grew more tranquil. As he had perfect confidence in Uncle Richard's judgment and forethought, he came to the belief that they had made their escape before the house was attacked. I wished again to set out in search of them, either by myself or with Mr Laffan, and to bring them back into the city. My father, however, not being so confident as many other people that the place would not be again attacked, said that they were safer among the mountains than they would be did they return to the city. "Uncle Richard," he said, "would probably make arrangements to obtain provisions from his small farm, which, being away from the highroad, the Spaniards would probably have passed by without destroying." He settled, however, to send Paul Lobo with a mule loaded with warm clothing for the ladies, wine, and other articles which they were likely to require.

"Depend on me, massa. I find dem out, wherever dey are, and bring back word," answered Paul, as he prepared to set out.

I occasionally saw Dona Dolores. Juan, too, whenever disengaged from his military duties, spent most of his time in her society, and, imbibing the principles which animated her, became more and more attached to the Patriot cause.

We had generally great difficulty in obtaining intelligence of the movements of our friends in different parts of the country, as the Spaniards did their best to capture, and invariably shot, every messenger or bearer of despatches. Indeed, they treated Patriots as banditti beyond the pale of the law. It must be owned, however, that our party often retaliated on them in a fearful manner.

We were anxiously waiting for Paul's return, when information was received that the Pastucians—the inhabitants of the province of Pasto, some way to the south of Popayan, who, being completely under the influence of the priests, had always opposed the Patriots—had risen in arms, and were marching northward in large numbers. They had been induced to rise by no less a person than Don Salvador Ximenes, the Bishop of Popayan; and it was said that that illustrious prelate, armed cap-à-pie, and accompanied by his stalwart secretary, was at the head of the Pastucian army. At first the report was not believed, but our spies corroborated it; so, as doubt no longer remained on the subject, it was settled that the Patriot forces must immediately march to repel the enemy, in order to prevent the southern part of our province being overrun. Our troops, now pretty fairly drilled, were eager for the expedition. We had a good body of infantry; our artillery was represented by the three guns we had captured; and we had five hundred cavalry, including Don Juan's troop—to which both I and Mr Laffan were now regularly attached.

Early in the morning we marched out of Popayan, and as we surveyed our forces, we, from the oldest to the youngest soldier, felt confident of victory.

But I must rapidly pass over this time. A march of several days brought us in sight of the enemy, who lay encamped about two leagues from where we halted. They were posted in an advantageous position close to a small village, with inaccessible heights behind them, a rapid stream in front, and a defile on the south which could be held by a few men, through which they might retreat if defeated. We occupied a less formidable position, but one which would enable the whole of our force to act at once, should we be attacked. Our men were in high spirits, and as ready to attack the enemy's position as to defend their own, should the Pastucians, taking the initiative, assault us. Instead of doing so, however, a flag of truce was sent into our camp from the bishop, expressing his wish to prevent bloodshed by an amicable arrangement of matters. Our general replied that the surest way of bringing this about was for his followers to return to their homes and disarm.

Several priests and others came with the flag of truce, under the pretence of visiting their friends in our camp; and wonderfully busy they were. It was thought that an amicable arrangement would be arrived at, and that both parties would march back without coming to blows. So friendly, indeed, were we, to all appearance, that the Pastucian officers sent an invitation to the officers of the flank company of the regiment of the Cauca to dine within their lines. An English officer, a Captain Brown, to whom I was paying a visit, and who was unwell at the time, begged that I would go instead of him, as I might be amused—the Pastucians having the credit of being a set of rough diamonds.

The next day about a dozen of us set out for the Pastucian lines, two leagues off—Captain Pinson, the commander of the company, being our leader. We were all in good spirits, laughing and joking, and expecting to be highly amused by our hosts. I promised to give Captain Brown an account of the party; but thinking it probable that there would be more drinking after dinner than I should like, I had arranged to ride back alone, and ordered my servant Antonio, who followed us, to have my horse in readiness at about four o'clock. The dinner-hour was to be two o'clock.

The Pastucian officers, who were more than treble our number, received us with every mark of courtesy, though a less attractive set of gentlemen I had never met. Indeed, they greatly resembled a party of banditti. Their complexions were swarthy, many of them having Indian blood in their veins. They all wore huge moustaches and beards, with their long black hair either falling over their shoulders or fastened behind in a queue, while their countenances were decidedly unprepossessing. They were, however, bland in the extreme, and had provided abundant fare, although not cooked in the most refined style. There was no want of wine and spirits, too, with which our hosts plied us. I remarked that there were two or three Pastucians between each of the Patriot officers.

Dinner went on as usual, though it was somewhat prolonged. Then speeches were made, chiefly complimentary to each other, both parties avoiding politics. Songs were then sung, and more speeches made.

I, however, began to grow very tired of the affair. I was seated, I should have said, opposite to Captain Pinson,—placed in that position, near the head of the table, in compliment to my father being an Englishman. While a song was being sung, I heard one of the Pastucian officers near me say to a companion, looking meanwhile at Captain Pinson, who had on a uniform with a large amount of lace about it, "I have made up my mind to have that fellow's coat for my share." As the Pastucian officer appeared already to be half-seas over, I thought that he had spoken in jest, or that I had misunderstood him.

On looking at my watch, I found that it was time for me to go, as the hour at which I had ordered my horse to be brought had arrived; rising from my seat, and going towards the window, I saw my servant leading my horse backwards and forwards.

I was on the point of moving towards the door, hoping to leave the room without being questioned, when I saw Captain Pinson start up; and turning to the other Patriot officers, he exclaimed, "Gentlemen, we are betrayed—treachery is intended—fly for your lives!" As he said this he drew his sword, when several of the Pastucian officers set upon him. By a natural impulse I sprang towards the window, while I drew my sword, intending to support my companions. Captain Pinson had moved in the same direction, that he might have greater scope for his weapon. I was soon convinced that he was not mistaken in his supposition that treachery was intended, for three of the Patriot officers by this time lay stretched on the floor, stabbed to the heart! The rest had endeavoured to rally near Captain Pinson, who called to them to make for the door and cut their way out. The Pastucians, who were mostly powerful men, set so fiercely on us, however, that I saw there was but little hope of this being accomplished, although Captain Pinson had already killed two of them. Pistols were drawn, and the bullets now began to fly in all directions. It would be difficult to picture a more fearful scene. The room was full of smoke; shouts and horrible oaths arose; while the Pastucians rushed again and again at our little band, on each occasion unhappily bringing to the ground one or more of our number.

I was fighting as well as I could by Captain Pinson's side, when he said to me, "Save yourself if you can—quick!—through the window; all hope is gone for us." This, I feared, was too true; for just then overwhelming numbers of Pastucians rushed into the room, armed with spears and bayonets. Half our number had already fallen dead on the floor; most of the others were desperately wounded, as was Captain Pinson. I saw him plunge his sword into the breast of a third Pastucian, who was making a lunge at me with a spear. This decided me. Though unwilling to desert my companions, I was convinced that the destruction of the whole of us was intended, and that I should fall a victim with the rest. With one bound I leapt from the window, and called to Antonio, who was on the point of galloping off. He immediately pulled up, and rode towards me. A shower of bullets, fired from the house, came rattling around; but in another instant I was on horseback, and, with my faithful servant, galloping for my life.

Chapter Six.

We pass through the lines—Bullets whistle past our ears—Dangers on every side—We approach a Pastucian outpost, and turn to the right to avoid it—Rough ground—A river to cross—Pursued by the Pastucians—A tearful passage—Fired at, and wounded—We get out of range—Antonio binds up my wound—Reach the camp—Meet Mr Laffan—Make my report—Carried to Captain Brown's tent—An attack expected—I crawl to a height and witness the fight—The Pastucians, led by the Bishop, fight bravely, but are driven back—Our army pursues—The wounded brought in—Captain Laffan among them—We are sent back in litters to Popayan—Unsatisfactory intelligence from the army, which marches southward—The city threatened by the Spaniards from the north—We again prepare for the defence of the city—The dominie seized with fever—My father and I are visiting at Don Cassiodoro's when the Spaniards enter the town—Antonio escapes with the horse of a Spanish colonel.

Antonio and I had escaped the volleys fired at us, but we had yet to pass through another shower of bullets. The house at which I had dined was not far from the lines, and the troops stationed there would endeavour to stop us. The gate, however, was open, to allow the passage of some mules bringing in provisions. The shots fired at us had scared the guards, who could not make out what was happening; but before they had time to close the entrance, we had dashed through. In little more than a minute the whistling of bullets passing our ears told us that the sentries had discovered their mistake in allowing us to pass. The rim of my hat was shot away, and two of the leaden messengers passed through my servant's jacket; but as neither ourselves nor our steeds were hit, we were soon beyond range of the Pastucian lines. We had, however, two leagues to ride before we could reach the Patriot encampment.

The horrible treachery of the Pastucian officers showed that, even though I had come under a flag of truce, it was very probable that other parties of the enemy whom we might encounter would not scruple to shoot us down. I saw, therefore, that I must endeavour to avoid any of their posts; not an easy matter, as all the roads would be guarded. At present, however, all we could do was to gallop on to the northward. I had fortunately noted the outlines of the mountains on either side as I came along, and was thus able to direct my course. From the unevenness of the ground, we ran, at the rate we were going, a great risk of falling; but it was not a time to stop at trifles. Not only our own lives, but the safety of the army, might depend upon our getting back. There was no doubt that the Pastucians intended to attempt surprising our forces; but this, if I should make good my escape, would be prevented.

Reaching the summit of rising ground, we now saw before us a Pastucian outpost. I could scarcely hope to pass through it without being questioned, as the firing from the lines would have been heard, and its cause suspected. Our best chance of escape, therefore, was to leave the road by turning to the right, and to make our way across the country. I looked behind, feeling sure that we should be pursued; but as yet no enemy was in sight in that direction, nor were we perceived by those ahead. At first the ground was sufficiently even to allow us to continue at full speed; but in a short time it became so rough that we had to make our way with more caution, and finally we were compelled to dismount and lead our horses over the rocks amid thick underwood. We had next to pass through a forest, which covered the side of a rising ground, but here we gained the advantage of being concealed from our enemies. On emerging from the wood we saw below us a broad stream, which separated the two armies; and once on the other side, we should be in comparative safety. My intention, therefore, was to gallop down the bill, and at once to ford or swim the stream, in the hope that we might reach the other side before being discovered by the enemy.

We had just remounted, when I saw to the left a considerable body of the Pastucians, watching, I concluded, a ford in that direction. To the right the river went foaming and roaring over a rocky bed, but there were one or two smooth-looking places, across which I thought it possible we might pass. The question, however, was whether we should be able to reach a practicable spot before the Pastucians could come near enough to fire at us. To escape their observation was almost impossible, so not a moment was to be lost.

"Now, Antonio," I said, "we must push on for our lives, and pray Heaven that we may reach the bottom of the hill without breaking our necks; then, at the first likely spot, we must push across the river. Can you swim?"

"Si, señor, like a fish."

"Then, the instant our horses lose their footing, we must slip from their backs and guide them across."

A momentary glance showed me that the Pastucians had seen us, and were hurrying along the bank of the river to cut us off. Keeping to the right, therefore, we dashed forward, our horses frequently descending several feet at a time, but alighting always on their legs. It was almost by a miracle that we reached the bottom of the steep hill. We then had to gallop along over rough ground until we came to a place which afforded some prospect of crossing. There was no time to survey it narrowly, and leading the way, sure that Antonio would follow, I plunged in—my horse stumbling forward some distance, so that I was afraid he would lose his footing and be carried down the stream. At length he made a plunge, and his whole body sank under the water. I instantly threw myself off and turned his head up the current, holding on by one hand to the saddle, while I swam with the other. Antonio, in the same fashion, followed close at my heels. Below us, to the right, was a roaring waterfall, threatening instant death to us should we go over; but the sagacious animals seemed to understand their danger, and did their utmost to keep away from it.

I could now see the enemy coming along the bank; they were holding their muskets ready to fire directly they got within range of us. The bank for which we were making was steep, but still our brave steeds might climb it, if not too much fatigued by their swim. I shouted to Antonio that we would lead them up, as we should gain in the end by it.

Most thankful was I when at length I found my horse beginning to walk, and I soon set my own feet on the ground. Even then it was no easy matter to get along; while there was the risk that my horse, in his struggles, would strike me with his hoofs.

We landed at last, and taking the reins, I dragged him up the bank. Antonio followed closely. Scarcely had we reached the top when we heard the rattle of musketry, and several bullets struck the ground around us. At some little distance, however, was a wood. If we could gain it, we should be in safety; for should the enemy attempt to swim across the stream their muskets and powder would be damaged, while we should get well ahead before they had time to construct rafts in order to ferry them over.

We threw ourselves upon our horses; but scarcely had I got into my saddle, when I heard a peculiar thud, and felt that a bullet had struck me—whereabouts I could not for the moment tell.

"On, on!" I shouted to Antonio.

"O señor, you are bleeding!" he exclaimed.

"I suppose so," I answered, "for I felt something strike me; but never mind—on, on!"

We dashed forward; and I was in hopes that I might retain my strength until we could reach the camp. Another volley came rattling after us, but we escaped being hit, and in a few seconds were in the midst of trees, among which we made our way as fast as we could, frequently having to leap or scramble over fallen trunks. But nothing stopped us. It was not likely that we should encounter any of the enemy on the side we had gained; but still it was possible, and it was necessary to keep our eyes about us.

I had been too much excited to feel any pain, but at length I began to experience an uncomfortable sensation, though I would not consent to stop and allow Antonio to bind up my wound. I did not fancy, indeed, that it could be very severe.

"Do, señor, allow me to bind your sash over the wound, or you will faint from loss of blood; then it will be difficult to get you back," said Antonio.

At length I yielded to his persuasions. We both dismounted; and having tethered our horses, he set scientifically to work to bandage my wound.

"It was high time to do this, señor," he observed; "a few more minutes, and you would have had no more blood in your veins."

He tore off a piece of my shirt, and with a pocket handkerchief made a pad, which he bound on my side. This increased the pain, but at the same time it stopped the flow of blood, which was running down my trousers into my boots. I then again mounted, though not without difficulty, and rode on, doing my best to keep my saddle; but I had to confess that I felt very weak. Most thankful was I, therefore, when we came in sight of our camp. Some of the tents were pitched on a long ridge, protected by mountains in their rear, while a steep bank sloped down to the valley. Other tents appeared to the right, also on elevated ground. Altogether, the position was one of considerable strength, and well chosen. Large numbers of troops were exercising in the valley below.

After passing the videttes, as we rode along the southern ridge, overlooking this valley, we saw a horseman approaching us. It proved to be my *ci-devant* tutor, Mr Laffan,—now holding the rank of captain.

"What has happened, my dear Duncan?" he exclaimed as he saw me. "You look as pale as death. Why, you must be wounded; no doubt about it."

I gave him a brief account of what had happened; with which he was, of course, horrified.

THE PATRIOT CAMP

"We must get the doctor to you, in the first place; then you can make your report to the general."

But just then we saw the general approaching, so we rode forward to meet him. He would at first scarcely credit the fearful account I had to give; but it was confirmed by Antonio, who described how he had seen me leap from the window, and how the Pastucians had fired at us.

"Have any of the officers escaped?" he asked.

I told him I was afraid every one had been killed.

"We must avenge them," he said; "such treachery deserves the most complete punishment. Now go, young señor, and get your wound looked to," he added.

As I rode off, he summoned several of his staff, and issued orders to prepare for an attack.

I was carried to Captain Brown's tent.

"I must look after you," said Captain Brown; "for had you not gone, I should most certainly have been murdered with the rest of the poor fellows."

The news I brought naturally excited the greatest indignation, especially amongst the officers and men of the regiment of the Cauca. All hoped that the Pastucians would attack us that night. The troops were got under arms, and every preparation was made for the battle, though the tents were allowed to stand, in order to deceive the enemy's scouts.

Juan, hearing that I was wounded, came to see me, and expressed his sorrow.

"I thought I should have had you by my side in to-morrow's fight," he said; "for, from what I can hear, if the Pastucians do not attack us we shall attack them, and I hope to punish them severely for their treachery. It is in keeping with their character, and our poor fellows should not have trusted them."

Neither Juan nor Mr Laffan could stay with me long, as they had to attend to their men, and every officer was needed. Captain Brown and Antonio looked after me, however; and the doctor assured me that, if I remained quiet, I might be able to sit my saddle again in a few weeks.

"A few weeks!" I exclaimed; "I thought a few days would put me to rights, doctor."

"For the sake of getting another bullet through you," he observed. "Well, I will patch you up as far as I can; you must do as you think fit."

I lay awake, expecting every instant to hear the rattle of musketry and the booming sound of our field-pieces, but the night seemed to be passing away quietly. At last I dropped off to sleep.

"If the enemy intended a night attack, they had thought better of it when they found that you had escaped and given us warning," said Captain Brown, when he awoke me in the morning and gave me the breakfast that Antonio had brought. "When they do come, I must go out with my regiment, whether ill or well; but you, Sinclair, must remain in camp—you will be unable to sit a horse for many days."

From the excessive weakness I felt, I feared that he was right, but I was much disappointed at the thought of being unable to take part in the expected battle.

I had been sleeping for some time, when I was awakened by the sound of firing. No one was in the tent, for, in spite of his illness, Captain Brown had joined his regiment and gone to the front. Weak as I was, I thought that I could manage to crawl up to some neighbouring height, from whence I might see what was going forward. The sound of the rattling of musketry now came up the valley, with the louder boom of our artillery, so I could resist the temptation no longer. Supporting myself on a stick, therefore, with a spy-glass hanging by a strap over my shoulders, I left the tent and made my way on, sometimes crawling on my hands and knees, until I reached a rock overhanging the camp, where I could lie down and rest the glass on a ledge just above me.

Our troops crowned the heights of the opposite side of the valley. It was not of sufficient elevation, however, to prevent me seeing over it on to the plain beyond, where the Pastucians were moving, endeavouring to force their way to the northward—their main body attacking our centre, while other divisions were marching to the right and left, evidently with the hope of outflanking the Patriots. I could clearly distinguish the different corps. The centre stood their ground. Juan with his cavalry drove back the enemy on the right; while the Cauca regiment, charging, prevented the body threatening our left flank from gaining the advantage they expected.

Frequently the Pastucians were so near that their shot came flying across the valley; but, their powder not being of the best, the bullets had by that time expended their force. Among their leaders I saw several friars; and, mounted on a fine horse, I recognised the bishop. He and his stalwart secretary had crucifixes in their left hands and bright swords in their right, which they kept vehemently flourishing. Now the bishop would hold up his crucifix, and now point with his sword at the Patriots. Then the enemy, with shrieks and shouts, would charge right up to our men; but on each occasion they were driven back with dreadful slaughter. Two or three monks were knocked over; still the bishop and his lieutenant seemed to bear charmed lives. Perhaps superstition had something to do with it, and our men were afraid to fire at a right reverend prelate.

At times I feared that the Patriots would give way, and on one occasion the bishop and his followers had nearly succeeded in breaking our line; but the regiment of the Cauca coming up, flushed with their previous success, charged the enemy and drove them back headlong—the bishop and his secretary, the ex-captain of dragoons, setting the example, and scampering off at a rate which made it difficult to overtake them. I expected to see Juan's troopers in pursuit, but he was meanwhile hotly engaged with a body of the enemy's cavalry, which after a sharp contest he defeated,—though they rallied again to cover the retreat of the bishop.

Soon after this I lost sight of the main body of our army, which had advanced; but small parties were seen coming to the rear, bringing in the wounded. I observed one party going towards the cavalry tents, which were directly below me. The men were carrying an officer on a stretcher, and as I brought my glass to bear on them I saw, to my grief, that the wounded man was Captain Laffan. Anxious to low whether he was much hurt, I immediately began my descent from the position, though in doing so, in my weak state, I nearly rolled to the bottom. Fortunately I met one of the camp-followers, who assisted me along, and by his help I got to Laffan's tent, and found my friend in the hands of the surgeon.

"You are where you should not be, young man!" exclaimed the latter when he saw me.

"But I want to know how my friend is," I said.

"What, Duncan, my boy!" exclaimed the captain, who recognised my voice. "I appreciate your kindness, but I wish you had remained in bed. I have only a bullet or two through me, and a sabre-cut on my arm dealt by one of those six rascals whom I was attacking. If there had been one less, I should have cut them all down. As it was, three bit the ground. Don't fear! I shall be all right, with a little plastering and bandaging, — shall I not, doctor?"

"Yes, yes, captain, you'll do very well; but you must keep quiet for a few hours. — And you, Mr Sinclair, must get back to your tent."

I endeavoured to obey the surgeon, but, overcome with exertions for which I was ill-fitted, I sank down in a dead faint.

"Now this is too bad of the boy, when I want to be attending his friend," I heard the doctor say, after he had poured some cordial down my throat, which somewhat restored me. On this, two men whom he summoned took me up and carried me back to Captain Brown's tent.

Towards evening, a portion of our troops returned to guard the camp, but the main body was advancing in pursuit of the Pastucians.

The next day less satisfactory news arrived. The enemy had been reinforced, and the Patriot army had had no little difficulty in maintaining its position.

The surgeons now advised that the wounded officers who could bear the journey should be carried back to Popayan; and as neither Captain Laffan nor I were likely to be fit for duty for some time to come, we gladly availed ourselves of the opportunity. We were put into litters hung on long poles, supported on men's shoulders; and the journey occupied several days, though I can give very little account of it. Some of the time, indeed, I was in a semi-somnolent state, caused by weakness.

The only striking scene I can recall was our passage on a bamboo bridge over a river in our course. The army had crossed by a ford lower down, where the water was shallow and the current slight. Here it was of great depth, and the banks of considerable height. As I looked at the slight structure, however, it appeared to me incapable of bearing more than the weight of a single man, while a few cuts with a manchette would have sent it into the torrent below.

I heard Captain Laffan, who was in advance of me, cry out to his bearers, "You don't mean to say that we are to go over that spider's-web affair! Why! it looks as if it would give way with the weight of that woman going along it."

"Have no fears about the matter, señor captain; cavalry have charged over it before now," was the answer. And, in spite of the captain's protestations, his bearers tramped on and crossed in safety.

I followed, and though the bamboos creaked ominously they held fast, and no accident occurred to any of the party. It was along such a bridge as this that the gallant Colonel Mackintosh rode at full gallop, when leading on his brave Albions to the capture of La Plata, some time afterwards.

The path we took would only allow of one litter passing at a time, and I had no conversation with the rest of the party; so, when we stopped at night, Laffan ordered his litter to be placed alongside mine. He was in excellent spirits, and seemed to feel his several wounds scarcely so much as I did the single one I had received.

"You are not so well accustomed to it, my boy, as I am. I have no extra flesh to be annoyed, you see; and my parchment-like skin soon unites," he observed, laughing.

At last we arrived at Popayan. My father looked somewhat horrified when he saw me and heard of my narrow escape.

"I am sorry I allowed Mr Laffan and you to go," he said. "However, you are here now, and I hope you will soon be brought round."

A BAMBOO BRIDGE

"Faith, doctor, but I'm mighty glad to have seen a little more service; and as soon as you can patch me up I'll be off again to fight for the right cause!" exclaimed our Irish friend.

I inquired for my mother and the rest of our relations.

"Paul Lobo," said my father, "discovered them in a hut among the mountains. They were all very well, and in tolerable spirits, only somewhat anxious about us. I have sent him back again with a load of necessary articles; and if we receive satisfactory accounts from the army, I trust that they will return as soon as they grow weary of their rough life. Uncle Richard, however, takes very good care of them, and obtains abundance of provisions; but they intend, at all events, shortly to return to the farm, from whence, should the Spaniards again overrun the country, they can make good their retreat."

Under my father's careful treatment Mr Laffan and I soon regained our strength, and we became eager to rejoin the army. My father, however, declared that I was not in a fit state to be exposed to the hardships which I should have to endure; but that Mr Laffan might do as he liked.

The news from the south was not altogether satisfactory. Although the Patriots had hitherto been successful, the Pastucians had doggedly stood their ground, and had retreated slowly — probably with the intention of drawing them into some defiles, where they might be attacked from the heights. At this period intelligence was received that the Spaniards were again advancing from the north. On hearing this, the commandant of Popayan immediately sent a despatch entreating the general to return. Instead, however, of the whole army coming, only a few made their appearance to assist in the defence of the town. At the same time, troops had been collected from all quarters, and every effort had been made to bring them into a state of efficiency. Our uncle, Dr Cazalla, was one of the most active in preparing for the defence of the place. He had established a manufactory for gunpowder, on a plan devised by himself. It was one of the articles most required. He had also taught all the blacksmiths who could be found how to repair muskets, and some of the most expert even how to manufacture them.

"It is a sad way of employing our strength and talents," he observed to my father. "The same exertions rendered to the cause of peaceful industry, might make this country rich and flourishing, instead of which all our energies are being expended in killing one another. Still, we are fighting for the advantage of our children; but the ruin this war has brought upon the country cannot be repaired during our lifetime."

The officer now in command of the city had seen no service. He may have been a very worthy man, but he was a bad general. I have described the chief square of the town. Most of the houses in it had been turned into barracks, the owners having fled, some because they were Royalists, and others in order to avoid the risk they would incur should the place be captured by either party.

I was now nearly quite well, as was also Mr Laffan, and he had determined to set off next day to rejoin Juan's corps. He had, however, over-estimated his strength; for that very evening, on returning home, he was seized with a fever. My father insisted that he should at once go to bed. "If you do not," he said, "I will not answer for your life."

The dominie obeyed, but very unwillingly. His illness however, as was proved in the sequel, was the means of saving his life. I had gone one afternoon with my father to visit some Royalist friends living in the great square, who had had the courage to remain in the town. My father had attended the family, and not long before had been the means of curing Don Cassiodoro de Corran of a dangerous disease. Though a Spaniard, he was very liberal, and, being respected by all parties, he ventured to remain, and the Patriots had not molested him. The young ladies of the family were playing on their guitars, and two or three other people having come in, we were proposing a dance, when we were startled by the sound of musketry. Presently we heard shouts and cries, and the trampling of horses coming down the principal street leading from the northern gate.

"The Godos! the Godos! the hated Spaniards! The enemy is upon us!" shouted the people, as they rushed across the square.

Unfortunately, the principal officers of the troops were in different parts of the town, paying visits or amusing themselves. The soldiers, without proper leaders, seized their arms and turned out, some coming without ammunition, others leaving their bayonets or swords behind them. They then attempted to form under their sergeants and such officers as remained, but, being ill-disciplined, all was done in a hurry and without order; and many, seized by a panic, made their escape.

Antonio, who, I should have said, had accompanied me, rushed into the house and begged me to fly. My father, however, insisted that I should remain.

"You can do nothing, and will certainly lose your life," he said.

Antonio, who was a brave fellow, hastened out again to join his comrades. I could not, however, resist going to the window to see what was taking place. Presently a large body of Spanish cavalry rode into the square, putting to flight the soldiers they first encountered, who, scattering in every direction, attempted to seek safety in the houses. Among others I caught sight of Antonio, who was making towards the house he had so lately left, hotly pursued by a Spanish colonel. I determined, if possible, to save Antonio, and asked Don Cassiodoro to speak to the colonel. He was about to do so, when Antonio stopped and cried out—

"I will surrender, señor colonel, if you will spare my life."

"Well, well! trust to me," was the answer.

But as the Spaniard spoke he drew a pistol from his holster; on which Antonio, expecting the next moment to be a dead man, made a lunge at him with his long lance, the point wounding the colonel, who the next moment rolled from his horse. Our hero, as may be supposed, did not stop to help him up, but leaping on his steed, galloped off, master of a good horse and all the colonel's appointments. As he passed our windows he waved his hand to me, and disappeared like lightning down the street. I had great hopes that he would make his escape before the main body of the Spaniards could enter.

Don Cassiodoro, on seeing the colonel on the ground, went out with my father and brought him into the house, that his wound might be attended to. The spear had torn his coat, but, excepting a slight scratch on the side, had not otherwise harmed him. He begged, however, that his wound might be dressed; when Don Cassiodoro advised that he should go to bed, which he appeared very willing to do.

I waited, in hopes that the Patriot officers would rally the troops and drive out the Spaniards before the arrival of the main body; for, after all, those who had entered formed but a small party, and were unaccompanied by infantry. So completely panic-stricken, however, had our men become, that it was found impossible to make head against the Spaniards; indeed, a considerable number of them had fled from the town. Most of the officers, as well as the men, saw that their wisest course would be to retreat to the southward, where they could join the army. Thus Popayan once more fell into the hands of the Spaniards.

Chapter Seven.

Don Cassiodoro conceals my father and me—Fearful treatment of the inhabitants by the Spanish soldiery—I visit our house in disguise—Mr Laffan's mode of preserving the house—I meet Paul Lobo in disguise—News of my relations—He goes towards our home—I visit the market—Nearly betray myself—Paul tells us that Dr Cazalla and the Monteverdes are made prisoners and sent to Bogota—Plans for rescuing them—I return to Don Cassiodoros—My father determines to send Mr Laffan and me to Bogota—The Spaniards search for my father—Our host conceals him and me—I return to our house and prepare with Mr Laffan for our expedition—I go back to Don Cassiodoro's, and assume the character of a young english milord—The dominie and I, attended by Domingo and Lion, start from the hotel—Journey along the valley of the Cauca—Stop at Calli.

A reign of terror now commenced in Popayan. The city was filled with Spanish troops, which took up their quarters in the houses lately occupied by the Patriots. A considerable number of the latter made their escape, but numbers were cut down in the streets, and others were captured and thrust into prison. The square was literally strewed with the dead.

My father proposed to return home, but Don Cassiodoro insisted that he should remain.

"You will be safe here," he said; "for no one will suspect me of being capable of harbouring disaffected persons; and I owe you a debt of gratitude, which I can only partially repay by concealing you from your enemies."

"But I am a non-combatant, and it is my duty to attend to the wounded," said my father.

"Can you say as much for your son?" remarked Don Cassiodoro. "Besides, you would have no opportunity of attending to your duties, as you would be immediately seized and sent to prison. General Calzada has been directed by Murillo to capture all suspected persons, and to forward them to Bogota for trial—and I may say, for execution. Be advised by me—remain in safety here. When you are not found at your house, it will be supposed that you have fled from the city, and the search after you will be relaxed."

My father at length consented to follow the advice of Don Cassiodoro, who promised to keep him informed of all that was taking place. There was, however, a risk that the Spanish colonel, whose wound he had dressed, would inform against him. The only hope was, that the colonel, who was a stranger, did not know who he was, as he spoke Spanish like a native, and Don Cassiodoro had introduced him as his family physician, without mentioning his name.

I had, by my father's directions, resumed my civilian dress, as had also Mr Laffan, who was, I should have said, at this time safe in our house. There was, however, much probability that the Spanish soldiers, on entering to plunder the house, might wantonly kill him, and burn it down.

That night, it may be supposed, was one of intense anxiety. We could gain no tidings of any of our friends, for had we gone out the danger would have been great, as the Spanish soldiers were ranging through the town, constantly firing at the windows of houses supposed to be inhabited by Patriots, and killing all the persons they met with in the streets. We were especially anxious about our uncle, Dr Cazalla, and also about Señor Monteverde and Dona Dolores. They had all been in the city on the previous day, and, we feared, could not have been warned of the entry of the Spaniards in sufficient time to make their escape.

All night long the sounds of shots were heard in different parts of the town, and fearful shrieks and cries arose as some of the unfortunate citizens were being dragged forth from their dwellings, including old men, women, and even little children, to be slaughtered by the savage soldiery; while here and there great sheets of flame shot up, showing that a number of houses had been set on fire. Such were the terrible scenes which took place, not only at Popayan, but in nearly all the principal towns of the province, when they fell into the hands of the Spaniards.

A guard had been placed at the door of Don Cassiodoro's house by General Calzada, under the plea that a Spanish officer lay wounded within. The house was thus, indeed, safe from attack, but we were effectually prevented from going out to obtain intelligence.

Towards morning the trumpet sounding recalled the soldiers to their quarters, and we could distinctly see them crossing the square laden with plunder. The Spanish general, having frightened the inhabitants into something like submission, was now endeavouring to restore order among the troops. Had the Patriot army been near enough to enter the city during the night, they might have retaken it, and captured or destroyed every one of their enemies.

The next day the Spanish colonel, feeling himself very well—indeed, his wound was of the most trivial nature—desired to go forth, that he might visit the general and report his proceedings. Don Cassiodoro, who was anxious to get rid of him, did not object, and the colonel took his departure. As soon as he was gone, I begged that my father would allow me to go and learn what had become of Mr Laffan, Dr Cazalla, and other friends.

"But you will run a risk of being captured, if not of being injured or killed," said my father.

I told Don Cassiodoro what I wished to do, and one of the young ladies suggested that I should put on the livery of a stable-boy who happened to have been sent away into the country sick some time before. I gladly accepted the proposal, and José's dress being procured, I found that it fitted me exactly. Don Cassiodoro charged me to refrain from answering questions; but if pressed, I was to say I was one of his servants. It was proposed that I should wait until the evening, as there would be less risk of being recognised; but dressed as I was, I thought that no one could possibly know me: besides, poor Mr Laffan might in the meantime be starving. Before leaving, I filled my pockets with eatables, supposing it likely that all the provisions in the house had been carried away.

Taking a whip in my hand, I went out by a side door when no one was near, and then walked along with as jaunty an air as I could assume. A number of people of the lower orders were moving about, but none of the citizens who had escaped were anywhere to be seen. There were also soldiers with parties of slaves or Indians, whom they were compelling to carry off the dead bodies in order that they might be buried outside the town. Foraging-parties had also been sent out, and were now returning, driving in the peasantry with provisions, for the general had given orders to establish a market in the place. The crowd was an advantage, as I was able to make my way without being noticed.

I hurried on, and soon reached our own house, which appeared not to have been entered. All the doors and windows were fast closed, though I saw that they had been struck by several musket-balls. Going round to the courtyard, I climbed over the gate, a feat I had performed often before. I knocked gently, when a bark from within assured me that Lion was acting as guardian of the house.

"Who's there?" asked a voice which I recognised as that of Mr Laffan.

"Duncan," I replied; and presently I heard the bolts withdrawn. Mr Laffan started back, for he did not recognise me; but Lion, rushing past him, began to leap up and lick my face and hands.

"For the moment I didn't know you, Duncan," said Mr Laffan. "Thankful I am that you have escaped; for I have been in a mighty fright about you and your father since the Spaniards entered the place. Come in, come in, and tell me all about it." I then went in, and he again closed and bolted the door.

"We have been equally anxious about you," I replied; "how did you escape?"

"By bolting all the doors so that the villains could not break them open without a battering-ram, then hanging a British flag out of the window and shouting, 'Vive el Roy! If any one comes in here, he will bring down the vengeance of England on his head.' I don't know which had the most effect, the flag, the loyal shout, or the threat of vengeance, but one party after another of the rascals turned away; so, you see, if you and your father had been here you would have escaped. Poor Lion and I, however, have been somewhat on short commons. I shared what I could find in the house with the faithful brute, as was but fair."

"I suspected that such might be the case," I said, producing what I had brought in my pockets; of which Mr Laffan eagerly ate a portion, and bestowed the rest upon Lion, who gobbled it up in a few seconds, showing how hungry he was. As what I had brought could do little more than stimulate their appetites, I offered at once to go out and buy some provisions, which I could do very well in my character of a stable-boy. Fortunately I had some money in my pocket. I started immediately, intending afterwards to visit Dr Cazalla, as also the house in which Señor Monteverde and Dona Dolores had been residing, although I did not expect to find any of them.

As I was proceeding along the streets, I saw an old black man. His only clothing was a broad-brimmed hat, and a pair of loose drawers fastened round his waist by a girdle, to which was hung his manchette. He came along driving a mule laden with bamboo-canes, such as are constantly sold in the town for piping and other purposes. I was going to pass him, when I saw him look very hard at me, and heard him utter my name in a low tone of voice, which I thought I recognised. A smile passed over his countenance, and on looking round and observing no one near, he said—

"I am better disguised dan you, Señor Duncan."

By his voice I at once recognised Paul Lobo.

PAUL LOBO

"Are my mother, sister, Don Ricardo, and the rest well?" I asked.

"Yes, yes, I hab a good account to give ob dem," he replied; "but tell me, has el señor doctor escaped, and is de house safe?"

"Yes," I replied.

"Den come on with me, for I hab much to tell you, and we may be discovered if seen speaking here."

I said that I had to go to the market and obtain some food, and that I wished to inquire about my uncle, Dr Cazalla, and the Monteverdes.

"Buy de food, by all means, but do not venture to make furder inquiries; I can tell you all you want to know," he said.

Seeing some one approaching, he drove on his mule, singing out, "Who wants to buy canes—sound straight canes?" though he did not stop for any one to answer him.

I hastened to the market-place. Provisions were but scant, the soldiers having appropriated most of what was brought in. However, I got as much as I wanted, although I nearly betrayed myself by the ignorance I displayed in making my purchases. With a basket on my shoulder, which I had bought, I returned homewards. Several persons cast inquiring glances at me; and a Spanish sergeant eyed me very narrowly, I thought. But I went whistling along, as if free from care, and he did not stop to put questions to me. I was thankful when I got back to the courtyard, where I found Paul Lobo standing by his mule. Both he and Mr Laffan, and Lion too, were very glad to get some of the provisions I had brought.

"And now, Paul," I said, "what information have you to give me?"

"Berry sorry to say, not good. I hear as I come 'long dat all de gates are guarded, so dat no one can go out ob de city; dat de general gib orders to take up eberybody in de place who can read and write, no matter who dey are. They hab already got hold ob el señor Doctor

Cazalla, Señor Monteverde, and his daughter. General Calzada, him pretty good man and not like to shoot people, so dey send dem all to General Murillo at Bogota; and he, dey say, kill for de pleasure ob killing. Depend 'pon it, dey come to look for señor doctor; so he mus' hide away, and not show his face till de Patriots come back—and dat dey do, I hope, 'fore long."

"This is indeed bad news; I will go back to my father and tell him what you say, Paul," I answered. "But do you think it would be possible to rescue Doctor Cazalla and the Monteverdes?"

Paul replied that they had already, from what he could learn, been sent out of the city, and were on their way to Bogota.

I proposed to hasten immediately to the army and let Juan know, in the hope that, by a forced march, he might be able to intercept the escort and rescue the prisoners. But both Paul and Mr Laffan declared that it would be impossible: that I could not obtain a horse, as the Spaniards had taken possession of all those found in the city; and that if I could get one, I should not be able to pass through the gates of the city.

We talked over the subject, but could think of no plan likely to succeed. I was in despair. I felt, however, that I must immediately return to my father and give him the information Paul had brought; he would, perhaps, be able to devise some plan more likely to succeed than any I could form. As it was certain that our house would be searched, I advised Mr Laffan to try and gain some place of concealment where he and Lion might remain, assuring him that Paul Lobo would find the means of supplying them with food.

"No, no; I'll stop and defend the house to the last. The plundering rascals will hesitate before they attempt to break-in," he answered. "We have four muskets and three brace of pistols, and I shall be able to give a good account of a dozen or move of them if they make the attempt. If they come with authority to search for your father, I intend that they shall find me seated at table writing despatches to the English Government; and I shall have the same flag I used before hung over my head. If they inquire for the doctor, I'll tell them the fact, that he left this house some hours before they came into the city; and that if he has a swift horse, he is probably leagues away to the north, south, east, or west, to join his family. If that does not satisfy them, I'll shrug my shoulders, send a puff of smoke in their faces from my cigar, and go on writing my despatches."

I could not help laughing at the honest Irishman's coolness. His plan seemed the best that could be adopted, and I hoped that it might succeed. Paul said he should remain with his mule in the courtyard, and should the Spaniards come to the house, he would move away crying his wares, hoping thus to escape being questioned.

Fortunately I had told neither Mr Laffan nor Paul that my father was at Don Cassiodoro's; although, seeing me in the livery of that family, they might have suspected where he was. As it was important to get back to Don Cassiodoro's without delay, and finding that no one was near, I slipped out at the gate, and passing along some back streets, made my way to his house.

My father was greatly grieved when he heard that Doctor Cazalla and the Monteverdes had been arrested and sent off to Bogota. He was too well acquainted with General Murillo's bloodthirsty nature not to feel the greatest possible fear for their safety.

"That Spanish tiger has sworn to stamp out every spark of liberty in the land, and to destroy all those who are capable of rekindling it," he observed; "we must, however, try what can be done. Let me consider."

He was silent for a quarter of an hour or more. At last, looking up, he said, "Duncan, I can trust to your judgment and energy, and also to those of Mr Laffan. I will send you and him to Bogota, with letters to various friends who are likely to interest themselves on behalf of the prisoners. They may be the means of preserving their lives for the present, and of ultimately obtaining their liberty."

"I am ready to start this instant," I replied; "so is Mr Laffan, I am sure, for the excitement he has gone through has cured his fever. We may push on ahead, and get there before them."

"Neither are you nor Mr Laffan in a fit state to make a forced march," he answered; "you must preserve your health, else you may be unable to render the service you desire. I intend that you should travel in the character of a young English gentleman, with Mr Laffan as your tutor. You must speak no Spanish; and he knows quite enough to get on perfectly well."

We had just arranged the whole plan, and I had agreed to go back and explain it to Mr Laffan, when Don Cassiodoro hurriedly entered the room.

"My dear doctor," he exclaimed, "some Spanish officials are at the door, and from the information I have received I fear that they have come to arrest you. Follow me instantly. Take up these writing materials and everything that belongs to you; there's not a moment to lose. Let your son come too; were he to be seen, they would at once conclude that you were here."

Don Cassiodoro leading the way, my father and I followed him to an upper story, and entered an unfurnished room. "If the don requires us to stay here, we shall certainly be discovered," I thought. But I was mistaken. Drawing aside a panel in the wall, he disclosed a recess; then pointing upwards, he showed us a broad shelf at the top.

"How are we to get up there?" asked my father.

Don Cassiodoro pulled down a small ladder. "Draw this up after you," he said, "and place it along the side. You will find that there is a cover which may be let down, and which will completely conceal you. Should those seeking you chance to discover the panel and enter the recess, they might search round it, and yet not suppose that you were within."

My father wrung the don's hand and expressed his gratitude. We immediately climbed up, and drawing the ladder after us, then let down the lid,—for so I may call it,—which made the surface look exactly like a broad beam running from one side of the house to the other. A more perfect hiding-place could scarcely have been devised, as no stranger, unless treachery had been at work, was likely to discover it.

We heard Don Cassiodoro's footsteps as he descended the stairs. Soon afterwards voices from below reached us. The door of the room had been ostentatiously left open. Don Cassiodoro's voice rose above that of his unwelcome visitors as he complained of the insult offered him, and at the want of confidence placed in his loyalty. The officers must have been, by some means or other, informed that my father was in the house, as they persisted in searching every room.

"He is nowhere below, but we shall probably unkennel him in the upper story," I heard one of them say as they mounted the stairs.

They at last entered the room.

"Where can that rascally English doctor be?" exclaimed one of them. "He was too wise to hide in his own house; but if he is not here, where is he?"

"Never fear, we shall catch him somewhere," observed another; "and we shall have the pleasure of seeing the Republican heretic shot, to repay us for our trouble."

From these remarks I knew that our house must have been searched directly after I left it, and that I had had a very narrow escape. I was in hopes that something would have been said to inform me of what had happened to Mr Laffan; but no remark was made on the subject. I could only hope that Mr Laffan's plan had succeeded, and that they had been afraid to touch him. The long-coated, grave-looking dominie would never have been suspected of having lately acted the part of a dashing lancer.

We lay listening and perfectly still, for as we could hear everything that was said, we knew that the slightest noise might have betrayed us.

"Are you convinced, gentlemen, that the English doctor is not here?" I heard Don Cassiodoro ask. "Now, I desire you to apologise to me for your intrusion. The general knows best whether it would be politic to shoot a skilful surgeon and an Englishman, who is willing and able to heal the wounds of the loyal subjects of King Ferdinand as well as of rebels. My belief is, that although he may love liberty in the abstract, he is too much engaged in his professional duties to interfere in any way in politics."

At length we heard the front door close, and Don Cassiodoro returned to the recess to tell us that we might come down, but that my father must be ready to return to his place of concealment at a moment's notice. "And you, young sir," he said, turning to me, "it will be wise in you to keep out of the way of General Calzada; for, should he find out whose son you are, he might seize you as a hostage for the doctor."

On this, my father told Don Cassiodoro that he was anxious to send me and my tutor to Bogota, and that under the circumstances it would be safer for us to travel under assumed names.

Don Cassiodoro at once agreed to render all the assistance in his power; for he saw that the sooner I could set off the better. So, in the first place, as it was necessary to obtain a couple of horses, he immediately undertook to supply us from his own stud, and also to advance any money we might require.

While my father was writing the letters, I hastened back to our own house, being still dressed as a groom. I found Mr Laffan seated at the table as he proposed, with a flag over his head. The house, as I had fully expected, had been visited and searched, but had not been plundered. Probably the officers had been forbidden to plunder it, in order that my father might be the more easily enticed back.

On hearing the proposed plan, Mr Laffan sprang to his feet, and declared that he was ready at once to proceed. The question was, What was to be done with the house?

"Leave dat to me," said Paul; "me find honest woman who fight like one panther 'fore she let any one come into de house."

As a precautionary measure, we concealed all the most valuable articles we could find; leaving, however, a few silver forks and spoons to mislead plunderers, who might suppose that they were the only things in the house worth taking.

The dominie—for so I may again call him—having dressed in as appropriate a style as possible, as the tutor of a young English milord, and Lobo having warned us that the coast was clear, we left the house to proceed to a posada where Don Cassiodoro had arranged to send the horses. I carried the valise containing Mr Laffan's wearing apparel. My own was in the provision-basket on my back. The load, I must say, was rather a heavy one. Lion rushed out with us. At first I thought of leaving him as a guard to the house, but he seemed to have made up his mind to come, and Mr Laffan advised me to take him. "The noble brute may render us good service on our journey, and I would sooner have him than half a dozen guards, who would be very likely to rob us, or run away if we were attacked." Lion wagged his tail and showed every sign of satisfaction when he understood that I intended to take him with me.

On arriving at the posado, the dominie put a piece of money into my hand, as if to pay me for having carried his valise; and I heard him tell the landlord that he was waiting for a young English milord, who was anxious to return home by way of Bogota. I then hurried back to Don Cassiodoro's, where I resumed my proper costume. To prevent my being recognised, my father had provided a pair of huge whiskers and moustaches, and by careful painting he made me look considerably older than I was. With the aid of a few additions to my costume, I certainly looked as I had never done before. Even the young ladies, when I came downstairs, did not at first recognise me. My father, having given me all needful instructions, supplied me with a purse and the letters he had written; while Don Cassiodoro put into my hands a passport, which he had obtained at considerable risk of implicating himself. He then ordered a servant to strap my valise on the saddle of my horse, while another mounted servant led the horse intended for the dominie.

"That man is as true as steel," observed Don Cassiodoro. "You cannot proceed without an attendant, and I have directed him to accompany you. You will find Domingo of the greatest use. He believes you to be what you profess to be. I have charged him not to let it be known that he is in my service, so as to prevent inconvenient questions."

We reached the posada without being stopped.

"I am so glad my dear young lord has come," said the dominie, turning to the host; "for though the Royalists have gained the day at present, we do not know how soon those dreadful Republicans may have the upper hand."

"Truly, truly," answered the landlord, bowing to me. "Milord will be glad to return to England, where all, I am told, are true Royalists."

"Milord does not understand much Spanish," observed Mr Laffan; "we must wish you farewell."

As we might have risked discovery by further delay, we rode forward; Domingo, armed to the teeth, following us. Mr Laffan, I found, had two brace of pistols in his holsters, and a sword, which he kept concealed under his cloak. I, of course, carried one in my character of a young gentleman of fortune, and I also had a brace of pistols; so that we were tolerably well-armed. Mr Laffan, who had taken the passport, produced it with a flourish at the gates, and begged that milord might not be troubled with unnecessary delay. The officer on guard bowed politely, and we were allowed to pass. I had little expected to get on so well, but no one seemed to suspect our character.

As soon as we were out of sight of the city, we pushed forward, anxious to get as far as we could before nightfall. Our road was to be due north for a considerable distance, along the banks of the Cauca. After this we were to turn to the right over the Quindio mountains to reach Bogota. Our great object was to push on to such a distance from Popayan, that I might not run the risk of being recognised by any persons who knew me. The letters I carried were couched in such language, that had they fallen into the hands of the Spaniards I should still have been safe. They spoke of me as a young Englishman of fortune who had come over to see the beauties of the country, and who proposed to spend a short time at Bogota on his way down the Magdalena to Cartagena, from whence he expected to embark for England. They requested that the friends to whom they were addressed would render him every assistance in carrying out the objects of his journey, especially in obtaining any information he might desire. They were mostly addressed to well-known Royalists, still better to conceal my real object.

I cannot stay to describe the numerous incidents of the journey. The first night we stopped at the house of the padre of a village. I found him to be a man of liberal sentiments, from what he said to Mr Laffan; though, keeping up my character, I did not venture to speak. At first I felt surprised at this; but I afterwards discovered that he possessed a Bible, which he constantly studied.

"You Englishmen appreciate the book," he observed to my tutor; "but I have, on several occasions, been compelled to hide it, lest I should be accused of being an enemy to Spain."

Continuing our journey, we travelled along the base of the Cordilleras, which towered to the skies on our right. The scenery was most magnificent. From a height we had reached we cast our eyes over the beautiful valley, with one or two large villages near us, and the pretty town of Calli in the distance. We made our way towards it, though it was somewhat out of our direct course. The inhabitants were generally supporters of the Liberal cause, and had suffered greatly from the Spaniards. As we got close to the bridge we stopped to inquire which was the principal inn in the place. Crossing the bridge, we rode through the streets of the neat little town in search of a posada, at which we agreed that it would be more prudent to stop than with a resident, as I might thus be able to gain much more information from the conversation of the visitors than I could at the house of a private person. Everywhere the town exhibited traces of the visit of an enemy. Many of the houses were deserted, others had been burned to the ground. Several were in ruins, and the walls, in many places, were bespattered with bullet-marks.

THE TOWN OF CALLI

Domingo took our horses round to the shed which served as a stable, while we entered the public room, the centre of which was occupied by a long table with rough benches on either side, at which several persons—merchants, small traders, and carriers—were seated. Mr Laffan requested to be supplied with food, and asked if we could have a room in which our hammocks could be slung up.

The landlord assured him that the whole house was at our command.

"Yes," said Mr Laffan, "but we would rather have a room to ourselves. This young English milord likes to be quiet."

The landlord examined me with a curious look, and said he should be happy to clear out a room at present occupied by some of his family.

I asked Mr Laffan to tell me what the landlord had said, and in reply begged to assure him that I would not on any account put his estimable family to so much inconvenience; that we would, therefore, sling our hammocks at the further end of the hall.

He was not long in placing a very fairly concocted olla-podrida before us. It consisted of beef, fowls, bacon, mutton, and a variety of vegetables, all cooked together, and tolerably free from garlic. The landlord remarked, as he tasted it before us, "I am aware that the English do not like much of that root, as I discovered by observing the expressions of disgust exhibited by the countenances of some British officers for whom I had prepared a dish with rather more, perhaps, than the usual allowance of seasoning. One of them declared that he was poisoned, and compelled me, at the point of his sword, to eat the whole of it; while another clapped the dish upside down on my head, and insisted on my producing some other food of a less savoury character. I have remembered ever since that Englishmen do not like garlic."

While the landlord was talking, I endeavoured to listen to the conversation going on at the other part of the table. I gathered from it some satisfactory news. Bolivar was again in arms, and at the head of a considerable force, with which he had been successful in Venezuela, and was marching towards New Granada. I earnestly hoped that he might capture Bogota before the Spaniards had put our friends to death. Once or twice I was tempted to ask questions, and only recollected just in time that I was supposed not to understand Spanish. Some of the men at the supper-table eyed me, I fancied, narrowly; but whether they suspected who I was, or were considering whether it would not be profitable to rob the young English milord, I could not make out.

Mr Laffan and Domingo having secured our hammocks, we turned in, with our pistols by our sides, while Lion took up his usual post under where we lay.

Chapter Eight.

Our journey continued — A snake killed — Abundance of animal life — Paucity of inhabitants — Black herdsmen — Vegetable productions of the Cauca Valley — Beautiful scene near Cartago — We enter Cartago — A wretched posada — Mr Laffan searches for carriers — A suspicious character — The Silleros — Arrangements for crossing the mountains — The officer tells us of the escape of Dona Dolores — A midnight robber — Lion keeps guard — We have cause to be uneasy — The Spanish officer starts before us — Our journey over the Quindio Mountains commenced — A ruined village.

We left Calli at daybreak, before the rest of the guests were astir. I was not altogether satisfied that we had escaped detection; and from the appearance of some of the characters at the supper-table, I thought it possible that an attempt might be made to rob us. How Domingo might act, I could not tell; but I was very sure that, in the event of being attacked by banditti, Mr Laffan would prove to them that they had caught a Tartar. The road we traversed was as bad as could be. Sometimes our horses descended the hills almost on their haunches; at others we were compelled to dismount and lead them up the steep inclines. We had several streams to cross; some we were able to ford, others were spanned by wooden bridges. One of these was thrown over a rapid river which flowed at the foot of some steep and huge rocks, above which was a level space with inaccessible-hills on either side.

"That would form a good military post," observed Mr Laffan, pointing to the spot. "Either our friends or our enemies will take possession of it one of these days, and it will prove a hard matter to drive them out."

I noted the spot, as well as his remark.

At the next stream we came to, which was a more tranquil one than the former, we had an adventure. As we were crossing it, we observed a large snake swimming towards us. On it came, with its head and part of its body raised out of the water. On nearing us it stopped, apparently watching our motions. I then knew, by the black cross which I observed on its neck, that it was of the species called aquis, one of the boldest and most venomous of the serpents of that region. Mr Laffan, not liking the creature's appearance, and naturally thinking it intended to attack us, drew his pistol.

"You had better not, señor," cried Domingo; "you are very likely to miss, and the brute will come after us. Let me take it in hand. Please hold my horse."

Domingo dismounting, ran a short distance, to a place where we saw a number of bamboos growing. He cut one with his sword, and then advanced to fulfil his promise. The aquis had all the time remained perfectly quiet, with its eyes fixed on us. As Domingo approached, the creature put out its forked tongue, and raised itself higher in the water, as if preparing to make a dart at its enemy. On this, Domingo retired to a distance; but he and the snake continued to watch each other for some minutes. Suddenly the aquis turned round, and began to swim to the other side of the river. The moment Domingo observed its head turned from him he rushed to the bank, and before it got beyond his reach gave it three or four tremendous blows with the bamboo, which made it turn on its back. Then following up the attack, he succeeded in killing the creature. On measuring it, we found that it was upwards of six feet in length.

"It never does to run from these creatures," observed Domingo, as he remounted; "they will follow even a horse for a league or more, and move as rapidly, provided the ground is not too dry."

In the meadows we observed large numbers of fine cattle.

"Ah, señor, you might have seen twice as many before the Spaniards passed by," said Domingo; "but they slaughtered all they could get, sometimes merely for the sake of their tongues. It is a pity that the people should have rebelled against their lawful sovereign; and this is the consequence."

Mr Laffan made no reply. It was as well, for our purpose, that Domingo should appear so loyal.

THE WAX-PALM.

In the woods, and often flying across the valley, we saw various kinds of birds, macaws and parrots; some of the latter had yellow plumage on the breast, wings, and tail, and red feathers on the head. We also met with wild turkeys, grouse, and partridges in large numbers; and we frequently caught sight of deer scampering over the hills. But sometimes, during a whole day, we did not pass a single house of any size, while the cottages of the peasantry were scattered at long distances from each other.

As we proceeded down the valley, however, we saw a number of neat country-houses and cottages; while the soil appeared to be fruitful in the extreme, and nothing could surpass the beauty of the scenery. The numbers of the cattle also increased. They were under the charge of black slaves, who were riding about looking after them. We saw neither Creoles nor Indians: the latter had made their escape to the forests and mountains, and the former had been carried off to serve in either the one army or the other. The appearance of the blacks on horseback was singular. On their heads they wore large straw hats, while their bodies were covered by a cloak made of rushes, which served to keep out both the heat and the rain. Their legs were bare, but their feet were protected by sandals, to which were fastened spurs of huge dimensions. Each man carried by his left side a long manchette, or sword-knife, secured to his girdle. They were all galloping as hard as they could go, wheeling their horses round and then halting in a moment.

"Those fellows would make useful cavalry, if they could be got to face the enemy; and I should like to find myself at the head of a thousand of them," observed Mr Laffan. "We should give a good account of any of the Spanish lancers we might fall in with."

Soon after this, on the shores of a small lake, we came upon a curious tree, which Mr Laffan pronounced to be the wax-palm, or the *Ceroxilon andicola*. From its appearance I should have supposed that it could only grow in the very warmest regions; but it is of so happy a constitution that it flourishes equally well in temperate and in cold climates. We afterwards found some on the mountains of Quindio. They are the most hardy of the Palm tribe: where others would perish, or assume a dwarfed or stunted form, the wax-palm raises its stem, in the form of an elegantly-wrought column, a hundred and fifty feet high, with a splendid leafy plume. From the leaves and trunk exudes a grey and acrid matter, which on drying assumes the nature of wax as pure as that of bees, but rather more brittle. I have seen tallow-candles surrounded by a thin coating of this wax, which, not melting as rapidly as the tallow, prevents the candle from guttering.

The valley of the Cauca abounds with bamboo-cane, which serves a variety of purposes. With the bamboo the inhabitants build their houses, and erect a pretty kind of fence around their farms. The peasantry make with it sweet-sounding flutes; it furnishes them also with drinking-cups, water-buckets, and bird-cages, chairs and baskets, blow-pipes and arrows. With the canes also large rafts are built for carrying cocoa and other produce down the rivers even as far as the ports of embarkation, where the rafts themselves are disposed of to advantage. As cattle abound, ox-hides are made use of for all sorts of domestic purposes. Tables are covered with them, and also sofas, chairs, bedsteads, doors, and trunks. Cut into strips, they form lassoes, greatly in use among the cattle-keepers of the plains. They are formed into bottles, too, for wine and chica; and with them also, stretched on poles, hand-barrows are constructed for carrying earth and rubbish.

We met in this region a number of horses and mules without ears, and others with their ears lying flat on their necks. On inquiring the reason, we found that this was occasioned by an insect like a wood-louse getting inside them, and which is as prolific as the chigua in the toes of human beings. These insects gradually devour the nerves of the ear, which then falls off. To prevent this, the muleteers rub the inside of the animal's ears with hog's lard, to which the insect has a decided aversion.

Even this paradise was not perfect. We caught sight of several tiger-cats, jaguars, and pumas, which come down and commit depredations on the flocks and herds; and occasionally a huge black bear will descend from his mountain lair and pay a visit to the hog-pen, though he runs a risk of being shot by the watchful owner.

BY THE SIDE OF THE CAUCA

Having all my life lived in the high regions of New Granada, I was not prepared for the perfectly tropical scenery I now for the first time beheld. I remember one spot by the side of the Cauca, just before we reached Cartago. The sepos, or rope-like vines, hung from the lofty branches of the trees, and beautifully-coloured parasitical plants were suspended in the air. Gaily-tinted macaws flew across the blue sky, and other birds of the gayest plumage flitted here and there. There were several plants of the cacti species on the borders of the stream, on the shores of which were seen the bamboo-dwellings of the inhabitants, with palms and other graceful trees rising above them; while long-tailed monkeys swung to and fro on the creepers, which seemed arranged specially for their amusement.

Soon after this we reached the town of Cartago, from which we were to strike upwards over the Quindio mountains. The town was of considerable size, and at one time, I have no doubt, was as flourishing as others in the province. The curse of war had fallen upon it. Many of the houses were empty,—their owners having been killed on their own thresholds, or carried off to be shot, or sent to work at the fortifications of Cartagena or other places on the coast. I saw here a larger number of slaves—negroes and negresses—than at any other place we had passed through. The latter were dressed in blue petticoats, without any other garments. They came in numbers from the river-side, carrying huge pitchers or leathern bottles of water on their heads, and walking gracefully and perfectly upright. I remember a group we passed in the outskirts of the town, who appeared to take life very easily: the women, in the most scanty raiment, with huge necklaces, were seated on the ground chatting and laughing; the men, their only garment a shirt, were lazily smoking their cigars. Forgetting that I was to be ignorant of Spanish, I spoke to them, when, turning round, I saw a person passing in the uniform of an officer. He looked at me for a moment, but making no remark, passed on, and I thought no more about the matter.

Only a very small remnant, I should say, of the ancient inhabitants now remain, though the traces of their former existence are everywhere to be seen, showing that at one time they must have been very numerous. They have been destroyed in vast numbers by the severity of their relentless and avaricious taskmasters. Thousands and tens of thousands of poor Indians have perished from famine, the sword, and the pestilence, or have died with hearts broken by the loss of liberty, or from being compelled to labour in the gold-mines with constitutions unequal to the performance of their hard task-work.

We were, of course, anxious not to stay an hour longer at Cartago than was necessary; and yet it might seem strange to the inhabitants that an Englishman, travelling for the sake of amusement, should not wish to remain a sufficient time in the town even to form a correct opinion of it. The posada was a wretched one, but there were few people in it. The old woman who kept it declared that the Spaniards had carried off all her property; indeed, except a few red earthenware plates, I could see nothing on which our supper could be served. I sat down in a corner of the room, and pretended to be reading an English book; while Mr Laffan went out to arrange for guides, silleros, and peons, to enable us to travel over the Quindio mountains. From what our old landlady said, I guessed that she was a Liberal; but, of course, I thought it best not to trust her. The silleros are chairmen, the peons carry the baggage. It was not necessary, we found, to leave our horses behind, though it might be dangerous to ride them. At the same time, if it had not been important to keep up our character as travellers, I should not have hesitated to push over the mountains with a single guide to show the way.

While I was waiting for Mr Laffan's return, a Spanish officer entered the posada, and in a dictatorial tone ordered supper, although it was an early hour for that meal. He then eyed me narrowly, and inquired of the old woman who I was. It struck me that he was the person I had seen while I was talking to the natives.

"An English milord going over the Quindio mountains to Bogota," was the answer—being the information Domingo had given her.

Turning towards me, he inquired if such were the case. I was very nearly replying, when I remembered that I did not speak Spanish, and I made signs to let him know that my companion would soon return and inform him all about the matter. Finding that he could make nothing of me, he paced up and down the room, his sword clanking on the hard mud floor. Whenever he came near me, Lion gave a low growl, and appeared as if about to spring on him. There was something in the tone of his voice, or the appearance of the man, which evidently the sagacious animal did not like. Soon after an orderly appeared, conducting a sillero and two peons—the sillero was a fine strong-built man in a loose dress.

The captain told them that he meant to start next morning at daybreak to go across the mountains, and that they must reach Ibaque in five days.

"Impossible," was the answer. "Six is the least in which the journey can be performed. Except with the greatest exertion, it requires seven."

"I must start at daybreak to-morrow morning, and my orders must be obeyed. Go! the sergeant will look after you."

The soldier retired with the men, who, I found, were his prisoners; and in a short time Mr Laffan appeared, and said that he had arranged with two silleros and five peons, three of whom were to lead the horses, and the other two to carry our baggage.

"Domingo will have to walk, and so must we, if we wish to push on fast," he observed. "They can go on ahead, and we can overtake them at the foot of the mountains," he added.

This was satisfactory intelligence. I then told him what I had heard the Spanish officer saying; that he seemed an ill-tempered fellow; and that we must be on our guard towards him.

The captain, after having discussed his supper, put the same questions to Mr Laffan that he had put to me.

A GROUP OF NATIVES

My tutor told him the story agreed on. "Oh!" he said, "you will follow me, for I must carry intelligence of the proceedings of the rascally rebels to Bogota."

"A pleasant journey to you then, colonel," said Mr Laffan, giving him a higher title than was his due. "We Englishmen, unaccustomed to your wild mountains, cannot travel so fast."

I begged Mr Laffan to inquire what news the officer could give us.

"Very satisfactory," he answered; "the rebels are everywhere defeated, and many of their leaders have been taken prisoners. The only unfortunate circumstance has been the escape of some of the prisoners who were being sent to Bogota by the way of La Plata. Among others rescued is that intriguing lady, Dona Dolores Monteverde."

I tried to keep my countenance as this was said.

"Never heard of her," observed Mr Laffan with imperturbable coolness. "How did it happen?"

"Suddenly, as the guards who had her and others in charge were emerging from a defile, they were set upon by a small party of horsemen who had remained concealed behind the rocks, and had allowed the larger force to pass. Most of the escort were cut down, for their bodies were found strewed on the ground; and the prisoners, including Dona Dolores, were carried off. Though hotly pursued by the cavalry, who, on hearing the shots, had returned, the rascals made good their escape."

I was delighted to hear this, and I had no doubt but that Juan by some means or other had heard of the capture of Dona Dolores, and had formed a plan for her rescue. I hoped also that her father had escaped with her, as he probably would be in her company. It relieved my mind of a great difficulty; for although I had resolved to attempt her liberation, I could devise no plan for its accomplishment. I advised Mr Laffan to ask no further questions, lest the officer might suspect that he had some object in view.

We slung up our hammocks as usual in the common room, and the dominie and I did our best to sleep soundly, knowing that Lion would awake us if necessary.

The captain had stowed himself away on a pile of straw and cloaks in the corner, and just before I closed my eyes I heard him snoring loudly. A small oil lamp on the table shed an uncertain light through the room, so that objects could be only dimly distinguished. Our valises, I should have said, had been left on the ground a short distance from the heads of our hammocks.

How long I had been asleep I do not know, but I was awakened by a low growl from Lion. He did not spring forward, however. Looking up, I thought I distinguished a figure stealing along the wall. Lion still growled. The person, if there was one, remained in dark shadow, or else had passed through some opening, which I did not remember to have observed. I lay awake for some moments watching, but could see no one. I tried to make out whether the Spanish captain was still asleep on his bed, but, at the distance I was from the corner, I could not be certain. He was not, at all events, snoring, though he might be there.

Supposing that I must have been mistaken, I once more fell asleep. Strange to say, the same circumstances again occurred; but this time, forgetting at the moment that it was supposed I could not speak Spanish, and suddenly aroused from slumber, I shouted out, "Who goes there? Take care, whoever you are, else I'll send a bullet through your head." There was no answer. Lion gave a suppressed bark, in addition to a growl, and moved forward to where the valises lay, where he couched down with his fore paws stretched out, and his head resting on them, watching our property. From this I was convinced that some one had attempted to steal them, or, at all events, to obtain some of their contents; for we had carelessly left them both partly open. I was, however, now very sure that Lion would take care not to allow any one to touch them without giving us abundant warning.

This time I remained awake for some minutes, and clearly distinguished a person creeping round to the captain's bed, on which he threw himself. It must have been the captain himself. Possibly his object was to obtain some money, which, supposing me to be a rich Englishman, he had concluded he should find; or he may have wished to get hold of our letters to ascertain who we were. He had, during the evening, frequently cast suspicious glances at my tutor and me, as if he were not quite certain that the account we gave of ourselves was the true one.

Overcome by sleep, my eyes once more closed; but I dreamed that I saw the captain reading our letters at the table, and making notes of their contents; and that then Lion jumped up and seized him by the throat. The dominie and I sprang to his rescue, but could not find the letters. I thought that he addressed us both by name, however, and appeared to know all about our affairs.

The captain got up at daybreak, and awoke us by shouting for his breakfast. During the meal, which he hurried over, he asked Mr Laffan a number of questions; then suddenly turning to me he said —

"How is it that you, who have been some months in the country, cannot speak Spanish?"

I looked at Mr Laffan and signed to him to reply.

"The young milord has no aptitude for learning languages," he observed. "If you were to go to England, it might be some months before you could make yourself understood."

The Spaniard, smiling grimly, said, "That's strange, for I was awakened during the night by hearing him cry out, in very good Spanish, threatening to shoot somebody. I recognised his voice, and could not be mistaken."

I endeavoured to look perfectly unconcerned, as if I had not understood what was said.

"You must have been dreaming, señor captain," observed Mr Laffan; "I was nearer to him than you, and did not hear his voice."

A SILLERO

He then, turning to me, asked what the Spaniard could mean.

"Tell him that the young English lord is indignant at having such remarks made; that he must apologise for venturing to say such things. It will be better to carry matters with a high hand."

The captain again smiled grimly, and muttered, "We shall see, we shall see."

Having finished his meal, without even offering to pay the landlady he left the house and joined his men, who were waiting for him at the door with the captive silleros and peons. I followed him out unobserved, and heard him remark "that they must push on as fast as they could go, and keep ahead of the two English travellers."

"They are not likely to start for a couple of hours," answered the sergeant; "and if you wish it, we may find means to stop them."

Some further conversation ensued, when the captain took out a paper, on which he wrote several sentences.

"Give this to Major Alvez, and if he thinks fit he will despatch a party to arrest them. You may accompany it, as you know them, and so there will be no mistake."

Not wishing to be discovered, I returned into the house before I could hear more. The captain, mounting a strong mule, rode off, followed by the soldiers and the prisoners.

As soon as they were gone, the men whom Mr Laffan had hired made their appearance. The two silleros were remarkably fine, intelligent—looking Indians, dressed in loose trousers and shirt, the universal poncho of small dimensions over their shoulders, and a large straw hat. They had long poles in their hands. The peons wore only hats and loose short trousers. The machine on which the latter carry the baggage is a sort of frame of bamboo about three feet long, with a cross-piece at the lower end, on which they rest the load. It is secured with straps, which first pass round the burden and then go over the shoulders and across the breast; another strap passes over the forehead, and is fastened to the top of the bamboo at the back.

The peons are careful to put a pad between the strap and the head and loins, to prevent chafing. The chair on which people are carried is much the same as the silla de cargo, except that the chair has rests for the arms, and a step for the feet. A peon will carry a load weighing a hundred pounds, but sometimes double that weight. Although neither Mr Laffan nor I intended to make use of our silleros unless in case of necessity, we thought it prudent to take them with us, that we might keep up our character as English travellers. The sillero who had been engaged to carry me was a well-informed fellow, as I judged from his remarks to Domingo;—of course, he did not address me.

Some time elapsed before the mules were brought to the door. Our horses were led by halters; and, that they might be as unencumbered as possible, their saddles and bridles were carried on the backs of peons. Everything being ready, we started; the porters, with the loads on their backs, keeping up easily with the mules. The road for about a league of the way was tolerable, but it then became so bad that we had frequently to dismount and trudge on foot. So steep were the hills in some places, that there was no little danger of our animals rolling over. The mules, however, accustomed to the ground, inspected it narrowly, then, planting their four legs together, slid down on their haunches. All we could do was to sit well back in our saddles, and trust to the sure-footedness of our animals.

Our first stopping-place was in a ruinous village at the foot of the mountains—the last we were to see until we reached Ibaque. We occupied a room in one of the houses, while our attendants formed sheds, and covered them with large plantain-leaves, which they had brought from Cartago. From one or two of the very few people we met we learned that the Spanish captain had gone on ahead, the soldiers we had seen with him having returned to a fort in the neighbourhood. He must have trusted to the terror which the Spaniards had inspired by their fearful cruelties. The Godos had indeed so cowed the natives that they would not have dared to molest him, else he would scarcely have ventured alone on such a journey. He, of course, had no luggage or animals to impede his progress, and would be able to travel faster than we could. As, however, Mr Laffan and I agreed that he very likely suspected us, we resolved to push on as rapidly as we could, so that we might, if possible, reach Bogota before he would have time to warn the authorities against us.

Chapter Nine.

Our journey over the mountains—Wild scenery—A ride on a Sillero's back—Fears for the safety of our servants and horses—Making progress—My Sillero and I get ahead—The cruel conduct of the Spaniard, and its fearful punishment—Our camp on the mountains—An adventure with a jaguar—I kill a turkey for supper—Our attendants rejoin us—Sounds at night—We begin to descend—Dangers of the journey—We part from our Silleros, and proceed on horseback—A visit to the Falls of Tequendama—Their magnificence.

The road was as bad as could be,—often so steep, that it was like climbing up steps; in some places, indeed, large trees had fallen across the path. But our peons skipped over the trunks with as much firmness as if they had been walking on level ground. Now on one side, now on the other, were tremendous precipices, down which the traveller, by a slip of the foot, might be hurled, and dashed to pieces. We had cloaks and blankets, which we required during the night, for as we ascended the atmosphere became very cold. We also maintained good fires to keep off the jaguars, which frequently, we were told, attacked the mules. We heard them roar during the night; while a dismal howling was kept up by the red monkeys which abound in these deserts. Added to this, our ears were saluted by the loud screeching of night-birds, which formed a serenade far from pleasing.

The mountains were clothed with gloomy forests, which ascend almost to the summit of this branch of the Cordilleras. In a few places, where there were openings, we enjoyed extensive views, on either side, of superb scenery—the mountain-tops concealed in the clouds. We also saw numerous birds perched on the trees, or flitting among their branches—many of the most brilliant plumage, such as I had never before seen in the neighbourhood of Popayan.

I generally kept ahead with my sillero, who led the way. One of the peons following carried the chief load; then came Mr Laffan;

Domingo and the rest of the people with the animals bringing up the rear. My sillero, though an Indian, was called Manoel; being, as he said, a baptised Christian. As I was anxious to gain information, which he seemed willing to impart, I was tempted to break through the plan which had been agreed on, and to speak a few words of Spanish, so that I might ask questions. I began in a broken, hesitating sort of way, until at length I forgot myself altogether, though Manoel did not appear at all astonished.

"El señor speaks Spanish better than I should have supposed possible from the short time he has been in the country," he observed.

"I can understand what you say, and that is all I want," I answered. "I have heard other Indians speak as you do, and so I am more ready to converse with you than I should be with a Spaniard."

I felt sure that I could trust Manoel, as, from one or two remarks he had let drop, I was convinced that he was a Liberal, and had no love for the Spaniards. While we were encamped at night, sitting round our fire, we all talked away until it was time to go to sleep; but while travelling, as we were compelled to move in single file, it was difficult to carry on a conversation, except with the person immediately in front or behind.

After we had proceeded some distance, we began to hope that I had been mistaken in what I had heard the captain say to the sergeant, and that we should escape any risk of being captured and prevented from continuing our journey. Still Mr Laffan continued anxious on the subject.

We had been travelling for some time, and I was beginning to feel more tired than I had hitherto done. I had not as yet, indeed, quite recovered my full strength, and was scarcely fitted to walk as I was doing.

Manoel at length persuaded me to get on the silla. "It makes no difference to me," he observed; "you are as light as a feather. You

English are very different from the Spaniards. They get on our backs as if they were riding mules, and will often use a stick if we do not go fast enough to please them."

I consented unwillingly, for I did not like the idea of any one carrying me.

From the position I had now attained, I could look down the steep ascent we had mounted, and I had an extensive view. I saw Mr Laffan standing gazing back along the path we had come; the rest of the party were nowhere, in sight. We shouted, but no reply came. Could the Spaniards have acted as the captain had advised them, and captured our people?

"Stop, Duncan," cried Mr Laffan; "I do not like the look of things." He soon overtook me, and expressed the same fears I entertained.

I asked Manoel what he thought.

"Very likely," he answered; "those ladrones would as willingly rob English travellers who honour our country by a visit, as they would the unfortunate Patriots or us poor Indians. The best thing we can do is to push on."

The peons carried our valises, the most valuable part of our property. We had our money in our pockets, with a brace of pistols apiece; and I had my gun, which I had brought in case I should see anything to shoot.

"But what shall we do for provisions?" asked Mr Laffan.

"We shall find game enough on the road to supply all our wants," answered Manoel.

We agreed, therefore, to move forward as fast as we could. Domingo, with the peons and our animals, if not captured, could easily follow and overtake us at night.

THE ASCENT OF THE MOUNTAIN.

"We are coming to the steepest part of our journey," said Manoel; "the Spanish soldiers will have a difficulty in climbing up the path ahead."

Every now and then Mr Laffan looked back, and I kept looking occasionally down the valley,—but not a sign of our attendants could I discover. In a short time Manoel said that he observed the marks of footsteps ahead. "They are those of a sillero carrying some person. We shall soon overtake them."

Manoel, in his eagerness, soon distanced the other peon and Mr Laffan, whose anxiety made him stop to ascertain whether our attendants were coming. We were at this time mounting an excessively steep and narrow path, with a tremendous precipice on one side, down which it made me giddy to look: had I not had the most perfect confidence in my sillero, I should infinitely have preferred to walk. I begged him, indeed, to let me get off; but he always answered, "You are no weight; it makes not the slightest difference to me. I feel my footing more secure with you on my back." Shortly afterwards I heard him exclaim, "There they are!—the savage brute!"

"Of whom do you speak?" I asked.

"Of the Spanish officer. He is digging his spurs into the side of my poor brother, to make him go faster."

I glanced round, although it was somewhat difficult to do so; and there, sure enough, I saw the captain whom we had met at the posada, seated in a silla, and striking, now with one leg now with the other, at his carrier, occasionally hitting him over the head with the back of his hand. The Indian went on, as far as I could perceive, without complaining; but the captain shouted "Go on—go on faster," and again dug his spurs into the poor Indian.

Manoel groaned. I could hear him grind his teeth.

"How can you bear it?" he muttered. "The Spaniard may repent his cruelty, though."

At the foot of the precipice, I should have said, rushed a fierce torrent, roaring and foaming down the side of the mountain. Presently I saw the sillero buttress himself, as it were, firmly with the iron-shod stick with which he supported his steps. Again the Spaniard dug his spurs into his side, asking him what he was doing, and, with a fearful oath, shouted to him to go on. The Indian answered by a vigorous jerk of his back, when I saw the Spaniard shot off, as from a catapult. The next moment he was falling headlong down into the gulf, several hundred feet below us. One fearful shriek rent the air; it was the only sound the wretched man had time to utter before the breath, by the rapidity of his fall, was taken from his body. It was the work of an instant. I shut my eyes. It seemed like some terrible dream. The Spanish captain was gone, though his voice still sounded in my ear.

Manoel stopped. "He has met the fate he deserved," he said.

"But the sillero will see you, and suppose you will inform against him."

Manoel answered with a low laugh. "He is my brother, and knows that the secret is safe in my keeping. Can I trust you? No other creature saw what has occurred."

"God saw him, and he is the avenger of blood," I answered.

"Would you have had my brother patiently submit to the cruelties inflicted upon him?" asked Manoel.

"We have no right to take the life of a fellow-creature, except in self-defence or open warfare," I replied. "But the secret is safe in my keeping. I did not even see the face of the man who committed the deed, and I know not who he was. I love the Spaniards as little as you do, and I promise you I will not reveal the dreadful crime I have just witnessed."

"I am grateful," answered Manoel; "for, to tell you the truth, had I thought you capable of informing against my brother, I might have been tempted, though much against my inclination, to serve you as he served the Spaniard; but had I done so, I never should have been happy afterwards."

I scarcely thought that Manoel was in earnest, and yet I believe that he was so. His fidelity to his brother sillero would have been paramount to every other consideration. Manoel was advancing as he spoke, but when I looked round the sillero had disappeared, though I afterwards caught a glimpse of him bounding up the rocks on the left, having hurled his chair over the cliff.

It was some time before I could recover from the horrible scene I had witnessed; and I debated in my own mind whether or not I should have given the promise I had made to Manoel. One thing was certain, however—I was bound to keep it.

When the path became less steep, I insisted on walking. Manoel, too, though he had boasted of his strength, was obliged to stop and rest; and at length the peons and Mr Laffan rejoined us. The latter was still anxious about the rest of the party, and declared that it would be impossible for the horses to mount the steep path by which we had come. He thought that even the mules could scarcely do it, supposing that they had not been overtaken by the Spaniards.

I had not, of course, told him how our chief cause of anxiety was removed, and that we need no longer fear discovery on our arrival at Bogota.

"When the Spaniards are driven away, and a Liberal government is established, we must have a good road over these mountains," exclaimed Mr Laffan. "It is a disgrace to a civilised country, that no better means of communication exists between the capital and her most fertile districts."

At last, as evening approached, Manoel selected a spot for encamping, and we made the usual preparations. We enjoyed a magnificent scene. As far as the eye could range were mountains clothed with immense forests, into which man had never penetrated. About a couple of hundred feet below us ran a sparkling stream, towards which, while the peon was employed in collecting wood for the fire, Manoel made his way, to fill a leathern bottle with water. I accompanied him with my gun, followed by Lion, hoping to shoot some birds for supper.

We had gone a little way along the bank, when a wild turkey got up. I fired, and brought it to the ground. Manoel ran forward to secure it, but just before he reached it he stopped and beckoned to me. As he did so I saw a huge jaguar, which had been drinking at the stream, not two hundred yards from us. I had, as a sportsman should, reloaded my gun before moving. The only weapon Manoel possessed, besides the manchette at his girdle, was his sharp-pointed staff, —not calculated for an encounter with so powerful a beast. The jaguar, having seen the turkey fall, crept on to seize it. I advanced as rapidly as I dared, keeping my gun ready for instant use. Lion would have rushed forward to get the bird had I not ordered him to remain at my heels, for, powerful as he was, a blow from the jaguar's paw would have been too much for him.

The jaguar seemed determined not to be disappointed of the turkey, and would probably, I thought, spring at Manoel. The difficulty was to avoid wounding him in shooting at the jaguar. Manoel stood ready for action, with his staff in his hand. He dared not for a moment withdraw his eye from the jaguar, which, had he done so, would immediately have sprung upon him. I called to him, telling him I was coming, in case he might not have heard my footsteps. The jaguar was all the time creeping up, threatening at any moment to spring, and I was about twelve yards behind Manoel when the brute began to bound forward. Manoel leapt on one side. Now or never, I must gain the victory, or both my companion and I might lose our lives. I fired. The jaguar bounded into the air, then fell over on its side.

Manoel dashed forward and plunged his stick into the creature's neck, pinning it to the ground; then drawing his manchette, he quickly terminated its existence. We left it where it lay, for we could not have carried its skin, even had we taken the trouble of flaying it.

Near the top of the hill we met Mr Laffan, who had witnessed the encounter.

"Bravo, Duncan! you behaved famously; and Manoel too—he is a fine fellow. All the same, the turkey is welcome, for I am terribly hard set."

We soon had the bird roasting before the fire. It was, however, but a moderate supper for four people and a dog, and I was sorry that I had not succeeded in killing another turkey.

Mr Laffan kept constantly jumping up and looking down the path by which we had come, in the hope of seeing our attendants; and just as the shades of evening were creeping over the mountains, he exclaimed, "There they are!—I hope I am not mistaken."

I could see several persons and animals winding round the side of the hill, so I called to Manoel, and asked him if he thought they were our friends.

"If they are Spaniards, señor, we shall be wise to move forward, for they will treat you with but little ceremony, I suspect."

Manoel descended to a point from whence he could observe the approaching party without being seen, and in a short time returned and relieved our anxiety by assuring us that they were our friends. It was some time, however, before they reached our camp.

They had been delayed by their efforts to rescue one of the mules which had slipped over a precipice and got pitched in a tree; from which, wonderful to relate, it was drawn up uninjured. The Spanish commandant, we therefore concluded, had not thought fit to send in chase of us.

During the night we heard the roar of jaguars and other wild animals; but as we kept up a blazing fire, we were not molested. In the morning, just as we were about to start, I shot two wild turkeys; and had we had time to spare, I might have killed several more. As we proceeded we saw several tracks of bears and jaguars, perfectly fresh.

The next day we reached the Paramo, on the summit of the Cordilleras, thirteen thousand feet above the level of the sea. We caught sight of numbers of wild asses, which inhabit this mountainous region. The hoof of the animal is divided like that of a pig. They are very shy, so that even the Indians are seldom able to approach near enough to kill them; and they are also very swift of foot.

We crossed the Paramo in safety, and continued our journey for several days without any further adventure.

The views, as we descended the mountains, were magnificent. We could see the Cordilleras on the opposite side of the plain of Bogota, seventy or eighty miles off; while north and south rose prodigious heights, with apparently perpendicular sides, their bases covered with thick, gloomy forests, which appeared perfectly impenetrable. As we looked back, it seemed impossible that we should have crossed the range. Frequently we passed through dark gorges piercing the forests, two miles in length, and not more than three or four feet wide, the vegetation on either side being most luxuriant.

We had to be on our guard against bruising our legs by pieces of rock; or getting our clothes torn by the long thorns of the bamboos; or being knocked off our mules—for we had again mounted—by the branches of trees. We met a party of peons conveying salt on the backs of oxen to Cartage. The cargoes were small, and placed in such a manner as to enable the animals to pass through these narrow places. Fortunately there was an opening near the spot, or we should have been unable to pass each other.

THE "SALTO"

At last we reached a tambo, or shed, built for the use of travellers —
the first sign of civilisation we had met since we left the western side
of the Cordilleras.

We were now once more in a warmer region. Butterflies of large size, covered with orange-coloured spots, fluttered about; and red monkeys leapt from tree to tree, frequently coming down to make grimaces at us. Another day's journey brought us to a cottage inhabited by peasants, who gave us a satisfactory welcome.

At length we reached the place where we were to part from our silleros and peons, and continue our journey on horseback.

"I hope that we shall meet again," I said to Manoel, who had won my regard.

"We shall, señor, it may be, if you do not soon leave the country," replied Manoel, looking earnestly at me.

"I may stay longer than I at first intended," I said.

Manoel and the rest of our attendants were well satisfied with the payment we had made them.

Mr Laffan and I, with Domingo, now continued our journey on horseback, the roads being tolerable. But, eager as we were to reach Bogota, we agreed that it would be wise, the better to keep up our assumed character, to visit the waterfall of Tequendama, which was not far out of our direct road. It is formed by the river Bogota, which is hereabouts sixty yards in breadth.

As soon as we got within a mile or so of it, we obtained a guide to show us the way. At a height of six hundred feet above the plain of Bogota, we enjoyed a magnificent view, embracing the various windings of the river, several large lakes, and enormous forests — the city in the distance, backed by a range of bold mountains. Thence we began to descend towards the waterfall, the sides of the hill being abrupt and slippery. We passed through a grand, gloomy forest, the lofty boughs of the trees sheltering us from the rays of the hot sun. All was silent, except the deep, fine note of the tropiole, which was occasionally heard; while through the openings we caught sight of other birds of brilliant plumage, which here live unmolested.

Leaving our horses, the dominie and I descended a couple of hundred feet to a spot where the "Salto," as it is called, burst on our view, rushing down between two mountains until it attains the edge of a precipice, whence the vast body of water is precipitated into a mighty abyss below. The chasms through which such falls issue are known in the country as barancas. The sides, consisting of reddish granite, rise almost perpendicularly. The height of the whole fall may be nearly one thousand feet, but the single fall in front of us was calculated to be about six hundred feet.

We stood on the bank of the precipice for some minutes, not daring to speak: indeed, the sound of the falling water completely drowned our voices when we made the attempt; the sensation in our ears being as if a thousand pieces of artillery were discharged close to us. The ground trembled beneath our feet, our eyes were dazzled by the sparkling spray, and our senses felt confused, as the mighty volume of water rushed down before us, between the perpendicular rocks, into the chasm at their base. The overwhelming body of water, as it left its upper bed, formed a broad arch, smooth and glossy. A little lower down it assumed a fleecy form; and then shot forth in millions of tubular shapes, which chased each other more like sky-rockets than anything else to which I can compare them. The changes were as singularly beautiful as they were varied, in consequence of the difference in gravitation, and rapid evaporation, which was taking place before the waters reached the bottom. Dense clouds of vapour rose for a considerable height, mingling with the atmosphere, and presenting in their descent the most brilliant rainbows. From the rocky sides of the immense basin hung shrubs and bushes, while numerous springs and tributary streams added their mite to the grand effect. The water at the bottom then rushed impetuously along a stony bed, over which hung various trees, and was lost beyond a dark turn in the rock. From the level of the river where we stood, the hills, completely covered with wood, rose to a great height; while through the only opening amid them we observed the distant mountains in the province of Antioquia, their summits clothed with perpetual snow. Hovering over the fearful chasm were various birds of the most beautiful plumage, peculiar to the spot, and differing from any I had seen before. Our guide told us that some philosophical gentlemen, in order to ascertain the tremendous force of the torrent, had once compelled an unfortunate bullock to descend it; but that, excepting a few bones, not a vestige of the animal could afterwards be found at the bottom.

"It is worth coming all the way from England to behold such a scene as this," observed Mr Laffan to our guide, as he put a piece of money into the man's hand. "The young milord is highly pleased."

The guide took care to inform some persons whom he found at the top of the hill, and who were going to Bogota, of the opinion I had formed; and they of course entertained no suspicion that I was any other than a young English lord travelling with his tutor. This was a great advantage to us, as it prevented puzzling questions being asked.

Mr Laffan, however, continued to express his fears that the Spanish captain might have preceded us, and given notice to the authorities of our coming.

I, of course, said nothing of having witnessed the man's terrible end, as I had resolved to keep the fearful secret locked in my own bosom. Probably, even had I mentioned it, very little trouble would have been taken to search out the culprit and bring him to justice.

Chapter Ten.

We overtake an escort with prisoners on the road to Bogota—Dr Cazalla among them—He makes no sign of recognition—We next see Uncle Richard—How Lion nearly betrayed us—We speak to Uncle Richard in English—Antonio among the guard—Has he turned traitor?—Hurrying on before the escort, we fall in with a body of volunteers for the Spanish army—At a posada—Cock-fighting—The sergeant and his recruits arrive—Entering Bogota—Description of the city—The Great Square—At the house of Don José—The children's remarks—We are kindly treated—The death of Dona Paula Salabariata—Don José's sympathy—Some other patriots shot.

Having made a circuit to the southward, we reached the highroad which runs between the capital and La Plata. As we did so, we saw before us a considerable body of men both on foot and horseback; and on inquiring of some peons who were coming in our direction, they told us that they were soldiers escorting a number of Republican prisoners to Bogota. Could any of our friends be among them?

Mr Laffan and I determined to ride up and ascertain; and by assuming a bold front, we hoped to escape detection.

We soon overtook the party, but found it impossible to pass them on the road; and although we saw some prisoners in their midst, we could not find out who they were. The escort, however, at length halted in the plaza of a village, which, being of considerable width, enabled us to ride past them. Pretending not to be much concerned, yet eagerly scanning the countenances of the prisoners, I saw several whom I knew, but among them my uncle, Doctor Cazalla, who, with the rest, had been compelled to walk, his hands secured behind his back with a rope. He was now, with his companions in misfortune, seated on a log of wood. I felt sure that he knew me, though he made no sign of recognition, and I dared not make any to him; but my appearance showed him, I trusted, that every effort would be made for his liberation. Further on was another group of prisoners, some lying on the ground, others seated on a stone bench. Fearing that the account the Spanish captain had given might not be true, I half expected to see Dona Dolores and her father. The Spaniards, of course, would not have treated her with more consideration than they did their other prisoners; but I could see neither her nor Señor Monteverde.

At that instant Lion rushed forward towards one of the people seated on the bench, and what was my dismay to discover Uncle Richard! Fearful lest the dog should betray us, I loudly called him back, pretending that I thought he was about to fly at the prisoners. Though always obedient, on this occasion he did not seem to heed me, until Uncle Richard spoke to him in a stern voice, when the sagacious animal returned to my side and remained there, as if he had never before seen Uncle Richard. He, I saw, immediately recognised Mr Laffan and me, by the glance he cast at us; but retaining his presence of mind, he made no sign to show that he had done so.

I rode close to him, and turning round to Mr Laffan, I said aloud, —"I wish he would address us as Englishmen, which he might easily do without causing suspicion; we could then learn all we want to know, and form a plan for helping him."

Directly I had said this, Uncle Richard shouted out, "I am sure those are Englishmen! Have pity on me, noble gentlemen; I am your countryman, made prisoner by the Spaniards, and shall very likely be shot if I am not rescued."

He turned to the soldiers standing by, and said in Spanish, "Those are English travellers—my countrymen. Allow them to speak to me; they are always generous, and will reward you."

Without waiting for leave, we turned our horses towards the bench; and leaning over, I asked Uncle Richard after our families, and how he had been made prisoner,—trying to assume as unconcerned a tone as possible.

"They are all safe," he answered. "Your father's black servant—I won't mention his name—has charge of them, and they are still safe in the mountains. I was unfortunately tempted to leave our retreat, in the hope of raising a body of Indians and others to be ready to aid a projected attack by the Patriots on the Spaniards, when I was surprised and taken prisoner. It will go hard with me, I fear, as, though I am an Englishman, Murillo will not stand on ceremony on that account."

"Do not be cast down. We will try to find out where you are imprisoned, and will do everything we can to rescue you," I answered.

"I am sure of that," he said. "By what wonderful chance are you here?"

I then told him the object of our journey, and how I had letters to a number of persons of influence in Bogota, so that I might hope to be of effectual service to him.

"You will do your best, I am sure," he said; "and, depend upon it, I do not intend to be killed like a rat in a hole, but shall try to gnaw my way out. You had better not stay much longer, or some of those fellows may possibly recognise you. Bestow a gold piece or two on me, if you have any to spare; in truth, I am greatly in need of money, as every dollar I had in my pocket was taken from me when I was made prisoner. And do not forget to bestow your promised gift on our guards—it will incline them to favour me. Two or three of them seem very good fellows, and have been attentive to me on the journey."

"Now," I said, "if you have an opportunity, tell my mother's brother—I will not mention his name—why I have come to Bogota, and that every effort will be made for his liberation."

After a few more words, I took out my purse and put a few gold pieces into Uncle Richard's hand. I then turned to Mr Laffan, who had been standing by, occasionally joining in the conversation, and begged him to distribute some money among the men. As I glanced my eye over them, what was my surprise to see my servant Antonio in a corporal's uniform, and apparently in command of the party! I was sure it was he, although he looked at me in the most unconcerned manner possible, returning only a military salute as Mr Laffan handed him the money. Could he have deserted to the enemy? I had considered him a faithful fellow, as he certainly was a brave one. He must have had some object in joining the Spaniards; what it was, however, we could not now ascertain.

A PARTY OF RECRUITS.

Uttering our farewells, we mounted and rode on, followed by Domingo. As we did so, Lion turned and cast a lingering glance behind; but the stern look Uncle Richard put on, told him that he must not take any notice of him.

It now became more important than ever that we should reach the city without delay. We had not gone far, when we saw a party of recruits marching from a large village to the eastward. Mr Laffan, however, thought that they were prisoners,—which they certainly resembled more than soldiers, except that each man carried a musket on his shoulder; for they were all secured together by a long rope, the end of which was held by a ruffianly-looking fellow on horseback. They were dressed in broad-brimmed hats, loose trousers, and ponchos over their shoulders; but the rest of their bodies, legs and feet, were bare. The sergeant had on a very unmilitary-looking hat of large dimensions, with wide leggings, and huge spurs.

"Faith, I wonder the fellows don't turn round and shoot him," observed Mr Laffan.

"Probably, to save the risk of that, they are not supplied with ammunition," I rejoined. "This is the way in which the Spaniards obtain their recruits. The poor fellows are thus marched off to be slaughtered; unless they can contrive to run away, which they certainly will do if they have the opportunity."

Saluting the sergeant, who only scowled at us in return, we rode on ahead of the party. We found, on inquiring the distance we should have to go, that we could not reach Bogota that evening, and accordingly stopped at a posada three or four leagues from the city. It was a large straggling building, at which small traders and merchants generally put up. People of more consequence were accustomed to proceed further, or stop at the country-houses of their friends.

As we rode up, we found all the inhabitants and guests assembled in the yard witnessing a cock-fight, their eager countenances and excited exclamations showing the interest they took in the brutal pastime. The birds, armed with steel spurs, flew at each other and fought desperately. When one was killed or hopelessly wounded, the owner tore his hair and swore fearfully at his misfortune—by which, probably, he had lost no inconsiderable sum.

We turned away disgusted and entered the inn—Domingo having taken our horses into the stable—but it was some time before we could get anybody to attend to us. At last the landlord appeared; and Mr Laffan having explained who we were, or rather who we pretended to be, begged that we might have a private apartment. On this the landlord laughed, and said that even for an English milord this was impossible, but that we might have a corner of the public room for ourselves. He then inquired what we would have for supper, assuring us that anything we might ask for would be provided. As usual, when Mr Laffan mentioned one thing after another, it was not to be had. At length, however, a tough fowl, with some salt beef and fried eggs, was placed before us, together with some plantains and various fruits, off which we contrived to make a very satisfactory repast. The scene at night reminded me of that at the posada on the opposite side of the mountains, the arrangements being very similar. On this occasion, the greater part of the floor was covered by recumbent figures.

We had already turned into our hammocks, when a loud voice demanding admittance was heard outside the house; and—by the light of the only candle left burning—on the door being opened I recognised the sergeant and his recruits. This individual in an authoritative tone ordered several of the sleeping people to get up, in order to make room for his party. He then called for supper, while his men lay down, with their muskets by their sides, to rest their weary limbs. Having quickly finished his meal, he took possession of a vacant space; placing, I observed, his pistols under the saddle which served him as a pillow, and unsheathing his sword, so as to have it ready for instant use. He had probably no great confidence in his recruits, and thought it not unlikely that one of them might get up during the night and plunge a cuchillo in his heart.

On awaking next morning, I proposed starting immediately.

"Take my advice, and stow away breakfast first," observed Mr Laffan. "It is a sound rule to follow when travelling, unless one knows that a substantial meal is waiting one at the end of the stage."

We got off at an early hour, however, and again passed the sergeant and his so-called recruits on the road. We pushed on before them, wishing to get into Bogota as soon as possible. As we rode on, the towers and steeples of the city appeared before us, glittering in the rays of the rising sun. On one side was a range of lofty mountains, running in a semicircular form; the city itself covering an elevation slightly above the vast plain extending before it. Here and there we caught sight of the river Bogota, which runs through the plain in a serpentine form at about three leagues from the city. The surrounding country was generally uncultivated, except in the immediate neighbourhood of villages or quintas, though there were large enclosures for grazing cattle. On the summits of the mountains which rise immediately above the city were perched two white buildings, which we ascertained to be convents. We could see the domes and towers of others, and were told that thirty-three of them occupied the best sites in the city. They were, indeed, the only fine-looking buildings to be seen.

I was much struck with the appearance of the town as we entered it. All the streets appeared to be built at right angles, while a stream of water flowed through the centre. We passed, also, a number of handsome public fountains. The streets through which we rode were much crowded, making us suppose that something unusual was taking place. The handsomest street we saw was the Calle Real, or Royal Street. The ground-floors of the houses were occupied by shops; with a story above, and a large wooden balcony painted green. On either side of the street, which was well paved, was a foot-path; and as there were no vehicles of any description, the traffic being carried on by mules, it was free from ruts, and remarkably clean.

No one seemed especially to regard us, though we were occasionally favoured with a stare from persons who fancied they were looking at Englishmen—some of them scowling ominously at us, and bestowing curses on our heads for being heretics. Beggars of all descriptions swarmed in the streets, exhibiting their sores, and demanding rather than soliciting alms. Many were afflicted with that dreadful complaint known as elephantiasis—their legs being swollen to an enormous size. Still more numerous were the galenachas, or black vultures. As we reached the great square of the city, into which the Calle Real led us, we saw them hopping about, acting as scavengers, engaged in devouring the filth and offal left on the ground; and so tame were they, that they would scarcely get out of our way.

THE CALLE REAL

On riding forward, we found ourselves in the midst of a large market being carried on in the great square. It was filled with people vending their provisions—some sitting before pyramids of fruit piled up on the ground; others at low stools, on which articles of all sorts were exposed for sale. Among them were Creoles, Blacks, Sambos, Indians—indeed, every hue was represented—all jabbering in loud voices. On one side of the square was the town-house, and on the other the cathedral, with two convents, and other public buildings.

We inquired our way to the house of Don José Lagano, which we found looked into the great square. Though a noted Royalist, he was a friend of both my father and Don Cassiodoro, who were satisfied that he could be thoroughly trusted, even although he might suspect who we were.

Don José was at home; and on hearing from the servant that a young English milord had arrived, he politely came out to receive us. As he read the letter I delivered him it struck me that his countenance changed.

"You are welcome, at all events," he said; "and I will endeavour to forward the object you have in view."

He introduced me to his wife in the character I had assumed, and Mr Laffan as my tutor. Soon afterwards, several nice boys and girls of various ages entered the room. While refreshments were preparing, I endeavoured to amuse the children by playing with them. Though I spoke a word or two of ill-pronounced Spanish—not being supposed to understand their language—they were very free in their remarks, and I could scarcely refrain from laughing as I heard what they said. The lady spoke French; and as I knew the language pretty well, we could converse without difficulty. She somewhat puzzled me by the questions she put about England; but, as I found she had not been there, I gave her the best account I could of such places as I had heard my father and Uncle Richard describe.

Don José's countenance wore a puzzled expression as he heard me talking, but I believe he from the first suspected who I was. I found him an amiable, good-natured man, and really anxious to save the lives of such prisoners as fell into the hands of the Spanish general.

I had been directed to plead for Dr Cazalla on account of his scientific attainments, and as it would be a disgrace, whatever his political opinions were, to put such a man to death.

Don José shook his head when he heard what I said. "That is the very reason why Murillo will desire to destroy him," he observed. "His intention is to rid the country of all men of superior intelligence and influence; and he has especially vowed to put to death every lawyer who falls into his hands."

As a last resource, I had letters from Don Cassiodoro to Murillo himself, which I was to deliver in person—bearding the lion in his den—with my tutor to act as interpreter. It was considered that there would be no danger in this—that the doing so would rather tend to confirm him in the idea that I was a young English nobleman; and I should, on leaving the city, be able to proceed in any direction I might think fit. My only fear was lest Mr Laffan and I might encounter some person who had known us at Popayan, in which case we should be placed in a very dangerous position.

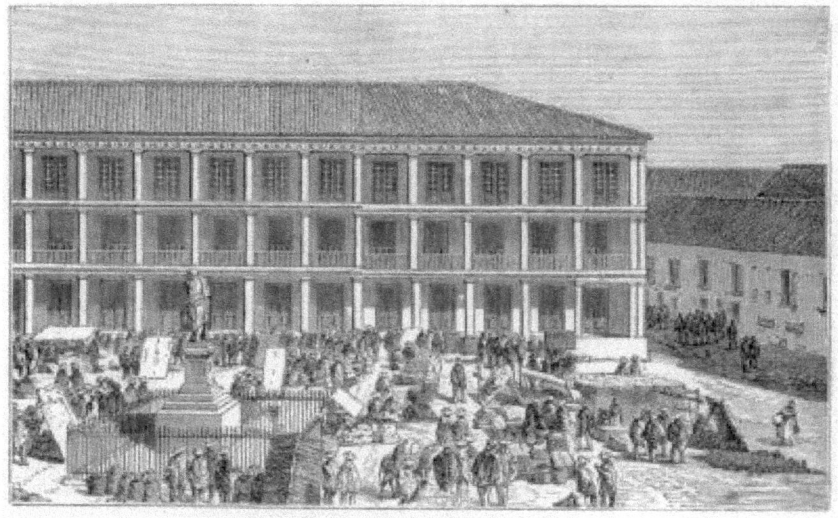

THE MARKET IN THE GREAT SQUARE.

Next morning the sound of muffled drums was heard, and on going to the window with our host I saw a body of troops marching from the direction of the prison. In their midst walked several persons, each between two priests. I was struck by the appearance of one of the unhappy persons—who were evidently prisoners—a young lady of graceful figure and features, who appeared to me singularly beautiful.

"Who are they, and where are they going?" I asked of Don José in French, for he spoke that language as well as his wife.

"That lady is Dona Paula Salabariata; and she is going to her death."

"To her death!" I exclaimed.

"Yes; in a few minutes she and those with her are to be shot. She is a determined Revolutionist, and has long been engaged in inciting the people to rebellion. Her correspondence with the Republicans has at length been discovered; and at her trial, which took place yesterday, she acknowledged her principles, and confessed that she had written the letters."

"So young, and so beautiful!" I exclaimed.

"Yes, my friend; and she is gentle, and possesses a woman's heart, though with the spirit of a man. She was engaged to marry a young Republican officer; but neither her youth nor her beauty will avail her with our stern viceroy."

"The cruel tyrant!" I exclaimed.

Not noticing what I said, he continued: "Do you think that anything will induce him to spare the learned doctor?" —and here he fixed his eyes on me—"or any young man who falls into his power?"

I could make no reply; indeed, our attention was absorbed by the mournful procession passing through the square. My eyes were fixed on Dona Paula.

"My heart will burst, if I do not go out and fight for her!" exclaimed my tutor, who was standing close behind me; and he clapped his hand to his sword.

"My friend," said Don José, "be calm. Although I do not hold her principles, I would join you if it would avail, but any attempt of the sort would only result in our certain death."

My heart was swelling with indignation, and I felt as did my worthy tutor, but I saw the folly of acting as our feelings prompted.

The rest of the prisoners walked with firm step; but I confess that I scarcely noticed any of them, nor, I believe, did my companions, our whole attention being absorbed by the lovely girl who formed the prominent figure. I remarked that she was dressed in black, and that she advanced with a firm step, her small head erect on her graceful neck; the only ornament she wore in her glossy black hair being a spray of orange-blossom, as if she were going to her bridal. She carried a book in her hand; and when the friar presented the crucifix to her, she gently but firmly put it aside.

The party moved forward until they reached the centre of the vast square, when they halted in line, the other prisoners being made to stand on either side. The lady knelt down, and was allowed to remain for a few minutes in prayer; she then rose, and handing the wreath and her shawl to some of her weeping female friends who had followed her, she stood alone, holding a handkerchief in her hand. Then exclaiming, "Success to the cause of my oppressed countrymen!" she let the handkerchief drop. At that moment the firing-party, a few paces off, discharged the fatal volley; and as the smoke cleared off we saw her stretched on the ground, not a movement to indicate that she lived being perceptible. An officer advanced and took her hand, to ascertain that she was dead, after which her attendants approached and bore her away; the only favour which the savage tyrant had been induced to grant being that her friends should be permitted to commit her body to the grave.

Such would have been the fate of Dona Dolores, had she not escaped, I thought. I was nearly expressing my opinion aloud, when I happily remembered in whose company I was. The two ladies, I had no doubt, had frequently communicated with each other; and since such women, full of intelligence and enthusiasm, were labouring in the cause, it must, I felt sure, in the end be successful. Would that all the men were like them, so disinterested, so self-sacrificing, so devoted,—ready, like Dona Paula, to lay down their lives for their country's good! But, alas! too many even among the Patriots were self-opinionated—seeking their own aggrandisement, and how to fill their coffers, without regard to the public weal; yet among them were many true Patriots, such as Bolivar, Paez, Arismendez, Santandar, and many others.

The rest of the prisoners were now brought forward; but Don José and myself, shuddering, retired from the window, unwilling to see our fellow-creatures slaughtered, while we were without the power to help them. The dominie, however, kept his post; but I saw that he was grinding his teeth and clutching the hilt of his sword, while his bosom heaved, and expressions escaped his lips, which, although I could not even catch the words, showed how deeply he was agitated.

"Sad, very sad, that such things should be," observed Don José; "but the general believes that the only way of overthrowing the Republican principles which have gained ground in the country, is to exterminate all who hold them."

"Does he remember the tale of 'the dragon's teeth'?" I asked. "The blood of that young girl cries for vengeance, and I feel assured that thousands will rise up to answer the call."

"What! do you Englishmen side with the Liberals?" he asked.

"My countrymen are ever ready to espouse the cause of the oppressed and suffering; and such, Don José, you must acknowledge the inhabitants of this country have long been," I answered boldly, for I was sure that my worthy host would not be offended. Indeed, I suspect that he himself leaned towards the independent side, although a professed Royalist.

"Time will show," he remarked; "but I wish that all this bloodshed could be avoided."

I remarked that every time a volley was fired he shuddered.

Chapter Eleven.

An interview with Murillo—We gain nothing for our
pains—I still endeavour to rescue the prisoners—Meet
Antonio, who belongs to the guard at the prison—My
conversation with him—He promises assistance, but gives
me bad news—Our plan arranged—Don José suspects us,
and requests us to leave his house—We remain till the
following day—Dr Cazalla and Señor Monteverde, with
many others, shot—Domingo brings me a disguise, and
advises me to escape without delay—Don José requests me
not to see him again—Mr Laffan and I separate—He starts
for Honda; I go towards the prison, followed by Lion—
Outside the prison walls—Joined by Uncle Richard—Our
escape from the city—We reach the mountains—Our arrival
at a river—No means of crossing—Spanish soldiers in
pursuit—A tarabita or rope-bridge—Dangerous crossing—
The bridge cut—Our escape—Sounds of firing—We find
shelter in the hut of an Indian, whose son undertakes to
guide us.

By the aid of Don José and other friends to whom I had letters, I
ascertained that Dr Cazalla and Mr Duffield had been brought into
Bogota, and were confined, with several other persons whom I
knew, in the chief prison of the city—although they had not yet
undergone the mockery of a trial, which would precede their
execution. Don José had made every exertion to obtain their
liberation, but in vain. The savage Murillo, it was said, had resolved
to shoot the whole of them. As there was no English Consul at that
time in Bogota, and no one who dared openly to take Uncle
Richard's part, I determined, according to the advice I had received,
to beard the lion in his den, and threaten him with the vengeance of
England should Mr Duffield be injured. I was also to point out to
Murillo the disgrace of destroying a man of such high scientific
attainments as Dr Cazalla, and to plead that he might be banished to
England, where he could render service to the human race.

Mr Laffan was quite willing to accompany me as interpreter. "We may bamboozle the scoundrel, and succeed where others have failed," observed the dominie. "There is nothing like impudence, — or a bold bearing, as some would call it, — when one has to deal with a fellow of this sort."

We set out, accordingly, for the viceroy's palace. On our arrival we found numerous officers hurriedly coming and going, but most of them merely glanced at us and passed on. In the ante-room there was a motley assemblage of persons of all ranks. Some had come with petitions, others had been summoned to undergo examinations; and several — informers, I have no doubt — were hoping to obtain a reward for their treachery. I sent in my card by an aide-de-camp, requesting an interview with his Excellency. To my surprise, we were almost immediately admitted. The general was seated at a table covered with papers — two or three officers standing near him. His countenance did not belie his character. Although the expression of his mouth was concealed by his huge moustache, the dark eyes which gleamed forth from under his shaggy brows, and the frown which wrinkled his high forehead, betokened his savage disposition.

"Who are you, and what do you want?" he asked abruptly in Spanish.

I turned to Mr Laffan and begged him to interpret what the general said.

"Tell him that I am English, and how, hearing that a countryman of mine has been imprisoned unjustly, I have come to demand his release, and permission for him to accompany me back to England."

"Of what profession is he?" asked the general of Mr Laffan. "Is he a lawyer?"

"No," I replied; "he is a British naval officer who has resided for some time in this country, but is still under the protection of the English Government, to whom it would be my duty to give information should any harm happen to him."

"Had he been a lawyer, whether a British subject or not, he should be shot," answered Murillo. "As it is, I will consider the matter."

He turned to one of the officers, who handed him a paper.

"Ah! I see he is married to a lady belonging to a rebel family; and he himself was found inciting the peasantry to take up arms. I care not though he is under British protection. He shall die."

"My countrymen will avenge him," I answered through Mr Laffan, who assumed an authoritative tone and manner, which I thought would produce some effect. "You know not whether the accusation is true or false."

Judging that it was best to leave what I had said to produce its effect, I stopped for a minute, and then continued, — "Well, your Excellency, I need not speak further about Señor Ricardo Duffield. I have now to plead for another person, who, although not an Englishman, belongs to all civilised countries in the world, and all will equally stigmatise those who injure him; I allude to the learned Dr Cazalla. I beg that he may be allowed to accompany me to my own country, where he can prosecute his scientific studies without molestation."

The general's brow grew darker than ever.

"He is one of the pests of this country. He taught the rebels how to make gunpowder and arms, to be used against their rightful sovereign. He shall die, even although the whole British army, with your Lord Wellesley at their head, were to endeavour to rescue him."

"That's an ungrateful remark, your Excellency, considering the service he has rendered Spain," observed Mr Laffan; "but it's just what may be expected."

"Go out of my presence—this instant!" exclaimed the general, irritated by this imprudent remark. "The prisoners shall die; and let me tell you that your errand is bootless."

I felt, indeed, that such was the case. In fact, I heard the general, turning to the officer who acted as his chief of police, direct him to keep an eye upon us. His suspicions had, I saw, been aroused.

We did not consider it necessary to pay any special mark of respect as we took our leave. The general was talking to the officers at his side, scarcely deigning to notice us. With heads erect, and as calm countenances as we could command, we passed through the crowd in the ante-room, and made our way into the street. We then hurried back to Don José's, to tell him how fruitless had been our visit to the viceroy.

"I was afraid so," observed our host. "If Murillo has made up his mind, no power on earth can turn him from his purpose."

I had not forgotten Antonio, and had formed a plan to try and rescue Mr Duffield and Dr Cazalla, should other means fail. As Antonio had not already betrayed me, I had great hopes that I could rely on his assistance. Always accompanied by Mr Laffan, I went about endeavouring to discover him. I at length ascertained that he belonged to the guard stationed at the prison. In all probability, then, he would at times have charge of the prisoners inside; and if so, he might be able to aid in their escape.

Before long we fell in with him off duty, and near the prison itself. It was late in the evening, but there was sufficient light for us to recognise each other. I made a sign, and he followed us to a dark spot under the prison walls.

"You know me, Antonio?" I asked.

"Ah yes, señor, the moment I saw you, while we were on the march here. I joined the Godos as the only means of saving my life—having obtained the uniform of a corporal who had been killed. My intention, however, was to desert on the first opportunity."

"Will you venture to assist the escape of Don Ricardo and Dr Cazalla?" I asked.

"Don Ricardo has already spoken to me, and promised a reward. I will do what I can without the reward, although the money would be welcome. He has promised me three hundred dollars."

"And I will give two hundred more when he is safe away from the city, and five hundred for Dr Cazalla."

"Ah, señor, that is more difficult, for he is strictly guarded, and, it is said, is to die to-morrow."

"To-morrow!" I exclaimed; "then he must escape to-night."

"Impossible!" answered Antonio; "ten thousand dollars would not effect his liberation. And besides, in endeavouring to free him I might be suspected, and thus be unable to help Don Ricardo."

"I know that I can trust you, Antonio," and I put some gold pieces into his hand. "Perhaps you can bribe your comrades; and promise them any further reward you think fit."

"They would take the money, and betray me," he answered. "I will employ some of it, however, but it will be in supplying them with abundance of strong wine; that will give me a better mastery over them than any bribe. Trust to my discretion."

After some further conversation, I arranged with Antonio that he was to try and effect the escape of Uncle Richard, and, if possible, that of Dr Cazalla. The following night he was to be on guard inside the prison, and he would then have the keys in his possession. The most likely time was about ten o'clock; and I arranged to be in the neighbourhood to assist, if necessary, in the escape of my friend.

Mr Laffan approved of the plan, but thought that it would be imprudent for him and me to be seen again near the prison, although we might afterwards join the fugitives. I proposed, therefore, having horses in readiness, and making our way down to Honda, whence we might embark on the river Magdalena; and the current being rapid, we should not occupy more than five days, and might at

Carthagena get on board the first vessel about to sail. If we could once reach any of the British West India Islands, we should be safe.

On our return Don José met us as we entered, with an expression of anxiety on his countenance.

"I fear, my friends, you are not exactly what you represent yourselves to be," he said. "You are honest, I doubt not, and well-conducted, and I wish to fulfil my engagement as far as I can to assist you; but I must advise you to leave this house and the city as soon as possible, or I shall be compromised by your remaining."

"I am deeply grateful for all your kindness, and will do as you advise," I answered. "I shall be thankful if I have ever the opportunity of proving my sincerity."

We should at once have left Don José, but that it was too late to seek a lodging; and as he did not express a wish that we should do so, we remained, promising to bid him farewell the next morning. I sincerely hoped that he would not suffer in consequence of his kindness to us.

We were about to start on the following day, after breakfast, to which our kind host insisted we should remain, when, on looking from the window across the square, we saw, as we had on the morning of our arrival, a body of troops marching from the prison. There was to be another execution, then. My heart sank within me. Was Murillo about to carry out his threat? As they approached I could scarcely support myself, for I saw my uncle, Dr Cazalla, with several other prisoners, nearing the spot where so many of the Patriots had already yielded up their lives for the liberty of their country. There were four other persons. It was certainly some relief not to see Uncle Richard among them; and my whole attention was now concentrated on Dr Cazalla. I pointed out the doctor to Don José, in the vain hope that something might even now be done to save him.

"I know him. He is talented, learned, and noble-minded," said Don José.

"The world will suffer if he dies," I said.

"I know it, my friend," answered Don José; "but his doom is sealed." He took my arm as he spoke. "I would not have you seen," he continued. "Be warned by me, and remain concealed until nightfall. Your horses are in my stable, and your servant is prepared for the journey."

Even while he was speaking the rattle of musketry was heard, and Mr Laffan, who had, notwithstanding Don José's advice, gone back to the window, exclaimed, "They have murdered our friend! I hope they will not treat the other in the same way."

"Do you speak of my uncle?" I asked in English.

"Too truly—I do. There he lies, like a clod of earth; and there, too, will lie many more, in a few minutes. There is another! I did not notice him at first. Poor Dona Dolores! what will become of her?"

"What! has Juan been captured?" I exclaimed, my thoughts running back to my friend, who might, I feared, have fallen into the hands of the enemy.

"No, not Juan; but Señor Monteverde.—Yes, I am sure it must be he, though he is poorly dressed, and walks with a tottering gait. Yes; they are leading him up to the place of execution."

Forgetting Don José's caution, I sprang forward to the window and caught a glance—it was but a momentary one—of our poor friend. It was sufficient, however, to convince me that I was not mistaken. Don José again took me by the arm and led me back; but a moment afterwards a volley was fired, and an exclamation uttered by Mr Laffan told me that Señor Monteverde was among those slaughtered by the savages.

"It will be sad news to carry to my mother and father, and to Dona Dolores. What will become of her? Her father dead—her property destroyed; but, probably, she herself is by this time in the hands of the Spaniards, and may ere long share the fate of Dona Paula. Shall I ever meet them again?" I murmured.

Other volleys of musketry, which sounded horrible in our ears, too plainly told us what was continuing to take place.

By Don José's advice, we kept close in our room during the remainder of the day; and it was growing dark when Domingo appeared, with a bundle under his arm.

"I have been provided with this for you to put on, señor," he said, producing a serving-man's dress, similar to that which I had worn at Popayan. It was curious that the same disguise should have been chosen. "You are suspected of being a Liberal; and whether you are so or not, you are to be arrested to-night, and probably share the fate of those who were shot this morning. I am desired to tell you, therefore, that you must make your escape as soon as it is dark—you taking one direction, while Señor Miguel and I take another."

Before I had time to ask further questions, Domingo retired.

I began to put on the dress he had brought me, and was quickly changed into a serving-man. While I was thus engaged Mr Laffan came in, and I told him what Domingo had said.

"But I cannot desert you, Duncan!" he exclaimed. "I will stick by you, whatever happens."

I soon convinced him that we should thus only increase the risk of being arrested, and advised him at once to make his way to Honda, as we had told Murillo we intended doing. If not molested, he might thence, instead of embarking on the Magdalena, travel over the mountains westward to one of the towns on the Cauca. As he had no proposal to offer against this plan—indeed, there was no other to be pursued—he agreed to it.

"But how will you be able to travel alone?" he asked.

"I do not intend to travel alone, if I can help it," I answered. "I believe that Antonio will succeed in liberating Uncle Richard, and that I shall be able to help him to make good his escape."

I was unwilling to leave the house without wishing Don José and his family farewell; and as I was thinking how I could best manage to do so, I discovered a slip of paper pinned on to the front of the jacket, on which was written in a feigned hand, — "I know your feelings, and what you would desire to say; but it is safer that we should not again meet. Farewell. Destroy this when you have read it."

The paper was not signed, but I guessed it came from Don José.

Domingo having now reappeared, and announced that the horses were ready, we descended to the courtyard. "It will be safer for me to slip out first," I observed.

To this Mr Laffan agreed.

"You had better take Lion with you," I said; and I ordered my faithful dog to remain with Mr Laffan. But on this occasion the usually obedient animal was disobedient. When I had made my way out of the yard I found him following me, and I had not the heart to send him back.

I resolved at all risks to join Uncle Richard, should he be able to make his way out of prison; so towards that gloomy building I at once directed my steps. As the town was in total darkness, there being no lamps in the streets, I ran little chance of being detected, while Lion could not be seen a few paces off. In a short time I reached the spot where I had had the conversation with Antonio; and there, crouching down, I awaited the hour he had named. There was but one clock in the city which struck the hours. The time appeared to go very slowly by. Perfect silence reigned through the streets. Neither Royalist nor Republican were at that time inclined to move about in the dark, as assassins too frequently plied their deadly trade, and several persons of both parties had been murdered.

At last ten o'clock struck. I sat with my hand on Lion's head, listening attentively. The prison door opened; the sentinel challenged, "Quien vive?" and the countersign was returned. Then the door closed, and I heard the sound of footsteps approaching, but they did not seem those of persons attempting flight. My hopes sank. After all, some officer might have visited the prison, and was now leaving it with a guard. I was afraid, consequently, to move; but in another instant Lion rose to his feet, and, though he uttered no sound, bounded forward towards one of the persons approaching.

"That must be Uncle Richard," I thought. "The dog knows him."

I was not mistaken; and I was quickly by his side, when I found that he had on the cap and cloak of an officer. The other person who followed close behind him was, I guessed from his uniform, which I could but indistinctly see, Antonio.

Uncle Richard divined who I was, and he put out his hand and grasped mine. I returned the pressure; but we did not venture to speak.

Antonio led the way to the western side of the city. "We must make for the mountains immediately; there will be less risk of the Godos looking for us there," he said, when we had got between some high convent walls, where no one was likely to overhear us.

One thing was certain, we must get to a distance from the city before daybreak. On that point we were all agreed.

When there was no risk of being seen, we moved as fast as possible; but as we drew near the guard at the entrance of the city we had to walk at a dignified pace. Antonio had given the sign and countersign to Uncle Richard and me, so we passed through without question; it being supposed, in all likelihood, that the officer was on his way to visit some outpost attended by an orderly, while I concluded that I was taken for a guide.

Long before morning dawned we were well among the mountains. Antonio had thoughtfully filled his knapsack with provisions, which, in addition to those I had brought from Don José's, would serve us for several days. The corporal had also furnished himself with a remarkably good rifle, and a quantity of ammunition. Our intention was to make our way to some place occupied by a Patriot force, of which we hoped to gain intelligence from the peasantry, either Creoles or Indians, the greater portion of whom were likely to prove friendly. It was most important, however, to put as great a distance as possible between the city and ourselves, for as soon as our flight was discovered parties would certainly be sent out to scour the country in search of us.

We rested for a couple of hours under an overhanging rock—to take some food and regain our strength—just before daybreak, and then once more pushed on. None of us, unfortunately, had any exact knowledge of the country. We had therefore to steer by the sun, and to follow the tracks which appeared to lead in the direction we wished to go. Occasionally, when we reached a height from which a view eastward could be obtained, we looked back to ascertain if any one was following. A party on horseback, by galloping over the more level ground, instead of climbing the mountains on foot, might even now overtake us.

The sun was still shining over the hills to the westward, but would shortly disappear behind them, when we saw before us a rapid river rushing between lofty and precipitous cliffs. How to cross it, was the question. We could see no bridge or canoe, and it ran too furiously for us to breast its foaming billows; while it would be dangerous to cross on a raft, even if we could find materials for forming one.

We made our way over the rough ground down the stream.

"I should think we must be safe from pursuit here; but I will just take a look-out from yonder height," observed Uncle Richard.

He had scarcely got to the summit of the hill when he shouted out, "Here come some suspicious-looking fellows; but they are a good way astern at present, so that we must somehow or other leave them on this side of the river." After taking another look, to assure himself that he was not mistaken, he rejoined us, and we hurried along the bank.

We had not gone far when Antonio exclaimed, "I see a tarabita! It will serve our purpose; and we must take care that it does not help our enemies across."

He pointed, as he spoke, towards a long thin rope thrown across from one cliff to the other. On getting up to it we found the bridge — for so it might be called — consisted of a long rope made of hides, the ends secured by stakes driven into the earth; to this a sort of basket was suspended, with two smaller ropes fastened to it — the one reaching to the side we were on, the other to the opposite bank, where a man — apparently the guardian of the so-called bridge — was seated on a log smoking. Antonio shouted to attract his attention; and getting up, he made a sign for one of us to enter.

"You go first, Señor Ricardo," said Antonio to Uncle Richard.

But the latter insisted on going last, and made me and Lion get into the basket. The bridge-keeper immediately began to haul away, and I soon found myself dangling over a fearful chasm. I was, however, quickly across; and, by means of a rope passing through a block on the side I had left, the basket was immediately drawn back.

Antonio was passed over in the same way, and joined me.

Uncle Richard had, in the meantime, gone to the height overlooking the path behind us, but he soon hurried back and took his seat in the basket.

"Tell the old Indian to be smart in hauling me across," he shouted out.

The man obeyed; but Uncle Richard was not more than half-way over when we saw a party of soldiers on the height above the river, and I clearly made out that they were Spanish soldiers. Should they reach the end of the rope before Uncle Richard was safe, they might, by threatening to cut it, compel us all to come back; so we hastened to seize hold of the tackle, in order to assist the Indian in dragging the basket over more quickly.

A TARABITA

"Take care, señores; you will break it, if you pull too hard," he observed.

We were not aware whether he had seen the Spaniards coming.

"Haul away," shouted Uncle Richard.

We obeyed him, and he was soon able to spring on to the ground. His first action on doing so was to grasp Antonio's sword, and to hack away at the rope, to the great astonishment of the old Indian, who loudly expostulated, and attempted to stop him. But Antonio and I seized the bridge-keeper and held him fast while Uncle Richard finished the operation, and soon the rope swung across to the opposite cliff.

"Now," said Uncle Richard, "we shall have to make the best use of our legs, or we may chance to have some bullets whistling about our ears."

We hurried on, hoping to get beyond the range of the firearms of our enemies before they had reached the bank; and we had completely lost sight of them when we heard a volley fired. We only hoped that the poor old Indian had hidden himself in time, and that it was not aimed at him. Whether there was any ford, or other means of crossing the river, further down, we could not tell; it was therefore important to make as rapid progress as possible. A moon was in the sky, about half full, which, in that atmosphere, allowed us to see our way for some distance, so we took great care to profit by it.

At length we saw a light ahead of us. It proceeded from an Indian's hut, in the centre of which a large fire was blazing. We made our way towards it, hoping to obtain a guide; besides, we required rest, and it was necessary to obtain it at all risks.

The owner of the hut was seated before the fire boiling a pot of cocoa, and he did not appear to be surprised on seeing us.

"Travellers are constantly coming this way, and I was getting some cocoa ready lest any should come in," he observed.

Uncle Richard said that we should be glad to rest for a few hours, and inquired whether he would guide us over the mountains.

"I cannot do so myself; but my son, who will be here shortly, will willingly do so. He has guided many travellers across the Paramo," was the answer.

We took our seats around the fire, and the Indian cooked some plantains, which, with the cocoa, served us for supper.

In a short time the son of whom our host had spoken made his appearance. He was a fine, strong youth, and seemed well fitted for acting in the capacity of guide.

He told us that as he was coming over the mountains from a village on this side of the river, to which he had escorted some travellers, he had heard firing, and concluded that there had been a fight between some Liberals and the Godos. "I hope the last were well beaten," he muttered, looking at Uncle Richard's military cap.

"So do I," I observed. "You do not take us for Godos?"

"I judge of people by their conduct, and as yet I have had no opportunity of learning how you behave," answered the young Indian, with a laugh.

"He is the right sort of fellow," observed Uncle Richard; "we may trust him."

I asked him if he had any food for my dog; and going out, he at once returned with some pieces of flesh, off which, although somewhat odorous, Lion made a substantial supper.

"It is the remains of a bear we killed some days ago," observed the young Indian.

We all lay down round the fire,—Lion sleeping between Uncle Richard and me, and both of us feeling assured that he would give us timely notice should any danger be at hand.

Chapter Twelve.

Our journey continued—Beautiful scenery—Preparing to cross the Paramo—Description of a Paramo—Commence the passage—Skeletons of men and mules—Intensity of the cold—Antonio suffers greatly—He recovers by drinking a draught of cold water—Darkness—Our sufferings on the increase—A strong inclination to sleep—I sink to the ground—Lion arouses me—We reach the Tambo—A night in the hut—Intense cold—Daylight at last—Our passage across the Paramo—Sad sights—The descent of the mountains—Reaching a forest—Padillo goes off to obtain intelligence—We build a hut, and go to sleep—Our hut on fire—A narrow escape.

For several days we had been travelling westward over the mountains. The young Indian, Padillo, as he called himself, had proved a faithful guide. If we were pursued, we had evaded our enemies, and, we hoped, had done so effectually. The scenery through which we passed was extremely wild and grand. Round us appeared mountains piled on mountains, rocks heaped on rocks; and when we fancied that we had reached the summit of an elevation whence we could look down below, another mountain, more grand and terrific, appeared through the veil of mist which before had shrouded it from our sight. It seemed as if we should never escape from this chaos of rocky pinnacles and snow-covered heights. The sky above us was of a clear, bright blue; in some places beautifully streaked, and varied with a silvery hue or pale straw colour, but not a cloud dimming its lustre. Severe as was the cold, as we were in constant exercise we scarcely felt it; while the rarity of the air imparted wonderful lightness and elasticity to our frames, so that sometimes I could scarcely help leaping and bounding forward. At night we generally found shelter in a cave or under an overhanging rock—always keeping up a blazing fire, to scare wild beasts, as well as to afford us warmth.

At last we reached the entrance of a gloomy valley, between lofty and snow-topped mountains, their sides in some places almost perpendicular.

"We must be prepared to push rapidly across the Paramo," observed Padillo. "It is late in the year, and I do not altogether like the look of the weather. We shall require two days at least to get to the further end. Frequently three days are occupied by persons on horseback, but you march so quickly that we may do it in less time; and there is a tambo about midway where we can obtain shelter."

"Cross it we must, at all risks," answered Uncle Richard, who was especially eager to get back to the neighbourhood of Popayan, to ascertain how his family were faring. He intended also to try and raise a corps.

It was not without reason that we dreaded passing across this bleak region. The name of Paramo is given to those inhospitable desert-regions high up among the mountains, of which there are so many in the Andes. No human being can exist in them without keeping in incessant and violent motion. Artificial means are incapable of sustaining life while a person is exposed to the inclement air. Ardent spirits are entirely void of any good effect, and generally increase the evil consequences. These Paramos are usually long deep valleys between lofty elevations, so shut in and obscured by the neighbouring hills as to possess all the severities of their extreme height, while not a ray of sunshine can enter to shed its gentle influence through them. Death almost invariably overtakes those who attempt to rest in them unsheltered at night. The extent of some of them is so great that it requires two or three days to cross them; and in these small houses have been erected, in which cooking utensils and other articles of convenience are kept for the accommodation of travellers, as well as stabling for their mules. Here, by means of large fires, they may manage to keep themselves warm, though even then people suffer greatly.

In consequence of the highly rarefied air, the traveller at first experiences great difficulty in breathing, accompanied by a sharp, piercing pain at each inspiration. This increases until he becomes what the natives call "emparamento,"—when his extremities are benumbed, and he can no longer continue in motion. Soon after this he is seized with violent raving and delirium; froth issues from his mouth; he tears the flesh from his hands and arms with his teeth, pulls his hair, and beats himself against the ground, meanwhile uttering the most piercing cries, until he is quite exhausted. The cold then deprives him of all motion and feeling, his body becomes much swollen, and fearful distortion of the features is produced by the dreadful convulsions he is suffering, while the surface of his skin becomes nearly black. The only remedy the natives know of is to scourge each other, and to drink the cold water from the springs, which are found here and there in most of the Paramos.

We had all of us heard this account of the Paramos, and were fully prepared for the danger we must encounter. Being on foot, we should the better be able to keep ourselves warm; at the same time, we should be the longer exposed to the piercing wind. Already, as we mounted towards this fearful region, we began to experience unpleasant sensations when breathing.

Having taken an ample breakfast, we determined to push on to the tambo, where we must rest until the following morning. It was most important to reach it before dark, for should we be benighted our position would become critical in the extreme. Nerving ourselves for the undertaking, we marched forward. Providentially there was but little wind. As we advanced we saw the skeletons and carcasses of numerous mules; some perfectly blanched by the wind, others still partly covered with flesh, on which numberless galenachas, or black vultures, were busily feasting. The stench proceeding from others not long dead, close to which we had to pass, was most offensive.

"At all events, no human beings appear to have died here," I observed to our guide.

"Don't say that, until you have got further," he answered.

In a few minutes we came in sight of a grinning skull placed on the top of a rock, the body lying below it. A few steps further on we came upon the skeletons of several persons lying with their legs across their mules; both the animal and its rider having evidently succumbed at the same moment.

"This does not look pleasant," observed Uncle Richard; "but we must not allow it to depress our spirits."

In spite, however, of the severe exertions we were making, we felt the cold every instant becoming greater. Antonio, though apparently as strong as any of us, became so benumbed that he could scarcely walk. He had brought a small flask of aguardiente, which he confessed he had drained to the bottom, but it had apparently had a bad effect on him. At length his sufferings became so great that we began to fear we must leave him behind, as to carry him on to the tambo would be impossible; though, if left behind, he would certainly die in a few minutes. While he was in this state, Padillo volunteered to go forward, recollecting that there was a spring in the neighbourhood, and urging us to try and reach it. In a short time Padillo returned with the information that the spring was only a little way on; so, while Uncle Richard took one of Antonio's arms, I took the other, and Padillo, with a stick, kept beating him severely about the body. Whenever Antonio cried out, Padillo answered, "Never mind, friend, never mind; it's all for your good." At length, what with pinching his arms, and Padillo's flagellation, he was kept alive until we reached the spring. Here we compelled him to drink a draught of water, though at first he showed a great unwillingness to swallow it, like a person afflicted with hydrophobia. In a wonderfully short time, however, he perfectly recovered, and declared that he felt warm and comfortable.

Uncle Richard and I then tried the experiment, as we were beginning to feel the sensations Antonio had at first complained of. The attempt, however, was extremely painful; indeed, I felt as if I had swallowed a handful of needles, the which were pricking and tearing the whole interior of my throat in their passage downwards.

Directly I had swallowed the water, however, I began to feel a comfortable glow, which in a short time spread equally over me.

The delay, however, might have been fatal to all of us, as darkness had already begun to spread over the deep valley, and we could see no tambo ahead. From the experience we had had, we were sure we could not rest anywhere for an instant, while the danger was great in proceeding in the dark. Still Padillo said he could find the way, and led us on at a swinging trot, we doing our utmost to keep up with him; often, however, I felt a strong inclination to sink down and enjoy a short sleep, if only for a minute or two. I thought that I should soon catch up my companions. The wind had increased, too, and a thick sleet drove through the air, which made us feel as if pins and needles were sticking in our faces.

"This is very unpleasant," cried Uncle Richard; "but it won't last for ever, that's one comfort."

The darkness increased, and the thought that we should have to go on through such weather as this during the whole night was terrible.

Padillo was leading. Uncle Richard made Antonio walk before him; I, with Lion, who kept close to my heels, continued talking to Uncle Richard for some time, until the desire to stop suddenly overpowered me.

"I hope we shall soon reach the hut," I said.

"Cheer up—in a few minutes we shall be there," I heard Uncle Richard say, and at that instant I sank to the ground. I heard the footsteps of my companions as they moved on; but, seized with a kind of insanity, I flattered myself that after a few minutes' rest I should be able to get up and follow them. For some time, as it appeared to me, though it may have been only for a moment or two, my senses completely left me; then I became conscious that Lion had placed himself above me, and was licking my hands and face. Then I heard him utter a loud bark; after which he began to pull at my clothes, and bark louder and louder, until he succeeded in arousing me. Mercifully, I had still strength sufficient to get up; and as I did so, Lion still pulling at my trousers, I heard Uncle Richard's voice shouting out, "Duncan! Duncan! come along." Presently he appeared through the gloom; when he took my hand, and I stumbled forward.

Soon afterwards we heard Padillo shout out, "The tambo, the tambo!"

Though we could not see him, guided by his voice we made our way to the hut. Antonio had already got in and thrown himself on the ground, but Uncle Richard roused him up, and compelled him to assist in lighting the fire. We soon had a genial blaze, at which we warmed our chilled limbs. I saw Lion looking up in my face, as much as to say, "Master, that was a foolish thing you did just now; in another minute you would have been dead, had I not kept some warmth in you with my body." I patted his head, and he wagged his tail, and smiled as dogs can smile when pleased. In spite of the blazing fire we kept up all night, we felt the cold greatly. Indeed, I had never felt so chilled in all my life; it seemed to pierce to the very marrow. Lion lay down close to the fire, and almost singed his hair, showing that he too was suffering from the cold.

Fearing that the fire might go out, Uncle Richard insisted that one of us should remain awake; and he himself undertook to keep the first watch. We first took our supper, but I fell asleep with a piece of food in my mouth. The training Uncle Richard had had at sea enabled him to keep awake, although I dare say he was as sleepy as any of us.

He at last aroused me, and charged me not to let the fire get low. "I can trust you better than I can Antonio or the guide," he observed. "However strong may be your impulse to sleep, do not yield to it, as our lives may depend on the fire being kept up."

I promised to keep a faithful watch, and, rising to my feet, began to walk about. In a moment more Uncle Richard was fast asleep. So strong was the desire I felt to lie down and close my eyes, that I was afraid of stopping, and kept pacing up and down the hut, rubbing my hands together, and every now and then putting on an additional stick, or scraping up the ashes. The time passed slowly by; the wind moaned amid the bleak crags which overtopped the hut, and I fancied I heard the cries of wild beasts. The sleepers, overcome with fatigue, did not even move, and as I gazed at them they looked as if stretched out in death. Every now and then, however, Lion lifted up his head, as if to see that all was right; and just as my watch was over, and I was about to call Antonio, he got up and stretched himself. "Now, Lion, if Antonio drops asleep, remember to call me or Uncle Richard. I will trust you, good dog. You understand?" Lion wagged his tail, and gave a low bark; and I felt confident that he would do as I had ordered him.

I then called Antonio, and gave him the same instructions and warning which Uncle Richard had given me.

"Do not fear, señor," he answered—giving, however, an ominous yawn; "I'll keep my eyes open."

Trusting more to Lion than Antonio, I lay down, and in a few seconds was again fast asleep. How long I had remained in that state I could not tell, when I heard Lion bark close to my ear, and felt him pulling at my clothes. On sitting up, I saw that the fire had burned much lower than it was when I gave up my watch, and that Antonio was asleep. I quickly roused him up.

"It was but for a moment, señor; my eyelids are so very heavy."

"Look at the fire!" I exclaimed. "It must have been a very long moment since you put anything on. Now, help me to make it up."

We soon had the fire blazing brightly again, and Antonio promised to keep awake until daylight. Had it not been for Lion, I should not have trusted him. He probably was not aware that the dog had aroused me.

Again I heard Lion bark loudly. The fire, as before, had burned down, and Antonio was again asleep; but on looking out of the door

I found that day had broken. I was convinced that Lion had been observing the fire rather than Antonio—considering it his duty to watch it—and that he had called me simply because he saw that it ought to be made up.

I now awakened the whole party, and by the time we had eaten a hearty breakfast the light had increased sufficiently to enable us to continue our journey.

We encountered the same sad sights as on the previous day. There were fewer animals, but many more dead bodies,—some evidently, from their dress, being those of women and children.

"They are those of unfortunate people who were attempting to escape from the Godos," observed Padillo. "The mountains hereabouts are full of the skeletons of those who have thus perished. But Heaven will punish our oppressors."

All we saw must have died on their first day's journey across the Paramo. Those only who had strong mules, or who had found shelter in the tambo, could have escaped. But it would not do to allow our thoughts to dwell upon the subject. Our business was to push on as fast as our legs would carry us. Directly we felt any of the sensations we had experienced on the previous day, we drank at the nearest stream we could reach, but we did not stop to take food.

At length the fearful Paramo was passed; and yet this was only half the size of many which exist in the country. Before dark we reached a tambo situated at a lower level and exposed to the free air, but even there we felt it very cold. In a few days we were rapidly descending, and at last found ourselves almost on a level with the valley of the Cauca, enjoying a tropical temperature, and on the borders of a dense forest. By keeping more to our left we should have continued along the road to Antioquia, but we were uncertain which party then possessed that town. Padillo, however, volunteered to ascertain this while we remained in the forest. We had already paid him his well-deserved reward, with which he seemed highly satisfied.

He had been absent some time, and we were anxiously waiting his return.

THROUGH THE FOREST

"I am afraid he has been seized by the Spaniards, or compelled to conduct one of their parties over the mountains," I observed.

"He'll not come back, depend on that," remarked Antonio. "He has fulfilled his engagement, and will not trouble himself further about us."

"I will trust the man; and if he can, he will return," said Uncle Richard. "Here he comes, too!"

Presently Padillo was seen hurrying towards us. "The Godos have possession of all the towns and villages in this neighbourhood," he said. "If you wish to avoid them, you must keep further down the valley before you cross the Cauca, and then continue up the other side. I wish that I could remain with you, but I know nothing of those western mountains, and should be of no use as a guide."

He now finally took his leave, promising not to forget us.

Following his advice, we commenced our journey through the forest,—often having to cut our way with our swords, and sometimes to wade across rapid streams which threatened to carry us off our legs. We ran a risk, too, of being bitten by serpents; several of those we observed being of large size, and others of an especially venomous character. Tribes of monkeys were seen on either side of us, leaping from bough to bough, and swinging on the sipos— sometimes running forward jabbering and grinning, as if excited with anger at our daring to invade their domains. As our food had run short, we were compelled to shoot a couple of the rogues for supper.

Night approaching, we made preparations for camping. We had to guard not only against human enemies, but against jaguars, pumas, prowling bears, and snakes. But having cleared a space of sufficient size, we ran some sticks into the ground, which were interwoven with smaller branches, so close together that no jaguar could thrust in its paw, or a bear its snout, nor could any but the smallest snake crawl in. We then thatched it over with large leaves of sufficient thickness to keep out the heaviest rain. As close to the entrance as we dared we piled up sticks, that we might keep a fire blazing all night. There was certainly some little risk in having a fire, as it might attract the attention of any Spaniards in the neighbourhood; but we believed that we were so far off a highroad that no enemies were likely to discover us.

Uncle Richard and I discussed our plans for the future, leaving Antonio to go to sleep, that he might be the better able to watch when it came to his turn. We alternately went to sleep for some hours, until we thought Antonio could be trusted to keep the regular watch.

I was awakened by Lion's loud bark, and by feeling him pulling at my clothes. Seeing that I was aroused, he next attacked Uncle Richard in the same way. On sitting up, what was my dismay to find that we were in the midst of a bright blaze! The hut was on fire. Antonio, in order to save himself trouble, had raked the embers close up to the entrance, and had then fallen asleep. Uncle Richard, seizing him by the shoulders, dragged him out; while I caught up his gun and the rest of our possessions, and sprang after him through the flames, followed by Lion, who would not leave the hut until he saw us in safety. The whole, however, was the work of a few seconds. Had we remained much longer, the roof would have come down upon us, and, at all events, have burned us severely. As it was, we got pretty well singed.

As we looked back and saw the flames ascending, we had good cause to fear that the trees overhead would catch fire; and if so, a fearful conflagration might ensue. It would be scarcely possible to cut our way through the forest so as to escape it. The danger, therefore, was imminent. Uncle Richard setting the example, we attacked the thatch, and brought it to the ground; while with our swords we cut the grass around wherever we saw the fire creeping along the ground.

A few minutes more, and we should have been unable to subdue the fire. Already some of the shrubs were singed in two opposite directions, but fortunately we saw the snake-like flames creeping forward in time to extinguish them.

As there was no appearance of rain, we scraped the ashes of the fire together, and placing on them a few unburnt sticks, sat ourselves down close to it to wait until daylight, without which it would be impossible to travel through the forest.

Chapter Thirteen.

A hard struggle to get out of the forest—Antonio finds some Cherimoias—Our escape from the wood—Dancing at a marriage-feast—Hospitable entertainment—Guides—Down the river in a canoe—The Spaniards ahead—We camp, and wait to pass them at night—Again embarked—The Spanish camp—A narrow escape—We reach the Cauca—We cross to the left bank, and see Juan with a party of cavalry on the right bank—Pacheco swims across the river, and returns with a note—Juan comes for me on a raft—Uncle Richard and Antonio proceed to Popayan—We reach a farm on the Llanos, and catch and train wild horses for Juan's troop—Mode of catching wild horses—Joined by Mr Laffan.

The morning found us hacking our way through the forest. As we could discover no path to follow, it was slow work, and the trees seemed to become thicker and thicker as we advanced. Under other circumstances, we might have stopped to admire the wonderful variety of shrubs and creepers which formed the undergrowth; as it was, we had to keep our eyes constantly about us, for at any moment we might have to encounter a huge boa or anaconda, or we might tread upon some venomous serpent, or a tree-snake might dart down upon us from the boughs above. Monkeys, as before, chattered and grinned at us. Parrots, and occasionally large gaily-plumed macaws, flew off from amongst the topmost boughs, startled by our approach.

Hunger and fatigue told us that we had been struggling on for some hours, so, coming to an open space, we determined to stop and dine. Uncle Richard, taking Antonio's gun, shot a monkey and a couple of parrots; and Antonio and I lighted a fire at which to roast them. But we had no water, and the food made us feel very thirsty. I proposed, therefore, looking for some cocoa-nuts, which, in that part of the country, grow a long way from the sea. We searched around in all the openings we could discover; at last Antonio shouted out that he had found something which would satisfy our wants, and he appeared with a huge melon-looking fruit under each arm. They were the wild cherimoia, which grow to a larger size than the cultivated ones, although not possessing their richness. The slight acidity of the fruit was, however, very refreshing; and, our strength restored, we were soon able to push on as before.

Another day of hard toil was about to close. To pass the night without a fire would be dangerous in the extreme, but as yet we had found no open space in which we could venture to make one. As long, therefore, as the light lasted we continued to press on, in the hope of discovering some suitable spot. Antonio climbed up a palm, by forming his sash into a belt which embraced the trunk—hoping to obtain a good view of the surrounding region from the top. He told us, on his descent, that he had seen the glittering of a river at no great distance to the south-west, and that we should soon be out of the forest. Our continued thirst, which even the fruit did not quench, made us wish to reach the river as soon as possible; so we pushed on, and at length had the satisfaction of getting out of the denser part of the forest, though trees and shrubs extended down to the banks of the river. Darkness overtook us; but the moon rose, and we were able to move forward without much difficulty, expecting every instant to reach the stream.

We were hurrying on, when strange sounds reached our ears. We advanced towards the spot from whence they proceeded, and, on an open space near the bank of the river, we caught sight of what at a distance might have been mistaken for a dance of demons or hobgoblins. But as we drew near we saw, as we had surmised, that they were Indians. Some of them were performing a wild dance in couples, holding their arms above their heads and snapping their fingers; while others were seated on the ground looking at their companions.

"There has probably been a marriage, and they are now performing the dance which usually follows the ceremony by the light of the moon," observed Antonio. "They are sure to be in good humour, and as they will have plenty of food, they will be ready to treat us hospitably."

On this assurance we approached the strange group, but the dancers appeared too much engaged in their amusement to notice us. The music was apparently produced by a sort of flageolet, accompanied by a calabash containing some hard seeds or stones, which was rattled in time to the wind instrument.

Some of those seated on the ground at last catching sight of us, advanced and inquired who we were and what we wanted. We told them that we were travellers—our object being to reach the western side of the valley; that we should be glad if one of them, well acquainted with the country, would act as our guide, and that his services should be liberally rewarded. This at once made them friendly; and begging us to sit down, they brought us a calabash of chica, with which they were regaling themselves, some venison, and a variety of cooked roots, and some fruit. The feast was abundant, if not served in a very civilised way, and we did ample justice to it.

We found that our new friends were, as Antonio had supposed, celebrating the marriage of one of their young men by a moonlight dance and feast. The happy bridegroom had just reached his eighteenth year, and his friends had helped him to build a hut and clear a spot in the forest for sowing maize. Being an expert hunter, he had bought mats and earthen pots with the produce of the chase, and had also made several utensils in wood, besides a store of calabashes; these, with a few other articles, served amply to furnish the abode to which he was to take his young wife. He had also, they told us, presented his father-in-law with a deer, part of which we were eating. The conjurer, who performs an important part on such occasions, presented himself to us. Of course he had been invited to the feast, since he acts as the officiating minister and declares the couple united. Our friends, who had already indulged somewhat freely in chica, continued passing the calabash round until they grew very noisy; the old conjurer especially, who, with several others, at length rolled on the ground and dropped off to sleep. The more sober of the party, however, assisted us in putting up a little hut, in which we took shelter,—while they, in spite of their scanty clothing, lay down round the fire, more for the smoke which kept off the mosquitoes than for warmth; indeed, we were now in a complete tropical climate, differing greatly from that of Popayan.

A DANCE OF INDIANS.

The provisions collected for the feast were sufficient to afford us a good breakfast; and having rewarded our entertainers, we expressed a wish to set out. Instead of one guide, three volunteered to come, saying that each of us would require one; indeed, none of them were disposed to go alone. We found, on reaching the river, that they proposed proceeding down it some distance in a canoe. This, too, would save us from fatigue; and there would be less risk, we hoped, of our falling in with the Spaniards.

We found, on conversing with the Indians, that they had anything but friendly feelings for the Godos, who had carried off several of their people, and on other occasions ill-treated them, compelling them to work without reward. We therefore felt ourselves perfectly safe in their company. Whenever we approached a spot—whether hamlet or farm—where they thought it likely the Spaniards might be quartered, one of them would go on ahead, and, keeping under shelter, creep up and ascertain if such was the case. On each occasion finding that the coast was clear, we continued down the stream.

Throughout its course the country on either side was wild and uncultivated, only small patches here and there being occupied by settlers, who owned some of the vast herds of horses and cattle roaming over the broad savannas which extend from the Cauca to the foot of the mountains.

In this region we met with three or four Indian families of the same tribe as our companions, and we learned from the last we encountered that a party of Spaniards occupied a spot on the bank of the river some way lower down, but whether they were marching north or south we could not ascertain. One thing was certain — we must either land on the opposite side to that where they were posted, or pass by during the night. Our Indian friends decided that the latter would be the safest plan to pursue, so we ran the canoe a short distance up a creek with reeds on either side and thickly wooded beyond; a place which afforded us ample concealment, while there was abundance of wild fowl to supply us with food.

The Indians had brought some network hammocks composed of fibre, which they hung up between the trees, and advised us to occupy while they prepared supper. No sooner had we landed than Uncle Richard shot a wild turkey, which we left with the Indians, while we went along the banks of the stream in search of ducks. Our friends' eyes sparkled in the anticipation of an abundant feast, as they saw us return with four brace of fat birds. The Indians had a big pot, into which they put some venison they had brought with them, and some of the birds cut up, with vegetables of various sorts. These they stirred over the fire, and made a very satisfactory mess, flavoured as it was with chili pepper and other condiments. We ate our turkey simply roasted, however, as it suited Uncle Richard's palate and my own.

We had still some hours to wait until the Spaniards were likely to be asleep, and the men on guard less watchful. At present, too, the moon was so bright that we should certainly have been seen had we attempted to pass their camp; but clouds were gathering in the sky, and we hoped that before long the moon would be obscured, when we might slip by on the opposite side unobserved. We therefore took advantage of the offer the Indians had made us, and occupied their hammocks; while they sat round the fire talking, and finishing the remains of the stew. Lion had come in for his share of the bones, and now lay down under my hammock with his nose between his paws. The moment I looked out he lifted up his head, showing that, if not wide awake, he was as vigilant as need be, and ready to give notice should there be any cause of alarm.

OUR HALTING-PLACE

We were completely in the power of the Indians, no doubt, who might at any moment have deserted us, or delivered us up to the Spaniards, or put us to death for the sake of our clothes and whatever valuables we carried. But we had entire confidence in them. It must be confessed that foreigners have occasionally been killed by the Indians, but in all the instances I have heard the former were the aggressors. We had from the first shown the simple-minded people that we trusted them, and their wish was to prove that our confidence was not misplaced.

The night was far spent when Pacheco, our chief guide, roused us up.

"The moon has kindly veiled her face to enable us to pass the Godos unperceived," he said. "Up, señors, up! we will start at once."

Jumping out of our hammocks, the Indians quickly rolled them up and carried them down to the canoe, on board which they had already placed the rest of their property. By their advice we lay down in the bottom. I kept Lion by my side, so that in case he should be inclined to bark I might at once silence him. Pacheco steered, while the other two Indians rapidly plied their paddles, and we glided at a quick rate down the stream. We soon approached that part on the northern shore at which the Spaniards were supposed to be posted, and we therefore kept to the opposite side. Not a word was spoken, and we all lay close; so that, had the canoe been seen, the enemy would have supposed that only three Indians were in her. We could hear the guard relieved, with the sentries exchanging the sign and countersign; and during the time this ceremony was going forward our canoe shot by the place without challenge.

In the hope that we were safe, we were about to get up out of our uncomfortable position, when a voice hailed us and ordered the canoe to be brought up to the bank.

"Paddle on!" I heard Pacheco say to his men; and directly afterwards a shot came whistling over our heads. "Don't be afraid of that," again whispered Pacheco—"we shall soon be out of sight of the Godos; although they may fire, they will not hit us."

The Indians, without uttering a sound to show that they felt any alarm, continued paddling away. Shot after shot was heard; but the Spaniards must have at length discovered that their prey had escaped them.

We continued our course until the morning, when we saw before us the Cauca, on the opposite side of which we wished to land. The Indians crossed the larger river, and pulling up for some short distance, we entered a creek thickly shaded by trees. Here there was no risk of being seen by enemies on the other shore. Pacheco, who had engaged to act as our guide, landed with us, and gave directions to his people to wait his return.

The stream by which we had entered the Cauca had carried us much further down the course of that river than we had intended to go; we had, therefore, now to make our way up it before we struck westward to Oro, the town at which I had arranged to meet Mr Laffan. Our guide advised us to continue along the bank of the river, as we should thus make our way more easily than by striking diagonally across the country. Having carefully husbanded our powder and shot, too, we were enabled to supply ourselves amply with food; and we were never in want of wild fruits which in most countries would be considered very delicious.

It was towards the evening of the second day, and we were about to encamp, when Antonio, who had gone down to fill a calabash with water at the river, came back saying that he had seen a small party of cavalry, who had come down to let their horses drink.

"Are they Spaniards?" asked Uncle Richard.

"No, señor; they appear to me, by their dress, to be Patriots."

On this we all crept down to the bank, keeping under shelter, to observe the strangers; and on seeing them we were convinced that Antonio was right. While I was looking I observed another horseman, who by his dress appeared to be an officer, join the people, and on watching his movements I felt almost certain that he was my friend Juan. So convinced was I of this, that I advanced to the water's edge and hailed him; but the noise of the horses prevented him hearing my voice. "What would I give to communicate with him!" I exclaimed. "Is no canoe to be found near, by which we can cross the stream?"

I explained my wishes to Pacheco.

"If you are certain that they are friends, I will swim across," answered Pacheco.

I assured him of this, and hastily wrote a note to Juan, begging him to wait for me, and I would try to get across the river to join him.

OUR GUIDE SWIMS ACROSS THE CAUCA

Pacheco placed the note inside his hat, on the top of which he fastened the short trousers and girdle he wore. He then cut two thick pieces of bamboo, with a still larger piece pointed at both ends, and taking them in his hand plunged into the water.

"Are you not afraid of the alligators?" asked Uncle Richard, under the idea that those creatures frequented the stream.

"There are few above the rapids, and those only of small size," answered Pacheco; "if one comes near me, he will feel the point of this bamboo."

Resting his chest on the stout pieces of cane, and striking out with his hands and feet, he made rapid progress towards the opposite shore. At length Juan saw him coming, and at the same time observed us waving, though he might not have known who we were. He probably guessed, however, that we were friends, and that the Indian was coming across to speak to him, for he rode towards the spot where our guide was about to land.

Pacheco gave Juan the note, and I saw him take a paper from his pocket and write an answer, which he delivered to the Indian, who, without stopping to rest, recrossed the river. Once I saw him give a dig with his bamboo, but the object at which he aimed was not visible. It might have been an alligator, or a water-snake, or a big fish; but it seemed to concern him very little, for he again came towards us, and landed in safety.

I eagerly took Juan's note.

"I will wait for you," it ran. "Come across, if you can find a canoe; if not, wave your handkerchief, and I will have a raft formed, and come for you. No time for more.—Juan."

As Pacheco assured us that we were not likely to find a canoe within a considerable distance, I at once made the sign agreed on, whereupon I saw Juan's men immediately begin to cut down with their manchettes a number of large canes which grew near. These they bound together with sipos, and in a very short time a raft sufficiently large to bear several persons was formed. The thick ends of some of the canes were shaped into scoop-like paddles, and Juan with four of his men at once embarked and commenced the passage of the river. As soon as the raft was sufficiently near the shore he sprang to the land, and embraced Uncle Richard and me. He looked paler and considerably older than when we last parted, and as if he had seen much hard work.

Uncle Richard's first question was, very naturally, for his wife and daughter; and I too asked after my family.

"They are still residing among the mountains, among some faithful Indians, with Paul Lobo as their guardian. Dr Sinclair thinks it prudent to keep in hiding while the Godos occupy Popayan, in case the monster Murillo should order his arrest. I lately heard that he was well, in spite of the trying life he, in common with so many other Patriots, is obliged to lead."

"And Dona Dolores?" I asked.

"She is safe with your mother and Dona Maria; I myself escorted her to their cottage, after I had the happiness of rescuing her from the Spaniards."

"Is she aware of her father's death?" I inquired.

"What!" exclaimed Juan, "has the tyrant dared to murder the old man?"

"I grieve to say so; as well as my poor uncle, Dr Cazalla, and many other of our country's noblest Patriots."

Juan lifted his hands to heaven, and prayed that their deaths might be avenged. What a change a few months had produced in him! Instead of the gay, thoughtless youth, he was now the stern soldier, ready to dare and do any deed full of peril. I told him of the murder of Dona Paula; at hearing which his eyes flashed fire, while he uttered expressions I dare not repeat.

I asked him what object he had in view in coming in this direction.

"I am proceeding to Llano Grande, for the purpose of collecting horses, and training them for our cavalry, as a large number of those in my troop have died from hard work and exposure on the Paramo of Purace, when we crossed the mountains to attack the Spanish convoy. I earnestly hope that you, Duncan, will join me; you will be of the greatest assistance, and I am certain that you are not required to help your father or mother. They are less likely to be molested than if it were known that you had joined them."

I felt a great desire to accept Juan's proposal, and put it to Uncle Richard whether I might not do so.

He considered a minute. "Yes; I see no objection," he answered. "I will continue my journey with Antonio, and try to communicate with Mr Laffan. Possibly he may join you, and be of service."

Accordingly, without hesitation, I at once agreed to accompany Juan; and wishing my Uncle Richard and his two companions farewell, I embarked with my friend.

"As soon as I have seen Señor Ricardo safe, I intend to make my way back to rejoin you," said Antonio. "If you are going to tame wild horses, you will find it a long business, and are not likely to have left the neighbourhood before I can get back to you."

Juan told me that he intended to ride some miles further before camping, as we were near a Spanish force; and should the enemy gain intelligence of us, they might attempt to surprise us.

When Lion saw me embark, he gave a look at his former master, as if to ask which of us he should accompany; but Uncle Richard pointed to me, and he immediately leaped on the raft.

By the time we landed, Juan's small troop were in readiness to move on. He had, fortunately, a spare horse, which I mounted; and I confess that I felt my spirits rise wonderfully when I found myself in the saddle, after so many days' journeying on foot.

We rode on until we reached the borders of a wood which would serve to shelter our camp-fires. There the horses were picketed, while patrols were sent out to give due notice of danger. Though in our native land, we had to act as if in an enemy's country. However, we invariably found the country-people ready to give us all the information we required as to the whereabouts of the Spaniards, and were thus able to avoid them. Had it not been for this, the Patriots would have been crushed by the superior force the Spaniards were bringing against them. While we could always learn the movements of our enemies, and obtain an ample supply of food, the Spaniards were unable even to trust their own spies; and it was only by means of strong foraging-parties that they could collect provisions.

We thus reached our destination,—a farmhouse situated on a slope at the foot of the mountains, with the wide llanos stretching out before it. Having an extensive view over the plain from this point, we could see the approach of an enemy from a great distance; and, according to the strength of their force, we might either prepare for resistance, or make our escape. An enclosure ran round it, formed by trunks of trees driven into the ground close together. It had been formed years before, for the purpose of resisting attacks by the Indians, and would still enable a body of men to hold their own against any small force of infantry or cavalry, though, for the present, we did not expect to be molested.

CATCHING WILD HORSES

The men Juan had brought with him were accustomed to the life of the llanos, and no time was lost in commencing the work for which they had come. The very next morning the whole party started off provided with lassoes,—Juan and I accompanying them. The herds of wild horses were accustomed to come close up to the farm, so that we had not to go far before we fell in with a herd. The men then separated into parties of two, forming a circle round the animals they wished to capture. The wild horses, seeing strangers advancing from all sides, closed up towards the centre, not knowing in which direction to make their escape; when the men galloped forward, lasso in hand, each singling out an animal, round whose neck he seldom failed to throw the noose. The horse would then dash forward, but was as speedily brought up by the rope; and the well-trained steed of the Llanero, throwing itself back, and pressing its fore, feet against the ground, effectually checked it, and threw it upon its haunches, or right over on its back. Another Llanero would then dexterously cast his lasso round the animal's fore-feet, and by a jerk bring it round its legs. By slightly slackening the rope round its neck, the horse was enabled to get up, when its first impulse was to dash forward; but it was brought to the ground by the lasso round its legs, with a jerk sufficient, it would seem, to break every bone in its body. The horse would then lie motionless while its hind feet were secured.

The first horse I saw caught in this manner, I thought was dead; but after a time it regained its consciousness, and, giving some convulsive plunges, again got on its legs. Before it had even time to look about, it was led off by some of the Llaneros to a post near the farm, where, in spite of its desperate struggles, it was saddled and bridled. Its strength regained, it began to bite, plunge, and kick in all directions, the Llaneros nimbly getting out of the way. One of the more experienced riders, watching his opportunity, then leaped into the saddle, and signed to one of his companions to cast off the lasso from its legs. The animal, finding itself free, darted off, and then commenced to back, plunge, and whisk round and round, sometimes dashing on for a few paces at a furious pace, and then recommencing its eccentric movements. The rider, however, stuck on; and another Llanero coming behind, administered a lash with his long cutting whip, which made the poor animal start off with a snort like a scream. No one but a well-trained horseman could have kept his seat in the way our men did. As it darted ahead, two other Llaneros rode on either side to keep the wild animal straight. Off it went across the level country for a league or more, occasionally stopping to back and kick; each time its efforts grew fainter, until at last we saw it come back, its eyes bloodshot, its whole body covered with foam and blood, and perfectly bewildered. It was then unsaddled and tied to a post, there to remain until hunger made it willing to accept the food and water offered to it. Thus, in the course of a day a number of horses were captured; but they were all young animals, and as yet scarcely fit for work.

Next came the operation of breaking them in, which occupied a much longer time. In this, Juan and I took a part. Every man we had with us was engaged from sunrise to sunset—or even later, when the moon shone brightly—as it was of the greatest importance to have some well-trained animals ready for service as soon as possible.

Fresh men continued to arrive, having made their way over the mountains to avoid the Spaniards, bringing their saddles and bridles, arms and accoutrements. Of course, they at once took part in catching and training the horses. The young animals were most easily broken-in, but they were less capable of enduring fatigue than the older horses.

We had been about a month thus engaged, when, as Juan and I were leaving the farm for an afternoon's sport, as we called it, we caught sight of a horseman—evidently, from his costume, not one of our own men—galloping across the plain towards us. As he drew nearer, I thought I recognised his bearing and figure.

"Hurrah!" I exclaimed; "I believe that's Mr Laffan."

"I hope so, indeed," answered Juan. "He will be a host in himself; and I suspect he will be able to train a horse as well as the best of us."

Mounting our steeds, we galloped forward to meet him; and with unfeigned pleasure I soon saw that it was no other than my former tutor.

"I am thankful to fall in with you again, my dear fellows," he exclaimed. "I thought at one time that I should never have got here. Mr Duffield told me where to find you, but those rascally Spaniards nearly caught me. I escaped them, but I had to hide away for several days until the coast was clear. However, here I am, and shall be mighty glad of some food, for I'm desperately sharp-set."

We returned to the farm with Mr Laffan, where we gave him our usual fare,—dried beef and plantains; for we were not living luxuriously. Except some chica, we had no beverage stronger than coffee or cocoa to offer him; but he declared that such provender would serve him as well as any other.

As soon as the meal was over, Mr Laffan begged to have a fresh horse, and insisted on accompanying us. "I have had a little experience in this sort of work," he said, "and may be able to catch a horse or two. At all events, I can break-in a few. I have no wish to eat the bread of idleness."

Mr Laffan was as good as his word, and took good care to select a first-rate animal for himself, which, by dint of constant practice, he got well broken-in. Juan and I were equally fortunate, and were much indebted to him for the training of our steeds.

As few persons came near the farm, which was remote from all thoroughfare, the Spaniards did not get notice of our proceedings; and we were thus, by dint of hard work, and the valuable assistance rendered by Mr Laffan, able to get together a very efficient body of cavalry.

Chapter Fourteen.

The campaign commenced—We join the Patriot army—
Orders to hold the fort of Guamoco against all assailants—A
thunderstorm—Survey of the fort from a height—The
enemy in the distance—We take possession of the fort, and
repair it—Spanish officers appear—Two of them shot by our
men—The Spaniards attack us fiercely, but are driven
back—They return, to meet with another repulse—The
enemy at length retire—We expect another attack.

Important events had meanwhile been taking place. Bolivar had
assembled a considerable army, of which upwards of two thousand
foreign troops—mostly disbanded British soldiers—formed the most
serviceable part. Whenever they met the enemy, the English
exhibited the hardihood and courage which they had displayed on
many hard-fought fields in the Peninsula, and lately at Waterloo. We
heard, too, that they were led by several experienced officers who
had taken part in those campaigns.

The fearful atrocities which had been committed by Murillo, Boves,
Morales, indeed by almost all the Spanish generals, had aroused the
spirit of the people throughout the country, and we looked forward
to the time when we should free our beloved land from the presence
of the hated tyrants.

At length being considered in an efficient state, with wild delight we
received orders to join the Patriot forces. Before long we had several
skirmishes with the enemy, and in a gallant charge—in which Mr
Laffan distinguished himself—we put to flight a superior force of
King Ferdinand's hussars. These hussars were the scorn of our wild
horsemen, and the contrast between the two was great indeed. The
arms and appointments of the hussar were a sad encumbrance in
this climate. He had his lance, sword, carbine, and a brace of pistols;
and his clothing and trappings were those of a Hungarian trooper.
He was obliged to have his horse's tail cut short, for on several
occasions a Llanero was known to have galloped up to the rear of a

trooper, dismounted in an instant, and seizing the horse by its long tail, by a sudden jerk contrived to throw it on the ground, and then despatched the rider. Our fellows, when charging, used to lay their heads and bodies on the necks of their horses, carrying their lances horizontally in the right hand about the height of the knee, so that when the Spaniards fired they seldom managed to hit them.

I was seated with Juan in the hut which formed our headquarters. We had not troubled ourselves with tents, for our men slept on the ground during the dry season, except when we were quartered in a farmhouse or a village. We had been talking over the prospects of the campaign, when an orderly, riding up to the entrance of the hut, delivered a despatch to Juan. He read it eagerly.

"We are ordered to ride on to the Pass of Guamoco, as no infantry can reach it in time to prevent the Spaniards—who are marching towards it—obtaining possession," he said. "Order the assembly to be sounded, Duncan."

While I hastened to carry out his order, he hurriedly wrote a few lines on a rough piece of paper, which had not a very official appearance, and gave it to the orderly, directing him to deliver it to the general. In a wonderfully short time we were in the saddle, and moving towards our destination.

Juan then told me that he had been directed to take possession of a fort of some strength, which guarded the entrance of a pass through which Bolivar intended to make his way, but which, if occupied by the enemy, would be impracticable. It was thus of the greatest importance that we should take possession of it. "The general orders me to hold the fort until an infantry regiment arrives to garrison it," added Juan.

"I hope they will put the best foot foremost, then, for I have no wish to be cooped up in a fort when we should be doing service in the open country," said Mr Laffan.

We pressed forward at a rate which none but light horsemen such as ours could have kept up. Nothing stopped us: up hills and across valleys we scampered; pushed through forests, or waded over marshes; forded or swam rivers when they crossed our way, without a moment's hesitation. We ran, indeed, a regular steeplechase. We were obliged to camp at night, however, to rest and feed our horses; but during the day we halted not a moment longer than was absolutely necessary. Hardy as were our steeds, they at length began to show signs of fatigue, but Juan encouraged the men to proceed.

"They will have time enough to rest when they get to the fort," he said,—"provided the enemy are not there before us."

We had gone on all day, and were still about four leagues from our destination when night overtook us. The road ahead, our guide informed us, was worse than any we had yet passed over, and that had been bad enough. It would be dangerous, he said, if not altogether impossible, to get our weary steeds over the ground in the dark. Still Juan, obedient to orders, would have continued the route, when a thunderstorm, which had been for some time gathering in the sky, burst over our heads. We were, fortunately, near a farm with a number of outbuildings and sheds about it, beneath which we took shelter. The rain fell literally in sheets of water, which quickly flooded the road; the lightning flashed with a vividness I had seldom before seen; and the thunder rattled and crashed as if huge rocks, rather than impalpable clouds, were being hurled against each other.

Juan now saw that it would be impracticable to advance until daylight; but he also knew that the enemy would not venture to march, so that, even if they were at an equal distance from the fort, we should get there first. He accordingly announced that he should remain during the night; so the men employed themselves in cooking their supper, rubbing down their horses, and in other ways, until they lay down to sleep in the driest spot they could find. The officers occupied one of the rooms of the house.

It was somewhere about two or three o'clock in the morning when Juan roused me up.

"I intend to ride on ahead of the party, in order to reach an elevated spot by daybreak, from whence I can take a survey of the fort and the surrounding country, and therefore learn the ground on which we may possibly have to operate," said he. "You will come with me, Duncan?"

I sprang to my feet. "I am ready to set out immediately," I answered, giving myself a shake.

Juan's servant brought us some cups of coffee, which we drank while our horses were being got ready, and in less than five minutes we had mounted. The storm had passed away, and innumerable stars shone out in the blue sky with wonderful brilliancy. We were obliged, however, to walk our horses, as it was with difficulty we could in many places see the road. Our last day's journey had been over ground of a considerable elevation, and we were still ascending.

Daylight broke while we were still on the road, and pushing on our horses, we reached the spot for which we were aiming. It was a lofty bluff with precipitous cliffs below us, beneath which there were several lesser elevations, and beyond, a wide valley opening into a vast plain. We here found ourselves far above the clouds, which spread like a canopy over the scene at our feet—a few tree-tops, the tower of a village church, and here and there, perched on heights, the roofs of some farmhouses. Immediately below us was the fort we were to occupy. It seemed as if we could almost leap down into it; though it was in reality too far off to be commanded from the height on which we stood, even had the enemy dragged up guns; but the path by which we had come was altogether impracticable for artillery, so we had no fear on that score. A short distance beyond the fort ran a rapid stream, which, descending from the mountains on our left, passed through the valley, and contributed materially to the strength of the position, as troops marching to the attack would have to ford it in face of the fire from the garrison. As far as we could see, the fort was still unoccupied; but the mist prevented us ascertaining positively if this was the case.

"I would that the clouds were away," said Juan, "to learn whether they are now concealing our approaching foes!"

ON THE LOOK-OUT

Here and there the mist appeared to be breaking or rising, and we watched eagerly for the moment when the whole face of the country would be exposed to view.

"Our men ought by this time to have got nearly round to the fort," observed Juan, looking at his watch; "and once inside, I hope that we shall be able to defend it against the Spaniards, though they may come only a few minutes after we have taken possession."

The sun now rose over the mountain-tops, his beams gradually dispelling the mists which had obscured the view. Still they hung over the valley, and we remained uncertain as to whether the enemy had had time to reach the fort below us. While we were thus eagerly watching, we caught sight of the head of our column rounding the foot of the mountain; but though visible to us, it could not as yet be seen by any one in the fort, and we were thus still in doubt as to the important fact we wished to ascertain.

"I gave directions to Captain Laffan to send forward and find out whether the fort was occupied, before exposing the troop to view," said Juan.

As he spoke we saw two of the horsemen ride forward, and Juan resolved to remain until the result was known. We now took a careful survey of the country before us.

"I can nowhere see a body moving which has the appearance of troops," observed Juan. "But there are so many woods and inequalities in the ground by which they might be concealed, that we must not trust to that. If, however, they have not already got possession of the fort, we shall have ample time to make such preparations as may be required for our defence. Duncan, take you the glass and see if you can discover anything which may have escaped my eye."

I did as he requested, and swept the surrounding country again and again. At last I saw what I thought looked like a dark shadow creeping slowly along over the brow of a hill from the westward, and descending towards us. Here and there was a slight glitter, as if the sun's rays were playing on polished steel.

I handed the glass to Juan, who was soon satisfied that what we saw was a body of troops. As, however, they were still some leagues away, and as they had a river to cross and some heights to climb, it would be several hours before they could reach the fort. We now felt sure that it, at all events, was not yet occupied. Dismounting, therefore, we led our horses down a steep path, by which we were at length able to rejoin our regiment. About the same time the scouts came back with the information that the fort was unoccupied. We accordingly rode forward and took possession.

It consisted of a strong stockade composed of whole logs of wood, with a deep trench in front of it. The huts were in a very dilapidated condition, but they would still afford some shelter to the garrison; while a stone tower in the centre, also surrounded by a trench, formed a sort of citadel as well as a storehouse. It comprised a ground floor, with a vault beneath, which served as a magazine, and two stories above without any divisions. In one of these were a few rough articles of furniture, which had been intended for the use of officers; and in the upper story, which had been used as an hospital, were a number of bedsteads covered with hides; while above the roof was a loopholed wall running all round, for musketry. Behind the fort was a wide space completely protected by impracticable heights and the fort in front, on which our horses could be turned out to graze. The Spaniards had most unaccountably left behind three guns, which, though spiked, were serviceable in other respects; and in the storeroom we found shot for them.

We had brought, I should have said, nearly two dozen horse-loads of ammunition—including powder for the guns which we had hoped to find—as well as the same number of animals laden with provisions. But, of course, as they had to travel as fast as our horses, they could carry but a very limited load.

Not a moment was lost in setting to work to repair the fort. Juan told the men how we had seen the enemy approaching, and consequently they laboured away with might and main. Trees were cut down from the hill-side above the fort, and dragged in to repair the stockade. The trench was cleared out; and shelter erected for the horses, which it would be absolutely necessary to retain inside in case of requiring them on an emergency. The men, accustomed from their earliest days to hard labour, toiled away without cessation. By night we had repaired the fort, and were ready for our enemies should they appear; but as yet we had not got a sight of them, and I began to fancy that Juan and I had been mistaken. Under Mr Laffan's directions, our farriers had contrived to extract the nails with which the guns were spiked, and all three were mounted and got into position during the night. A vigilant watch was kept, for should the enemy really have been approaching, they would very probably attack us before daylight.

Morning, however, came, and no sign of the foe being in sight. Though we had a flag with us, and a flagstaff stood in the fort, Juan would not have it hoisted; while the men were directed to keep as much under cover as possible, so that the Spaniards might not discover we had possession of the fort.

All the work outside had been finished, but we continued strengthening it, and making such, improvements as were necessary in the inside.

It was about noon when one of the sentries gave notice that he saw some people on the opposite side of the river. We watched them. Evidently they were Spanish officers reconnoitring the fort, and from their movements they seemed to doubt whether it was already occupied. At last, apparently satisfied that they were in time to take possession, two of them began to ford the stream. Before they had got half-way over, however, several of our men, without orders, fired, and they both fell, being carried down by the current. Juan rebuked his followers for this wanton act—at which the men seemed very much astonished. Several others who were following, and of whom we caught a glimpse, immediately retreated.

We now expected every moment to see the main body approaching to the assault, as it was not likely they would allow us to retain peaceable possession of so important a post, if they fancied they could capture it. Mr Laffan had charge of the guns, with the few men among us who had ever had any practice with artillery. There were, however, no more than two to each gun who had loaded and fired one before. Mr Laffan had to keep running backwards and forwards, to see that they put in the powder first and the shot afterwards, and rammed it home. In a short time the Spaniards advanced under cover, showed themselves on the bank of the stream, where they extended their line, and commenced a hot fire at the fort. We, keeping under shelter, did not reply to it until they commenced crossing the stream, when we opened on them with our guns. They evidently had not supposed that we possessed artillery; for they were at once thrown into confusion, and began to retreat, when numbers were brought down by our musketry, while our guns, being reloaded, again sent their shot among them.

We now ran up the Republican flag and shouted "Victory;" but we were mistaken in supposing that the enemy were put to flight. In the course of a short time a far larger body appeared, led by other officers, who behaved with great courage. At once they dashed across the stream,—we receiving them with a hot fire, our men loading and discharging their pieces as fast as they could, while our guns, considering the inexperience of the gunners, were well served. I could scarcely help smiling as I saw my old dominie spring from gun to gun, and point it at the thickest of the foe. One of the officers who appeared in command must have fallen, and although the others behaved with considerable gallantry, they failed to induce the men to come up to the stockades. Once more they retired across the stream, and many lost their lives.

After this they contented themselves with getting behind such cover as they could find, and firing at the fort. Had they possessed guns, the tables would, I suspect, soon have been turned, as our comparatively light defence must quickly have been knocked to pieces. The thickness of the stockades, however, prevented their bullets from entering, and a few only of our men who exposed themselves were hit,—two being killed, and three wounded. Out of our small garrison, however, that number was of consequence.

We continued firing away with the guns and musketry at the points where the Spaniards were concealed, but what damage we produced among them we could not tell. This style of fighting lasted several hours, while we every moment expected to be again attacked. Not a Spaniard who had fallen wounded was allowed to live, for our bullets quickly put them out of their pain.

At length the firing ceased, and we saw the enemy retiring—a round shot or two sent after them by Mr Laffan expediting their movements. The victory was decidedly on our side; but we knew full well that we might again be attacked by a superior force, and perhaps that very night. Therefore, as before, a vigilant watch was kept, so that, should they attempt a surprise, we might be ready to receive them.

Chapter Fifteen.

Captain Laffan and I go out to reconnoitre—A prisoner—
Gaining information—The Spaniards twice assault the fort,
and are repulsed with slaughter—We lose a number of
men—A council of war—Scarcity of ammunition and
provisions—Don Juan invites two of us to obtain
assistance—Laffan and I undertake the duty—We set out—
Narrowly escape the Spaniards—Enter a town lately sacked
by them—Obtain refreshment—Directed on our course—A
bivouac for the night—We proceed next morning—Laffan's
horse bitten by a snake—My companion trudges forward on
foot—We reach a farm—Obtain shelter and food, a horse
and a guide, and continue our journey.

Juan and most of our little garrison exulted in the idea that, after the
defeat we had inflicted on the Spaniards, they would abandon the
attempt to take the fort, and retire from the neighbourhood.

"Do not be too sure of that," said Captain Laffan; "they will watch
their opportunity, and attempt to surprise us if we are off our guard.
They know the value of the pass too well to leave us in quiet
possession. They may be looking all this time for a path over the
mountains, to try and take us in the rear; though they would find
that a hard matter, to be sure."

Juan, however, still persisted in his belief that the Spaniards had
retired, and turned their attention to some other enterprise. Fearing
that this opinion would make him and his followers less vigilant, I
volunteered to go out and reconnoitre.

"You shall not go alone," said Mr Laffan.

"No," I answered; "I intend to take Lion with me."

"I intend to go also," he replied. "I have done a little skirmishing in
my day, and three pairs of eyes will take in more than two. Indeed, I

do not think you should count much on the services Lion may render."

"He will, at all events, give us timely notice should we get near a sentinel, or should one of the enemy approach us," I remarked.

"You are right," answered Mr Laffan. "We will go together; and I am pretty strongly of opinion that we shall bring Don Juan word that the enemy are not far off."

"But shall we go by night or day?" I asked.

"At night we should have the advantage of being able to get up to the enemy without being seen," said Mr Laffan; "but we should be quite as likely to find ourselves in their midst before we had discovered where they were. Whereas in daylight, though we may find more difficulty in approaching them, we shall be able to see any of their men moving about at a distance. During the day, too, they will be less likely to be on the watch for scouts."

It was finally settled, after a discussion in which Juan and the other officers took part, that we should leave the fort just before dawn, and remain concealed until daylight, when we were to make our way in the direction in which it was most probable that we should find the Spaniards, if they were still in the neighbourhood. This plan was finally agreed on; and Captain Laffan, Lion, and I, at the hour fixed on, left the fort, and made our way across the river to a grove of trees which afforded us sufficient concealment; while, should the Spaniards themselves have sent out any reconnoitring party to ascertain what we were about, we should to a certainty discover them.

As soon as it was daylight we continued our route, Lion going on just before me, and turning round frequently to see if I was following. By his conduct, I was very sure that he understood the object of our expedition. We kept as much as possible under cover; occasionally when we came to open ground we ran across it in a stooping posture, so that, should we be seen by those at a distance, we might be mistaken for animals. We had gone nearly a league without observing a human being, when we caught sight of a small hamlet in the distance, with a wood on one side, and a stream partly encircling it.

"That's a likely place for the enemy to have occupied," observed Mr Laffan; "and if they are in the neighbourhood, we shall find them there."

We now approached more cautiously than before, while Lion showed a considerable amount of excitement, as if he believed that an enemy was near. Presently he stopped short, then advanced slowly, like a tiger stealing on its prey, glancing back every now and then to ascertain if we were following. Again he stopped, and then came running towards us, when, placing himself directly before me, he pointed with his nose in the direction he had before been taking.

We at once guessed that some one was concealed behind the brushwood; but if a sentry, he had not discovered us, or he would have fired. We accordingly determined to seize him and gain what information we could. Making a sign to Lion to keep behind, we cautiously crept on, bending almost to the ground, and completely hidden by the bushes. I made a motion to Lion to seize the man, if there was one. He understood me; and as he sprang forward we heard a half-stifled cry. The next instant we saw Lion struggling with a soldier, who had dropped his musket, and was endeavouring to draw his knife to thrust into the dog's body.

We grasped the fellow's arms, and quickly mastered him. It was at once evident that he had been sitting down, while we were approaching, to light his cigarrillo; or perhaps he might have dropped off to sleep. Releasing him from Lion, we threatened him with instant death if he opened his mouth or attempted to escape. Then, each of us taking an arm, we dragged him along towards the fort.

"If we carry this fellow with us, he will to a certainty be put to death," I observed to Mr Laffan.

"I don't like the idea of that," said he.

"Nor do I," I answered. "The best thing we can do is to get what information we can out of him, then bind him to a tree, and leave him. The Spaniards will discover him in time, and will yet be none the wiser."

"A good idea," said Mr Laffan.

The captive Spanish soldier looked imploringly at us, fully expecting that his minutes were numbered.

"We do not intend to kill you," I said, "if you will give us a faithful account of the number of troops in this neighbourhood, and what it is intended they should do, — whether they are about to attack the fort again, or to march away; and if so, where they are going."

"Have I your word of honour?" asked the Spaniard, looking at me, very much puzzled to know who I could be, as he heard me speak in English, and then address him in genuine Spanish.

"You have my word. We have no wish to murder our enemies," said I.

"That's more than I can say for my countrymen," he answered. "I will tell you frankly, señor. There are a thousand men in yonder camp. It was intended to attack you again to-night. Our officers have resolved to capture the fort at all risks, and they have told the men it must be done. If you will undertake, señor, to protect my life, I will follow you, and serve you faithfully. I would rather do that than have again to assault yonder fort."

"I believe what you say," I answered; "but I cannot venture to take you with me, for the Patriots would instantly put you to death, as they have vowed to do with every Spaniard who falls into their hands."

"I must submit to my hard fate, then," said the man.

"You will regain your liberty in a few hours," observed Captain Laffan.

"Ah, señor, if I am caught I shall be shot for sleeping at my post. If you will give me my liberty I will run away, and not again fight against you."

"The very best thing such a fellow as you can do. I think we may trust you," said Captain Laffan.

We led our prisoner on until within a short distance of the fort, when, instead of binding him, we let him go. He bolted away to the northward,—showing that he fully intended to carry out his promise.

On our return to Juan, he thanked us warmly for the service we had rendered.

As may be supposed, we were all on the watch; and about two hours before dawn we caught sight of the Spaniards advancing to the attack. As they crossed the river, we opened a heavy fire upon them; to which they replied, and then rushed forward, attempting to storm the stockades. The fort, from one side to the other, was in a blaze of light. Each man was fighting with desperation, and hurling back those who crossed the ditch and endeavoured to climb the walls. After the Spaniards had made several desperate attempts, they were driven back; and again getting under shelter, contented themselves with keeping up a hot fire at us. We, of course, replied in the same fashion; but, except that both parties expended a large amount of powder and shot, no great loss was suffered. In the attack a considerable number had been killed and wounded, and not a few of our own men had been hit.

We waited, fully expecting that with the return of daylight the enemy would make another assault. And we were not mistaken; but the result was the same as before, though I cannot say that, had they persevered, they would not have got in. Greatly to our relief, however, we heard the recall sounded. Once more they retired; and two of our men sallying out, traced them back to their former quarters.

We were for some time employed in repairing the damage done to the fort, and in attending to the wounded; and while we buried our own dead, we sent out a party to throw the Spaniards who had fallen in the river, as the easiest way of disposing of them. Several poor fellows who were found wounded were mercilessly bayoneted, in spite of all Juan, Mr Laffan, and I could urge to the contrary. Our men were generally sufficiently obedient; but when told to spare their enemies, who could no longer oppose them, they turned away with scowling countenances, not even deigning to reply—evidently resolved to carry out the fearful spirit of revenge which animated them.

Our men were again rejoicing at having repulsed our foes, when Juan summoned us to a council of war.

"Though we may rejoice at the victory we have gained," he said, "yet it has been dearly bought by the death of so many of the garrison, and by the expenditure I find, of nearly all our ammunition. Should another attack be made, we have not a sufficient supply to repulse the enemy. Still I know that you and all my men will fight to the last, and that we may offer an effectual resistance with our spears and swords. We are ordered to hold this post, and I am resolved not to quit it alive, or we might possibly cut our way through the enemy. After the losses they have received, they may not attack us for some time; so I propose to send off any two of you who may be willing to go, to endeavour to reach the general and obtain reinforcements, as well as a further supply of ammunition and provisions; though, in regard to the latter, we can live on horse-flesh, if need be, until assistance reaches us."

Juan looked at the other officers; but they made no reply. He then turned to Captain Laffan and me. "Are you willing to go?" he asked.

"With all my heart," answered Captain Laffan; "and I am sure I may say the same for Duncan. We gained some experience of the country in our reconnaissance the other day, and I feel sure we shall get off without being discovered."

"I am perfectly ready to go," I added; "but I am very unwilling to leave you, Don Juan, in so critical a position."

"Think not of me," answered Juan. "I have a duty to perform, and I may well rejoice if I am called upon to die for the sake of my country."

We accordingly settled that we were to set out about three hours before dawn, which would give us time to get beyond the enemy, and out of their sight, when we should have the advantage of daylight for seeing our way. I confess I felt more out of spirits than usual when I bade my friend Juan farewell. A presentiment of evil oppressed me, as I thought of the dangers by which he was beset.

It was shortly after two o'clock in the morning, when Mr Laffan and I, having our horses' hoofs muffled, and followed, of course, by Lion, led them down to the river; crossing which, we took the road we had before followed for some distance. We then turned to the left, along the base of the hills. Between these and the hamlet occupied by the enemy, it was possible that patrols might be met with, and if so we had agreed to mount and cut our way through them. As we were on foot, we hoped that we should not be perceived until close upon the enemy; we should then have a good chance of escaping. We trudged on, therefore, holding our horses by the left rein, so that we might mount in a moment.

We had got a good way to the westward, and, as we fancied, clear of the enemy, when, on doubling a high rock, round which the path led, we came suddenly upon a picket. Owing to the precautions we had taken, however, they did not hear or see us until almost within a dozen paces. To leap on our horses and dig our spurs into their flanks, was the work of a moment; and before the Spanish soldiers could spring forward and seize our reins, we had already got to a considerable distance beyond them. They immediately opened fire, but, owing to the darkness and their surprise, took very bad aim.

Possibly, not hearing any sound, they took us for phantom horsemen; but they continued to pepper away in the direction we had taken, long after the darkness had hidden us from their sight.

Not supposing that we should meet with another picket, we now dashed forward at full speed, the increasing light enabling us to see our way. Our horses, being perfectly fresh, went on for several leagues without flagging, and we now felt confident that there was but little chance of our being pursued. Not, however, being acquainted with the country, we knew that unless we could obtain a guide we should very likely lose our way, or take a much longer route than was necessary. With this object in view, therefore, seeing a small town on our right we rode towards it, to procure the assistance we required, and obtain refreshments for ourselves and steeds. Being uncertain who had possession of the place, I rode into the town, as I could pass there for an Englishman or a Spaniard, as the case might necessitate. I could thus obtain the information, while Mr Laffan remained on watch at some distance.

The place at first appeared deserted; but at length I saw three persons. One was lying in front of a door-step, another was apparently watching him, — both being badly wounded, — while a third, leaning against the wall, watched me as I approached.

"Friends," I asked, "what has happened lately in this town?"

"The Godos have passed through it, and as we were Patriots they burned down a large part, and killed most of us. Look at yonder woman; she alone survives of all her family. You see almost all the remaining inhabitants," and the speaker uttered a bitter laugh.

"I can feel for you, for I am a Patriot," I answered; "and I want to find my way to the army of General Bolivar."

"I would act as your guide, but I have no horse," answered the man; "and I could not sit one if I had; look here, señor," —and he showed me a severe wound on his side. "Nor can we help you," he continued, "for there is no young man left in the place who would be able to go; but I can direct you on your road. And you will rejoice to hear, señor, that the last news which reached us is that the general has beaten the accursed Godos; though whether it is true I know not. Good news never travels so fast as ill news."

I tried to cheer my new friend, and he undertook to obtain some refreshments for us.

"You may enter any of the houses you please, for most of them are empty; but to mine you are welcome."

While he went to find some food and fodder for our horses, I rode back to where I had left Mr Laffan.

On our return we found plenty of fodder for our horses, but the fare with which we were supplied was very scanty, almost everything having been carried off by the plunderers.

"If, however, we would wait," our host said, "he would find some fruit, and procure some fowls which had escaped."

As we were anxious to proceed, we begged that he would point out the road we were to take. This he did, and we bade him farewell.

We had still some hours to ride before nightfall, when we must, if possible, find shelter. As far as we could judge, it might take us three or four days to reach the Patriot camp, and some time must elapse before relief could be sent to Juan, —and what might not occur in the meantime?

Whenever we pulled rein, Mr Laffan stood up and took a survey of the country.

"It is wise to ascertain what's moving when traversing a country, or in our course through life," he observed. "We may thus know where to find our friends and avoid our foes."

A DESERTED TOWN.

Frequently, however, the view on either side was bounded by woods, the trees rising to a prodigious size. Many of them ran up to an amazing height in a straight line before they began to branch out.

From some of the fig species, various shoots descended perpendicularly, where they took root, so that we had no little difficulty in making our way through these woody columns. Between the openings we caught sight of the mountains rising to the skies; and occasionally a stream crossed our path, or ran foaming along on one side or the other.

We had hoped to reach some friendly village or farmhouse, where we might rest during the hours of darkness, and obtain better food for our horses than they could pick up in the forest; but though we pushed on until an hour after sunset, no glimmering window-light appeared to beckon us towards it, and we had at last to look about for an open space where we might bivouac. We accordingly dismounted, and tethering our animals, commenced searching for wood to light a fire. We ran no small risk, as may be supposed, of rousing up a venomous serpent, or disturbing a boa during its rest, while at any moment a jaguar or puma might pounce down upon us, or a bear make its appearance. We succeeded in obtaining fuel enough to make a pretty large fire, and by its bright flames we the more easily obtained a further supply of wood. We had, however, but scanty materials for a meal,—some fruit, and a few pieces of Indian corn bread. I gave part of my share to poor Lion, who looked up wonderingly at finding himself put on short commons in a land of plenty. There was sufficient grass, however, for our horses to obtain a feed, and as we had watered them a short time before, they were not so badly off.

Having collected fuel enough to last for the night, we cut a number of sticks, which we ran into the ground to form a shelter against any sudden attack of wild animals during the night; and then, pretty well tired out, lay down to rest. Every now and then Captain Laffan or I got up to change the position of our horses, but we dared not leave them far from the fire, lest some jaguar might spring out and kill one of them, although it might not be able to carry off its prey. Great as was our anxiety, we by turns got some sleep; and at dawn, again mounting, we rode forward. The sky, however, was cloudy, and we had greater difficulty than before in guiding our course.

We rode on for some hours, until the pangs of hunger and the necessity of resting ourselves made us resolve to stop. I was fortunate enough to kill a good-sized monkey, which was grinning down at us from a bough close above our heads; and we also found as much wild fruit as we required. So, having reached the banks of a stream, where we and our horses could get water, and where there was abundance of grass, we halted, and quickly had a fire lighted, and part of our monkey roasting before it. The other part I had given to Lion, who was quite ready to eat it uncooked.

We again moved forward, but we both felt very doubtful whether we were going right. For my own part, I know but few sensations so disagreeable as the idea that one has lost one's way. We were passing along a low sandy spot, with high bushes and trees on either side, when Captain Laffan's horse gave a sudden start; and looking down, we saw a small shiny snake gliding away. The horse had evidently been bitten, for we could see the mark of the creature's fangs above the fetlock, and soon the leg began to swell. The poor animal proceeded with the greatest difficulty. What remedies to apply we neither of us knew, but we had heard of the existence of a small snake called the aranas, the poison from whose fangs is so subtle that animals bitten often die within an hour; and even when remedies are applied, few are ever saved.

"The creature might have bitten either of ourselves," I observed.

"I do not think this species ever attacks man,—though I should not like to put the matter to the test," answered Captain Laffan.

There was no use in our stopping, especially as there might be other snakes of the same kind in the neighbourhood. We therefore, as long as the poor horse could move, pushed forward; but its pace became more and more sluggish, as the limb continued to swell. At length the animal stopped altogether, and my companion, feeling it tremble, leaped off. Scarcely had he done so when it came to the ground, and lay struggling in violent convulsions. Mr Laffan contrived to take off the saddle before it was damaged. In a few minutes, foaming at the mouth, the horse died, evidently in great pain.

"No use groaning over what cannot be helped," observed the captain. "You take the saddle, and put it before you; I'll carry the bridle; and I must try to get another horse as soon as possible."

The delay was serious, but it could not be helped; so we moved along, Mr Laffan trudging by my side. I asked him to get up, but he positively refused to do so.

The belief that we had lost our road was still further depressing. I thought especially of the serious consequences which might ensue to Juan should we not soon obtain the assistance of which we were in search. At length my eye fell on a papaw-tree, and what appeared to be a hut just below it. Riding on, we saw a Creole peasant-woman walking along and spinning, evidently near her home. At first, on seeing us, she seemed disposed to fly; but on our calling to her and assuring her that we were friends, she stood still, waiting for us to come up. Our wants were soon explained: we should be glad, of a horse, a guide, and especially of some food. Food she could give us. Her husband was out, she said, but he would soon return, and he would procure a horse, of which there were several broken-in on the farm; and perhaps he himself would act as our guide.

Eager to push on, our patience was greatly tried; though we waited and waited, the woman's husband did not appear. At last Mr Laffan proposed going out and catching one of the horses.

"But then you will not know in what direction to ride," observed the woman. "You have no right, either, to take the horse without my husband's leave."

"Might makes right," answered Mr Laffan; "however, we will not act the part of robbers, but will pay you handsomely for the horse."

This promise satisfied the poor woman.

Fortunately, just as we were setting out the husband returned, and was evidently well-pleased at the thought of getting a good price for one of his animals. He also undertook to guide us, if we could wait until the next morning at daybreak, and would promise him a reward. He took good care, indeed, that we should not start before then, as it was nearly dark before he returned with the horse. It was a tolerably good animal, though rather small, and we willingly promised him the price he asked. He described to us feelingly the terror he had been in lest the Godos should visit his farm; though, excepting a few cattle and horses, there was little they could have obtained. His wife had been in still greater fear lest they might carry her husband off as a recruit; but he had kept in hiding, and she had conveyed food to him from day to day, until the Spaniards had left the neighbourhood.

We managed to rest with tolerable comfort on heaps of Indian corn leaves, and slept securely, without the fear of being attacked by jaguars, bears, or other wild beasts, or being bitten by serpents.

Faithful to his promise, our host appeared the next morning with the horse for Mr Laffan, while he brought a smaller animal for himself. His wife insisted on putting up a supply of food for the day, and was evidently unwilling to receive any reward. After a good breakfast we started, thankful to find ourselves on the right road.

Chapter Sixteen.

Our guide complains of our rapid pace—He leaves us—We meet Captain Lopez—Our doubts as to his object—In a deserted hut—We meet Uncle Richard and a body of infantry—We turn back with him—A rapid stream—Finding a bridge—The Spaniards advancing—A rush to gain the bridge—We reach it first—A fight—The Spaniards defeated—No prisoners taken—We approach the fort—Captain Laffan and I ride on to reconnoitre—Signs of disaster—Our men fire—A flock of galenachas rises from the fort, which appears in ruins—Dead bodies scattered about—Discovery of that of Juan—We raise a tomb over his grave—The army of Bolivar—Description of the General—Treachery of Colonel Lopez—Attempt to assassinate Bolivar—Numerous engagements—Praise from the General—My return home—An interview with Dona Dolores—She joins the army—War the greatest curse that can afflict a country—Conclusion.

We endeavoured to make up for lost time by galloping as fast as our horses would go, whenever the ground would admit of our doing so. Every moment might be of consequence. Should the Spaniards again attack the fort, we knew too well that our friends would have a hard matter to hold it. Our guide frequently exclaimed that we should knock up our steeds, or bring them to the ground.

"Never fear, my friend," said Mr Laffan; "if we do, we must pick ourselves up again."

"But your bones, señors, your bones; you will break them or your necks," murmured our guide.

"Never mind—we must do the best we can; you don't know what we Englishmen are made of," said Mr Laffan.

"But I may break my neck, and then what will become of my poor Margarida?" cried our guide.

"We will do our best to console her, and find her another husband. On, on!" cried Mr Laffan.

In vain were all the expostulations of our guide. The dominie lashed his little steed, and up hill and down dale we kept on. Probably Tomaso would have left us to pursue our course alone and find our own way, had not my friend wisely kept back a portion of the price of the horse, lest such a trick might be played us. At last Tomaso pointed out what he called the highroad, and assured us that by keeping straight on we should in time reach the Patriot camp. How far off it was, however, he did not say. He now begged hard for the sum we owed him.

"Here it is, my friend; you have well earned it, I own," said Mr Laffan, handing him the amount.

He was profuse in his expressions of gratitude. "A fortunate journey to you, caballeros; and may the Patriot cause prove triumphant," he added, as, making a low bow, he turned his horse's head and rode back the way we had come.

We had not got far when we saw a horseman galloping in hot haste towards us; by his dress and accoutrements we knew him to be an officer. As he got nearer I recognised him to be Captain Lopez. He pulled up, and began to address us before he recognised either of us.

"Can you tell me, caballeros, if a division of the Spanish forces is stationed anywhere in the neighbourhood? I am told that such is the case."

"And what object, Captain Lopez, have you for wishing to know where to find the Spanish forces?" asked Captain Laffan, looking sternly at him. "Surely you are not going to desert to them!"

Captain Lopez now recognised us, and looked very much confused. He answered—

"No; desert to them, no! I am not a deserter, but I wish to ascertain their whereabouts, that the Patriots, who are advancing in this direction, may be prepared to encounter them."

Captain Laffan looked incredulous, but simply asked—

"Whereabouts are we likely to find the Patriots, as we wish to join them without delay, and possibly can give them the information you are going to obtain?"

I remarked that he said nothing about Juan, or that our object was to bring him assistance. Captain Lopez, however, inquired where Juan's troop had gone, observing that it was supposed he had joined Bolivar. Whether he really knew the true state of the case, I could not tell.

Captain Laffan was as reticent as at first. "Now, Captain Lopez, we must not delay; we possess all the information you wish to gain, and I would advise you to turn back with us, or you may chance to fall into the hands of the enemy."

In answer to this remark Captain Lopez made several excuses, and at last said, "I'll ride on for a short distance, and then follow you back. Farewell, señors, for a short time;" and he continued his course in the direction he was before going.

"The scoundrel!" exclaimed Captain Laffan as we galloped on; "I am very sure that he is on no good errand. We should have served the cause by shooting him."

We had very little time to make remarks, as we had generally to ride one before the other, but our suspicions of the object Captain Lopez had in view made it more important than ever that we should reach the Patriots without delay, and hurry them on to the succour of Don Juan and his hard pressed garrison.

Another night arrived, and we were still unable to ascertain how far off the Patriots were encamped. Had our horses been able to move, we should, in spite of the dangers of the road, have pushed on in the dark. There was just light enough for us to discover a deserted hut. At the back was a garden overgrown with grass, into which we turned our horses. A well in one corner supplied them with water, and we were sure that they would not wish to stray; while the thick hedge and trees which surrounded the garden concealed them from the view of any one passing. We ourselves were not likely to be discovered unless by a person entering the hut. The food with which our good hostess Margarida had supplied us afforded a tolerable supper, with something over for breakfast. We could not doubt but that early the next day we should fall in with the Patriots.

Scarcely yet persuaded that Captain Lopez was acting treacherously, as Captain Laffan supposed, I half expected to see him return.

"If he does, it will be with a party of the enemy," said my companion, "and we shall be made prisoners, unless we get due notice and can gallop off."

This idea made us more wakeful than we should otherwise have been, for Lion doing duty as sentry was sufficient protection. The morning, however, came, and no enemy appeared. I shared my portion of the remaining stock of food with Lion, who had been for some time on short commons, as vegetable diet did not suit his constitution.

We had gone some distance when, as we were stopping to water our horses at a stream, my ear caught the tramp of feet.

"There is a large body of infantry coming along the road," I exclaimed; "I trust that they may be friends, or we shall have to cut across the country to avoid them."

Captain Laffan listened, and was satisfied that I was right.

"We must approach cautiously," he said, "and be prepared to turn to the right-about if they should prove to be enemies."

We instantly mounted and rode on, and before long came in sight of the troops.

"They are Patriots, I am sure, from their dress, and the flags they carry," said Captain Laffan.

He was right. As we got nearer a mounted officer rode forward. To my infinite satisfaction I saw that he was Uncle Richard; while Antonio came close behind him, dressed as an officer.

"Hurrah! rejoiced to see you, Duncan; and you too, Captain Laffan," exclaimed Uncle Richard as he recognised us. "Where do you come from? Tell me all about it as we ride along; you will accompany me, for we shall soon halt to let the men dine, and you can then get what food you require."

We briefly told him the object of our journey.

"I knew that Don Juan was ordered to hold the fort, but I little supposed that he was so hard pressed. However, I hope we shall be in time to relieve him. You see these fine fellows?" and he pointed to the men. "I have been busy for some months, while you were away, raising and drilling them; and though I cannot say much for the uniformity of their appearance, I am pretty sure that, if well led — as I flatter myself they will be — they will do good service when we meet the enemy. I have had some difficulty in getting efficient officers, but I chose the best men I could find, independent of all other considerations. I have a Black, and two pure-blooded Indians, while the rest are Creoles. I found your former servant Antonio so intelligent and brave a fellow, that I gave him a company."

"I am delighted to hear it," I answered. "In a noble cause like ours there should be but one consideration, — to find the best men for every post; and if they have once been slaves, they are more likely to fight for freedom."

Our great object now was to march forward and attack the Spaniards before they could capture the fort. That we should come up with the enemy in time, I could not help thinking, was very uncertain. Our men, however, were well able to advance as rapidly as any troops could move. Except their muskets and powder, they were unencumbered with any accoutrements, or indeed with any superfluous clothing. They required but little food, and that of the coarsest description. Accustomed to the use of firearms from their boyhood, they had quickly been turned into efficient soldiers. We had intelligent guides, also, who knew the country, and were able to point out the best paths for our advance.

A short time only was allowed for the men to take their dinner, after which we marched on again until nightfall. At first it seemed somewhat strange to find myself seated round our camp-fire with Antonio, and to hear him addressed as "Captain;" but I did not allude to our former relative positions. In a short time, however, as he bore his honours well, and behaved in a thoroughly officer-like way, this feeling wore off, and it seemed quite natural to speak to him as an equal. He was only one of many who at that period rose from the ranks. One of the bravest generals in the Patriot army had been a slave. Indeed, General Paez had been a herd-boy, and Arismendez a fisherman. Bolivar was one of the few Patriot leaders of high family, for the Spaniards had put to death the larger number of the men of influence and Liberal principles, before the struggle for liberty began.

The next morning we recommenced the march two hours before daylight, when the men appeared fresh and in good spirits. We had again advanced some distance after our noonday halt when we came to a rapid river, running between high cliffs, over which, we had learned from our guides, a strong wooden bridge had been thrown. Had it not been for this bridge the passage of the river would have cost us great delay, as we should have had to descend by narrow pathways to the bottom of the cliffs, then to throw a pontoon across, and ascend on the other side. In the face of an enemy this would have been impossible.

I had ridden forward, curious to examine the structure of the bridge of which our guides had spoken. I found that strong timbers had been fixed on the ledges in the cliffs projecting over the stream, serving to support a platform; from this platform others were pushed forward on either side, the inner ends lashed to the first platform, while a centre one joined the two. Railings ran along on either side of this ingenious structure, which had a roof supported on poles—the object apparently being to prevent the wood-work from rotting with the wet.

AN INGENIOUS STRUCTURE.

I had got a short distance along the bridge, when I caught sight of a body of men coming over the ridge of a hill scarcely a mile off. Another look convinced me that they were Spanish troops; while the advance-guard of our force was nearly as far off on the other side. I waited for a moment longer, to judge whether, by the movements of the Spaniards, the latter had been seen; but I judged that they were concealed by the trees and rocks which lay between thorn, while they on their part had not discovered the enemy. The possession of the bridge was of the greatest importance, and I knew that the Spaniards, so soon as they should discover the Patriots, would make a rush down the hill to gain it. Partly hid as I was by the roof and railings of the bridge, I hoped that I had not been seen. To avoid the risk of being discovered, therefore, I slipped off my horse, and turning its head led it back until I got under shelter of some trees; when, mounting, I galloped as hard as I could until I met Uncle Richard, who instantly gave the word to advance at the double.

The Spaniards, who were already descending the hill, rushed down with headlong speed on discovering us, hoping to gain the bridge before our party had secured it. We at once dashed across to hold it against the Spanish advance-guard, which had nearly reached it. As the enemy saw us crossing they opened a hot fire, but, the distance being considerable, their bullets did no damage, and we were soon across without a casualty. Directly afterwards the head of our column appeared, and impetuously charged along the bridge. They came not a bit too soon, for already we were engaged with those of the Spaniards who had advanced ahead of their companions, whose numbers were every moment increasing, and who pressed us fearfully hard. In the meantime the Spanish troops, as they descended the hill, opened fire on our men, — those who were waiting to cross replying to it from the other side.

As I looked up the hill I feared, from the numbers descending, that we should be shot down before a sufficient number of the Patriots could cross to hold their own until our main body had got over. Our men, however, pressed forward and formed rapidly. In another minute we had secured our ground, and driven back the enemy a dozen yards or more, affording sufficient space for the main body to form up as they crossed. Several had been shot, and had fallen over into the torrent, which was already dyed with blood.

The order was now given to charge. The Spaniards, in their eagerness to reach the bridge, had been thrown into disorder as they descended the hill. Our left wheeled, turned their flank, and drove them down towards the river; while our right stood its ground. The contest was short, but sharp. In the course of a few minutes, it seemed, the larger number of the Spaniards were hurled over the cliffs; while the rest, in utter confusion, attempted to retreat up the hill, but were followed by our nimble-footed men, and cut down or bayoneted.

No victory could have been more complete. Not a Spaniard who was taken was allowed to live. Of the whole force, numbering some five or six hundred men, those only escaped who contrived to hide themselves in ditches or behind bushes or rocks, or whose activity enabled them to keep ahead of their pursuers. Our chief casualties had occurred while our men were crossing the bridge, but, in all, we had lost comparatively few.

The summit of the hill gained, we halted to reform our troops, and then once more advanced. Whether or not the Spaniards we had defeated were those who had attacked the fort, we could not tell, as not a prisoner had been saved. In vain did Uncle Richard call to his followers to spare the lives of those who yielded; his orders were not listened to. The men only followed the custom of that savage warfare, and the example of the Spaniards, upon whom they thus fearfully retaliated.

Once more we advanced. Another day passed; and it was late on the next before we reached the neighbourhood of the fort. I looked out eagerly to ascertain whether the besiegers were still before it, but as yet not a sign could I discover of the enemy. The hamlet occupied by the Spaniards appeared to be deserted. I now felt convinced that the body we had defeated was part of the force which had been besieging the fort, while the remainder had probably marched in an opposite direction. We had seen nothing of Captain Lopez, however, and he certainly was not with those Spaniards whom we had encountered.

Now came the question, What was the fate of the garrison? Had they been able to hold out until the Spaniards, growing weary of the attempt, had given it up? or had the fort been successfully assaulted, and its defenders cut to pieces? If so, the Spaniards must now have possession, and it would be our turn to attack them, and to attempt its recapture. This would not be so difficult a task to us as it had proved to the Spaniards, as Captain Laffan and I knew every point about it, and every spot from whence it was assailable.

The first thing to be done, however, was to make a reconnaissance; and Captain Laffan and I rode on for this purpose. With our glasses we saw from a distance that no flag was flying; and as we got nearer we discovered that the flagstaff itself was broken short off, and that the tower was fearfully shattered, while parts of the stockades were thrown down, and the whole fort seemed in the most dilapidated condition.

"A bad omen, that," observed my companion; "but, at the same time, it may have been shot through, and a puff of wind have blown it down."

My heart began to sink, as, still further lessening our distance, we could see no one moving in the fort. It appeared to be deserted. As this, however, might not be the case—for the garrison might possibly be keeping concealed—we advanced cautiously, halting again just out of musket-shot. We waited for some time, but not a moving object could we discern. By this time we had been joined by several men on foot. Captain Laffan ordered them to creep forward and fire, thinking that the salute might elicit a reply should an enemy be holding the fort. As the report went echoing among the rocks, a whole flight of galenachas winged their flight to the summit of the neighbouring cliffs, whence they could watch an opportunity of again descending to finish their horrible banquet. We knew now, to a certainty, that no living beings occupied the fort. What had been the fate of our friends?

Eager to ascertain the worst, we rode forward, and, fording the stream, made our way over a mass of ruins which filled the ditch, into the interior. The scene which presented itself told a sad tale. There lay, round the tower, the bodies of friends and foes in equal numbers, with limbs torn, clothing burnt, and countenances blackened. With a sickening heart I searched for one form, if it could be distinguished from the other disfigured remains of humanity. It was not long before I recognised the uniform my brave friend had worn. He was lying directly under the wall, while one hand still grasped the jewelled sword I had seen Dona Dolores gird to his side. Yes, it was he, my gallant friend! I knew him by his features, though scorched and blackened and fearfully changed, and by a ring he had worn, as well as by the watch in his pocket.

Captain Laffan found me kneeling by the side of my dead friend, unable to restrain my grief.

"It is the fortune of war, Duncan. A more gallant fellow never breathed; and he died a noble death—in discharge of his duty," said my late dominie. "Don't give way, my boy; he did not die in vain."

"But Dona Dolores!" I exclaimed; "her heart will break when she hears of it."

"It's of sterner stuff than that, I've a notion. But come, we must see at once about giving him a soldier's grave while there is yet time, for we may soon have other work to do."

Taking my dead friend's sword, and his ring and watch, that I might give them to Dona Dolores, I rose from the ground.

In a short time Captain Antonio came up with the advance-guard. On counting the slain, we found that they numbered more than half the garrison. The rest might possibly have cut their way out; if not, they must have been taken prisoners, and, to a certainty, afterwards shot. A still greater number of Spaniards had been destroyed. All that we could suppose was, that Juan, when he found that successful resistance was impossible, had blown up the tower, and perished with such of the assailants as had made good their entrance.

A grave was dug for Juan beneath a wide-spreading tree, some little way up the valley. We there laid him to rest; and a volley having been fired over his remains, a heap of unhewn rocks was piled up above them to serve as the young Patriot's tomb.

"When our cause is triumphant, and peace returns, I will erect a marble monument to his memory," I said. And I kept my word.

Our men, in order to save themselves trouble, cast the remainder of the bodies into the river,—caring very little for thus horribly polluting the pure water. I had before thought war a terrible thing, but the scenes I had lately witnessed impressed me still more forcibly with a horror of its fearful results. What hundreds—what thousands, I might say—of human beings had perished miserably within the last few months! How many more, too, were doomed to die! Then I thought of the towns and villages committed to the flames; the corn-fields, the orchards, and gardens destroyed; and, more than all, of the widows and orphans who, while bewailing the loss of those they loved, their protectors and bread-winners, were doomed to struggle on in poverty; and the numberless families, formerly in affluence, now reduced to absolute beggary. Such was the state of my native land. And yet no one complained—all were ready to struggle on in the cause of Liberty; blaming, not those who had risen to fight for freedom, but the tyranny of their oppressors as the cause of all they endured.

While we were encamped at a neighbouring hamlet, which afforded sufficient means for defence, and enabled us to watch the fort, a despatch arrived for Juan, ordering him to evacuate it. Alas! had it come sooner, he and his companions might have preserved their lives, as I believe he would have succeeded, had he made the attempt, in cutting his way through the enemy; but, influenced by a stern sense of duty, he had held it after all hope of successfully defending it had gone. This added greatly to my grief at his loss.

General Bolivar had heard of the corps Uncle Richard had raised, and now sent forward requesting him to join his army without delay. By forced marches across the mountains, in which both officers and men suffered not a little, we reached the general's camp, and I had the honour of being introduced to him. I little expected to see so young a man. In person he was small, but well-made and muscular, and able to go through astonishing exertion—frequently marching on foot over mountains and plains without exhibiting the slightest fatigue. His eyes were dark, large, and full of fire and penetration, denoting wonderful energy of mind and greatness of soul. His nose was aquiline and well-formed, his face rather long, and his complexion somewhat sallow. As Uncle Richard and I had the honour of being invited to his table, I had an opportunity of seeing him in his social moments. He was lively in his manner, full of anecdote and conversation; and it was said that, like Buonaparte, he possessed the power of reading at once a man's character, and placing him in a position where his talents and abilities would prove useful to his country. He was also thoroughly disinterested, and so little regard did he pay to himself under the most severe privations, that he was always ready to share what he possessed with his companions-in-arms, to his last cigar or his last shirt. He was always cool, and invariably displayed the most undaunted courage. He was, to be sure, hasty in his temper, and often made use of intemperate expressions, abusing in no measured manner those who had annoyed him; but, at the same time, he was ever ready to make atonement to the person whose feelings might have been undeservedly wounded. In his bosom revenge was never harboured, and it was owing entirely to the atrocities committed by the Spaniards on the Patriots that he was induced to carry on against them that fearful war of extermination which so long raged throughout the country. Bolivar might not have been a hero to his own valet, but by those who truly understand heroic qualities he should be deservedly placed on a high niche in the temple of Fame. I may add that he was temperate in his diet, drank but a very moderate quantity of wine, never touched spirits, and that he seldom smoked. Generally he was the last to retire to rest, and the first to rise.

Soon after joining the army, to my surprise I met Lopez, now raised to the rank of colonel. He appeared to be intimate with many of the officers, but kept aloof from Captain Laffan and me, as well as from Uncle Richard, whom I should properly designate as Colonel Duffield.

We had marched forward until we heard that Murillo, with a large force, was in the neighbourhood.

One night Captain Laffan and I had been invited to dine with several English officers, and our host told us that he expected Colonel

Lopez. However, when the dinner-hour arrived Colonel Lopez did not appear. A message was despatched to his quarters, but he was nowhere to be found.

"It's my belief," exclaimed Captain Laffan, "that the fellow has deserted! You will see that I am right; he was intending to do so when we met him."

Dinner over, we again retired to our quarters, and all was stillness in the camp. As I wished to take a few turns to enjoy the cool night air, I accompanied one of Bolivar's aides-de-camp who was about to visit the outposts, when we met a small body of troops marching towards headquarters. The officer in command gave the countersign, and they were allowed to proceed. Just then, who should we meet but Colonel Lopez, who informed my companion that he had some news of importance to communicate to General Bolivar respecting an intended movement of the enemy which he had just obtained from a deserter, and requested that he might be conducted to the general's tent.

"If you will remain here, I will immediately acquaint the general with what you say, and beg that you may be admitted," was the answer.

I returned with the aide-de-camp, but left him near Bolivar's tent to deliver the message. I had not got many yards off, however, when I heard a volley of musketry fired close to me, and directly, as it seemed, at the tent. An instant afterwards I saw a party of men, who must have followed close upon us, disappearing in the darkness.

"To arms!—to arms! the enemy are upon us!" was the cry, and soon general confusion ensued. The troops got under arms, and some fired in the direction taken by the fugitives, but in the darkness it was impossible to see whether any were hit. The fear was that the general must have been killed, and every one was in dismay until he himself rode round, quieting the alarm of the men. He had fortunately quitted his tent a few minutes previously, and was not many yards off when the firing took place. On examining his cot, it was found that three or four bullets had passed right through it, so that he must have been killed, or severely wounded, had he not providentially left his tent.

Few in the camp slept that night. A treacherous attempt had evidently been made to assassinate our general. When morning came we looked out in the direction of the enemy's camp. On the ground lay two bodies, and a party was sent out to bring them in. One of them was that of Colonel Lopez; and on his person was discovered a paper proposing a plan to Murillo for penetrating the camp with a party of Spaniards disguised as Patriots, and putting Bolivar to death. It was countersigned as approved of by the Spanish general. Such, then, was the fate of the rejected suitor of Dona Dolores.

I have not space to describe the several engagements which followed, but Colonel Duffield and Captain Laffan, who soon became a major, gained the credit they deserved for their gallantry on numerous occasions, and I had the satisfaction of being praised by Bolivar himself. However, the severe life we led at length affected both Major Laffan and me, and Colonel Duffield, in whose corps we served, insisted that we should return home to obtain the quiet and rest we required. The road was now open to Popayan, and we were able to travel with a small escort of invalids and wounded men, who, like ourselves, were unfit for service, and were anxious to return home.

With feelings of considerable anxiety we rode up to my father's house, for what might not have happened during our absence we could not tell. Great, therefore, was my joy when we were greeted at the entrance by my mother, Dona Maria, Rosa, and jolly little Hugh, who all threw their arms about my neck at once, and then bestowed a similar affectionate greeting on the major—who declared, as tears streamed down his cheeks, that it gave him as much joy to see them all well, as it had to beat the Spaniards in the last battle we had fought; while Lion, who had followed at my heels, was next saluted in nearly the same fashion, while he barked, yelped, and leaped about, evidently delighted to get home. Dona Maria looked very pale, and was evidently anxious about Uncle Richard, but we were able to give a very favourable account of him. Like many other wives, she had learned to endure her anxiety.

My father was out, but he soon returned, and expressed his satisfaction at the high encomiums which had been bestowed upon me by Colonel Duffield, and even by Bolivar himself.

"I have just come from visiting Dona Dolores," he said. "She has heard the report of Don Juan's death, but will not believe it; and I am afraid that it must be your painful task, Duncan, to convince her."

As soon as I could unpack the sword and the other articles which I had carefully preserved, I returned with my father to the house of the friend with whom she was staying. On hearing that I had come, she desired to see me alone. I felt more nervous than I had ever done in my life before, supposing that she would give way to her sorrow, and that it would be incumbent on me to endeavour to console her, impossible as that might be. What to say, indeed, I knew not.

I found her dressed in mourning for her father, and looking very pale. She was seated, but she rose when I entered, and advancing towards me, took my hand. Her eye fell on the sword, then on the ring on my finger.

"I know what you have to tell me, Duncan," she said in a deep-toned voice, but without a falter; "he died as I would have had him, — fighting bravely for the freedom of his country — for the same cause to which I dedicated my life. Give me that weapon: I would present it to you, but I must use it myself; not to avenge his death, but to take his place and wield it against the foes of Freedom. That ring — give it me; he sends it as a farewell token." She placed it on her finger. "Now, tell me the particulars."

I endeavoured to describe the circumstances of Juan's death, and how he had held the fort until all hope had gone.

She had remained standing during the time of our interview.

"Farewell, Duncan," she said at last. "I must prepare for a sterner life than I have hitherto led. As yet it has been one suited to a delicate creature like Dona Paula Salabariata—a mere scribe, endeavouring to incite others to do the task I should undertake myself."

I took my leave of Dona Dolores; and the next morning we heard that, attended by two servants, she had set out, habited in half-military costume, for the army. Some time passed before we heard of her again. She had joined a regiment, and taken part in every action. She seemed to bear a charmed life, too, for, although always in the thickest of the fight, the bullets passed her harmlessly by.

Years have rolled on since then, and the cause of Liberty has triumphed. When peace was obtained, I married my so-called cousin, the fair-haired Rosa; and my dear little sister became the wife of a gallant English officer who settled in the country.

I have described these scenes of warfare, not for the sake of encouraging a love of fighting, but for a very contrary object; and from the horrors I witnessed during that period, I am convinced that War is the greatest curse that can afflict a country, and I earnestly pray that the reign of Peace may soon commence on earth.